Myth-Understandings

Communication: the imparting or interchange of thoughts, opinions, or information.

Myth-Understandings

Edited by Ian Whates

NewCon Press
England

First edition, published in the UK March 2008
by NewCon Press

NCP 004 (hardback)
NCP 005 (softback)

10 9 8 7 6 5 4 3 2 1

ISBN: 978-0-9555791-1-0 (hardback)
978-0-9555791-2-7 (softback)

Cover Painting: 'Wayland's Smithy' by Anne Sudworth
Cover layout and design by Andy Bigwood

Invaluable editorial assistance from Ian Watson

Printed in the UK by Biddles of Kings Lynne

Contents

I Blame Liz Williams
An Introduction

It's all Liz Williams' fault. If not for her, this book would never have come into being.

Allow me to explain. I was in Glastonbury, visiting Liz at *The Witchcraft Shop*, which she runs with her partner, Trevor Jones. We were surrounded by all these wonderful and magical things, including racks of truly stunning gowns by the designer responsible for some of the costumes in the *Lord of the Rings* films. During the course of our conversation, Liz mentioned that Justina Robson had been approached a few years previously to assist with an 'all women authors' edition of *Interzone*, a project which came to nothing in the end. But that was enough to set me thinking.

Traditionally, speculative fiction, particularly science fiction, has been a male-dominated field. There remains a stubborn impression, akin to a lingering aftertaste which refuses to fade, that this holds true even today, when in fact there is a wealth of highly-talented women authors out there producing science fiction, fantasy, dark fantasy and horror that could knock your socks off – easily matching any written by their male counterparts.

What better way to demonstrate this fact than by putting together an anthology of exciting and original short stories featuring *only* women authors?

A few weeks after the conversation with Liz, I bumped into Justina Robson at an event in Cambridge, quite by chance. I couldn't resist mentioning the idea to her. She was suitably enthusiastic and promised to write something for the project should I go ahead, but then asked the telling question: "What's the theme?"

Theme? I hadn't thought beyond the 'all women' aspect. However, Justina was quite right. Of course the book needed a theme. I promised to get back to her.

By the time I returned home that evening an idea was already percolating, but I wanted to think it through, to make certain this was the *right* idea before mentioning it to Justina. So I mulled it over for the next couple of days, examining the concept from every possible angle. My two previous anthologies, *Time Pieces* and *disLOCATIONS*, featured themes that were both strong and broad: strong enough to provide a thread tying the constituent stories together, but broad enough to give the authors plenty of scope. The concept for this book would have to do likewise. I wasn't after a series of similar stories that told the same tale in a different way, but rather a collection of strikingly different stories that could trace their inspiration to a common root. The more diverse the tales and the more tenuous their link to the initial theme, the better; so long as the link was there. Whatever I settled on would have to encompass all of this and more. Finally, satisfied that it did, I emailed Justina, confirming the book's theme.

Communication.

Now all I had to do was recruit a suitably impressive battalion of female authors to the cause. The aim with these anthologies has always been to showcase new works from some of the biggest names in speculative fiction – people who have proved many times over that they can deliver the goods – while at the same time highlighting some of the excellent lesser known writers working in the genre, to introduce the reader to new voices.

To my delight, every author I subsequently approached and invited to submit for the anthology agreed to do so, providing me with a pool of fabulous stories to draw on.

I decided to do things a little differently this time around and almost immediately broke one rule that had been set in stone for the first two anthologies: I accepted a reprint. But what a reprint. Gwyneth Jones offered me her classic *The Grass Princess*, which won the World Fantasy Award for best short story in 1996. If ever there was a story that warrants breaking a 'no reprint' rule, this is surely it.

From the outset it was clear that this would be a considerably larger volume than either of its predecessors, and as the stories started to arrive another thing soon became apparent. Several of the most poignant and beautiful submissions had something in common over and above the underlying theme. All drew on one particularly rich vein of fantasy: they were steeped in the tradition of myth, giving them a very specific flavour.

This led me to contemplate setting another precedent. Whilst many of the accepted stories contained a distinctly mythical air, many others definitely did not. The sheer number of quality submissions I was receiving enabled me to divide the book into two sections, 'Myth' and 'Understandings'. Gwyneth's story, which draws on the tradition of the fairytale, intertwines it with myth and then seasons the result with a host of original ingredients, gave me the perfect anchor for the myth-related section. And so the form of the book began to emerge.

The cover presented something of a dilemma. I knew exactly who I wanted to do the artwork: Anne Sudworth. But Anne exhibits in art galleries and her original paintings sell for five figure sums. True, she has allowed her work to be used for book covers on occasion, but this has never been something she particularly relishes. So I bribed her. With chocolate. To my great joy, it worked, and I'm eternally grateful to Anne for allowing me to use her wonderfully evocative painting "Wayland's Smithy" for the cover of *Myth-Understandings*.

Thanks are also due to *disLOCATIONS'* cover artist Andy Bigwood, for designing the actual cover around Anne's painting. Andy and I, along with assistant editor Ian Watson, are the token males here. Every other aspect of the book has been produced by the more delicate female hand, even down to the layout, which is the responsibility of the multi-faceted Storm Constantine.

Myth-Understandings developed out of a desire to showcase the talent of women genre authors living in the UK. Of course, no single volume can contain all such, but this does include many of the very best, and its fifteen stories combine to produce a collection that achieves everything I had dared hope for. Though, of course, it's not really my place to say as much. After all, the only real judge of such things is you, the reader. With that in mind, thank you for buying, borrowing, or otherwise acquiring, a copy of *Myth-Understandings*. I trust you will enjoy the ride.

Ian Whates, January 2008

Myth

A traditional story dealing with supernatural beings, ancestors, or heroes that serves to explain the worldview of a people.

Owlspeak

Storm Constantine

In the 26th year of the Burnt Star, King Leonald defied Fate. Cenaggara, Lord of Destiny, became enraged and sent out his seventeen Slaughterers. Ten of the Slaughterers pursued the monarch through many levels of reality for several lifetimes; the rest imposed curses upon the Royal Family from which, to this day, it still reels and suffers. It is not prudent to displease Cenaggara. When he calls you, you bow and then dance to whatever tune he deigns to play. If you defy him, he will not forget you. It is in everyone's interest to be ignored or forgotten by Fate.

Shay was born into a family that followed the laws of Strixion. He did not go to the squat grey church with his mother every night, and said he did not follow her beliefs, but still he lived at home with her, and the family she controlled. Once he told me that when he was younger, he slept in a bed with six brothers, and on two occasions, in the midst of the winter, he had woken up to find one dead beside him. The first time, it had been from the Blacklung; the second , his eldest brother, who was fat, had slept on a young one and smothered him. Now Shay slept alone, because he was older, in his twenties, and it was therefore inappropriate to sleep with others.

The laws of Strixion are very particular. A human life, it is said, must not stray from the narrow path that winds between the cliffs of experience. The goal of our brief existence is to reach death, having reproduced as much as nature allows. We should not aspire to greater things, and to follow the instincts of the heart is not just folly but sinful. A devout Strix follows the footsteps of his or her parents, and their parents before them, way back through the generations, so that the footprints are kept perfect. Footprints in the mind. Shay was trampled from the day I met him.

Under normal circumstances, Shay and I would not have become friends; we were so different. I had no family of blood, but lived with others of my kind. We were followers of Lady Onyxx, which our detractors might say means we didn't follow very much at all, since Onyxx enjoys hedonism in her followers and despises anyone who bows a knee to her, never mind a head. But we did believe in destiny and magic, and that we could make a difference in the world. We believed that each person has a responsibility to evolve themselves as much as they are able, and that to retreat from life's challenges is weakness.

I had been taken in by my mentor, Dwine Estos, in my fifteenth year. Ten years had passed since. Dwine was in his forties even then, but a perennial dreamer who appeared far younger than his years. Dwine knew the state of the world, yet still he believed in its potential and had hope. From him, I had learned nearly everything I knew – how to shape reality, how to make dreams come alive. Ten of us lived in the house of Dwine, who had grown rich on the purses of gullible city folk needing guidance and magic. We, his younger followers, stayed up all night and slept all day. We did not want to grow old and scorned doing what we thought of as ordinary things. We scorned ordinary people too, and sniggered covertly at those who came to Dwine in despair, although he would have been disappointed in us if he'd known that, because we were supposed to be tolerant of others. But we were young then, somewhat arrogant I suppose, and determined to be extraordinary. When we were awake, we talked endlessly or created things together; works of art, stories, ideas, new systems of belief. Or else we worked our magic – shivery rituals beneath the midnight stars to make the world a better place. Sometimes we would have fires in the garden at the back of our house. We would get drunk on plum brandy and toast the most capricious of the spirits. My mentor later said to me that on one of these nights I had accidentally asked the universe for Shay to come into my life. Unwittingly, perhaps secretly desiring it, I had committed some magical act – perhaps a wish thrown with drunken joy into the night sky – that had made him happen to me. I had tempted Destiny. I can't remember doing so, but Dwine is no doubt right. He says we can trace everything back to an initial idea, when it was born.

As to how Shay and I met: well... It was during the Plague of Owls a couple of years ago. Conditions had been deteriorating in the city for several years. Our queen had gone senile and the ministers who now ruled in her name appeared to be mad. They instituted pettifogging laws constantly, some of which contradicted one another, while overlooking the greater ills that sorely needed a firm hand. While no one was now allowed to walk in the middle of a road because it was dangerous, the pavements were littered with rubbish, where vermin bred. Exotic new diseases were uncurling everywhere. People were becoming selfish and suspicious, and it was as if a plague of stupidity was taking over every mind, one by one. No one cared about anything any more, not the things that really mattered. Steadily, our once affluent society was falling into decay and no one truly knew why. Mismanagement, yes. Complacency, yes. But it was more than that. My friends and I talked about this a lot, how we had a duty to try and stem the inexorable tide, this nausea, this sickness. We called it the Yellow Wave, and it seemed unstoppable. Then the birds came.

No one knew where they came from nor why: a shadowy, whirring host of doom owls that brought twilight to the noon day. They came to roost upon the highest points of the city and turned the white towers to a midden. They were round-eyed in the daylight, perhaps wondering how they had got there and what to do next. The owl is a symbol of wisdom and of teaching. Why had these wise birds gathered in our stumbling city only to act like imbeciles, peering and blinking and uttering ugly cries?

People came in their hundreds to view the extraordinary sight. I went to look because it was phenomenal and beautiful and strange. I also went alone because my best friend, Theo, was called away by a boy she was in love with, seconds after we had put on our shoes to leave the house. I didn't mind. The experience was wonderful, whether shared or not. Poor owls. Had they come to teach, only to be horrified by what they'd found at journey's end? People pointing and making a noise, picking up the feathers that dropped, but no one really asking: why?

Shay was there with his family; they had brought the younger children to see. There were so many people. Easy to get lost in a crowd. A small boy ran into my legs, almost knocked me over. I was looking upwards, thinking how the wings that sometimes expanded from the towers above me looked as if they were trying to lift the city into the heavens.

"I'm sorry," a voice said.

And I looked into eyes that were like the sky. I didn't have to lower my gaze from the city summit that much; he towered over me. "For what?" I asked. It was then I realised I had a child attached to my legs.

"My kid brother," he said. "He ran off, nearly floored you."

Why had the child chosen me to cling to? I don't know. Cenaggara was in him. "There's no need to be afraid," I said to the child. He looked up at me with those wonderful eyes that belonged to his family. Strange how so repressed a breed could gaze upon the world through starlight. It was clear they were Strixes: the austere clothes, the cropped hair, the somewhat rigid body posture, even in the child, the skin that looked too scrubbed, almost raw. I noticed that their ears looked strangely vulnerable and naked. What they thought of me in my multi-layered clothing of many colours, the tassels, and bright rings and necklaces, I can only conjecture, but I doubt it was favourable.

"The birds are dark," said the child.

I smiled at him, touched his face. "That's just their colour. They're lost, that's all. They were going somewhere and forgot what they were doing. They are more afraid than you are."

The child's brother laughed then, in a not altogether pleasant way. My hackles went up. "Perhaps if he hadn't been scared, he wouldn't have run off," I said accusingly. "Do you teach your children to fear the natural world?" I disengaged the child and pushed him back towards his brother. "Yours, I believe."

It was the sort of moment when you should walk away, having ended the encounter, but unfortunately I was exactly where I wanted to be and had no desire to move.

We stood next to one another in uncomfortable silence, a pocket of stillness in a tempest of noise and activity. He did not move away and rather than wondering why, I simply found this annoying. But as the moments progressed, I realised I could feel a strong pulsating energy emanating from his body. That did not speak of Strixion; it tasted familiar to me, which was odd. As I was thinking about this, and what it might mean, he said, "Aren't you bored with this now? Shall we walk?"

I examined him for some moments. As I said, it had been clear to me from the start he was not of my kind, but there was something about him that was compelling. "Why do you want to?" I had to ask. It wasn't a coquettish question, just that usually his type avoids mine and vice versa.

He shrugged. "I just do."

If only I had said no. Why didn't I? He was a contradiction and that should have warned me rather than intrigued me, but then this must have been Cenaggara's influence again, sniggering away in his Halls of Torment. "Where shall we go?"

"Let me lose the kid first," he said.

"Again?"

He laughed, this time in a different way. It was altogether agreeable.

We went to the Swan's Neck Bridge, so named because, long ago, a princess had looked over the wall and had seen the Swan's Neck constellation reflected in the river water. She had seen ghostly birds fly out from it and they had spoken to her. She never revealed what they had said, but the bridge had been renamed. It is enormous, a suspended highway lined by stands selling food and trinkets. In summer time and the midst of winter there are fairs over the water, and a thousand fey lights mimic the heavens above us.

Shay told me his name and bought for me a cheap necklace made of metal swans. It would make my skin itch and presently be discarded, I thought. The sun was beginning to sink and the river turned to blood beneath its dying light. We leaned against the rosy stone, in a niche where benches had been placed, and gazed in the direction of the distant ocean that we could not see. The tide was coming in; the water seemed alive.

"Look," Shay said, and pointed up at the sky. The clouds there were multi-hued, as if fashioned by a painter of landscapes. "There are the tides and their king, riding into the light."

A shiver went through me at those words. They seemed to me wonderful. I looked at him askance. "I would not expect you to say such a thing."

He shrugged. "Why not?"

"Just that... well, you're a Strix, aren't you? Isn't such fancy against your laws or something?"

"I don't believe in anything," he said. "I can't help who raised me."

We stared at one another, and I thought that I would never again be able to break away from his gaze. "I think we were meant to meet," I said.

"I don't believe in fate," Shay said.

"I do. I believe in magic too."

"Of course," he said, "you're a Nixie. So there we have it. Meeting on a bridge." He laughed. "Ironic really."

"I'm hungry now. Let's eat."

He nodded. "Where do you suggest?"

Naturally, I took him to one of my haunts, which I hoped would impress him. It was a Nixie inn, decorated in vibrant colours, and filled with customers who had earnest things to say while getting very drunk. Even from that moment, I had a desire to reach Shay. I wanted to turn his head in my hands, so that he faced a different road in life. Perhaps if he heard the way my people talked, he would start to think. When he laughed, when his eyes lit up, I could see within him a shining light. It was like looking through the bars of a cage at something wonderful and winged that could not stretch or even breathe properly. But there was very definitely a cage and it was his sanctuary as much as his prison. For every step towards me, he retreated half a step. The creature in that cage was wild; suspicious of a coaxing hand.

After a few glasses of plum brandy I was ready to believe I could save this trapped soul. And so I wove with words my own philosophies on life. I spoke about that which we cannot see, that we are meant to see, even though the laws of his religion would forbid such things.

"Anyone can see there must be change," I said, "and it is our responsibility. We are ruled by fools."

"The ministers are doing the best they can," Shay said, somewhat too primly for my taste. "It is the people who are falling into decadence, not them."

Did he really believe that? "But can't you see the way people are manipulated? Yes, most of them are sheep who can't raise a bleat in protest, but in many ways they are innocent."

Shay snorted. "Some people spend too much time thinking and listening to their own voices, when they could be doing something useful. We are animals; we should live as animals do, and not in the way you're thinking right now. We should live our lives according to what is natural."

I wasn't completely sure what he meant by those words and in all honesty shrank from asking. I was sure the answer wouldn't please me. Instead, I put my head to one side and said: "Aren't you just the tiniest bit curious about what I do?"

He had taken drink too. "Actually, yes," he said. "I'm not sure I believe you can change the world, in any way, however big or small, but I'm curious about how you try."

"We could work magic," I said. "Are you brave enough?"

His responding laughter was nearly a coughing fit. "Brave enough? Is that a challenge?"

"It was you who said you didn't believe anything. What if I could prove to you that you *can* change reality through the power of your own will, and that it is the most natural thing in the world?"

He shrugged, grinned. "I'm open to having my mind changed."

I believed him.

And that was how our friendship began. At first, it was heady. When in his presence, I felt that together we would create miracles. There was power and huge potential inside him, plain to see. This appeared like flashes of starlight off moving water, almost too fleeting to glimpse, but when it did so, the light was amazing. It silenced me. Sometimes, when we were together, I would bring my work – poems or pictures – and when I was clawing my face in despair because I couldn't, just couldn't, get a detail right, and it threw off the whole work, Shay would just take a look at the piece. "Here," he would say, taking the charcoal from my hand. A few deft strokes later and there it was: the spirit of the picture brought to life. The same happened with words too, not just licks of pigment on a page. But when I suggested to him he should write or draw himself, he'd only laugh. "I can't," he'd say. "I'm not creative. I can simply offer ideas and solutions, that's all." He hadn't even tried. And why? I had no doubt this was because his mother would have considered such a thing fanciful and meaningless. He would be ashamed to be caught by her creating something beautiful with his own hands.

For Shay to lose himself in a life of Strixion – simply breeding, doing menial work, eating, sleeping and then dying, having achieved nothing – was obscene to me. It was up to me to fan the embers of his being into life. Surely, this was a vital task that had been put in my path. I took it very seriously.

My friends were not so enthusiastic. I let a few of them meet Shay a couple of times, but realised very quickly it was better to keep him apart from them until... until later. Theo, who never contains a thought if one pushes into her mouth, was most emphatic. "You're mad," she announced. "You really are. Why are you wasting time on that Strix? He's curious, yes, but there will come a point when he'll run from you. There is a line he will not cross. Don't get attached to him."

Dwine was not so caustic. I went to him for guidance and he listened to my impassioned description of Shay's potential without interrupting. Eventually I ran out of words and Dwine regarded me silently for some moments. Then he said, "If you feel you must pursue this path, then continue. There is always a lesson in everything we do."

As for what I showed Shay of magic, I opted for slow and gentle progress. We meditated together in places of beauty – the white stone fountain in the deserted Aurish quarter; the aspen copse on Sentinel's Tor outside the city; the Swan Pool in a corner of the City Park where no one ever goes. I tried to encourage visions within him, taking him upon guided journeys into fabulous landscapes. This was intended to open his mind to glorious possibilities. I think he enjoyed the experience but that was not really magic. After we meditated, we would drink watercress wine that we bought from a girl who made it herself, and who always sat at the gate to the park. Shay would come alive then. Even though we were so different, we discovered we were uncannily alike in many ways, saw humour in the same things.

We could only meet a couple of times a week, because Shay spent most of his time with his family, which was huge. He had duties and responsibilities at home, and his mother ruled him severely. I never met her, and never wanted to, but sometimes she was a third person at our meetings. There was a father, but he seemed to be like a ghost, a shadow, with hardly any presence at all. Shay rarely spoke of him. For all that Shay professed to be something of a rebel, it quickly became clear that in most ways he wasn't. Even if he claimed not to believe in the religion, he did believe in the narrow, restricted life he had been raised in and appeared to revere it. If the mother called, he ran, even if he had other arrangements planned. Once I listened, sickened, as he told me about the girl he would marry in several years' time and how he was looking forward to "settling down", as he put it. There would be no outside social meetings then, and he just accepted this as what should be. The girl was a clone of his mother, approved by her. He would run from one breast to another, without ever learning to feed himself. But still, he could not keep away from me and, I thought, was clearly fascinated by what I knew. I realised I had limited time in which to make him think for himself. I tried to make him aware of his own potential. He did not have to become a fully-fledged Nixie, but he could stand up for himself, do something different, have a rich life, both inwardly and outwardly. I did reach him to a certain degree. For a while, I think he too believed that together we could work to create positive change, even if this was only in our small corner of the world. Over the weeks I began to feel a certain impatience building within him and concluded the time was ripe to show him something more concrete. I told him this. "But first, we must establish a psychic link to enable us to work together properly."

He nodded, barely frowning. "Very well."

We were by the Swan Pool, because it had become our favourite place. The sounds of the city were muted there, as if we'd stepped out of time. The air smelled fresh, always with a hint of springtime, when all hope is renewed. "We must create a symbol," I said, "something that captures our very essences. This will bind us. We must sleep with it close by."

He agreed to this ritual act. Three nights later, we took parchment and the blackest of inks out to the Swan Pool, and beneath the light of a quarter moon and what seemed to be millions of stars, we created our symbol. Lines upon a page, some curling, some straight, delineating the essence of our friendship, the dreams we shared and those we might share in days to come. "Tonight, we will visit each others' dreams," I said. "Look out for symbols there. First we must call upon the Needles of Onyxx to empower our work. You know what they are?"

He shook his head. "No."

"They are servants of the Lady," I said. "But ruthless. They will serve us too, but it's important that they recognise you, so they do no harm." Something occurred to me then. "Shay…"

"What?" He was staring at our parchment, turning it in his hands to look at it in different ways.

"You must realise that through this act you will step upon the Path of Wyrd. You do understand that, don't you? If your eyes open to reality, if you ask for the Needles to work for you, that will be it. You won't be able to sleep again. By that, I mean you won't be a sleepwalker in life, not really *seeing* anything… the way… the way your church teaches you to be."

"I never was asleep," he said abruptly. "I've told you. It's not my church."

I sighed. "I don't think you get what I mean, but please just be aware this is a responsibility. There's no going back."

"Yes, I understand," he said, still looking at the parchment.

I dreamed we met in a garden. There were fruit trees on lawns, and snaking pathways of smooth slabs between them. It was winter time, very cold, everything rimed with frost. We sat on a bench together and I had a pile of papers on my knees, covered in scrawled writing, as if they were hastily scribbled notes. Despite the cold, my hands were fever-hot. I was trying to make Shay understand something; I can't remember what now.

He was speaking over me, not listening. "We can't do normal things," he was saying. "I can't take you to my home. You can't meet my relatives. That is what should happen."

"It doesn't matter," I said.

He looked at me sadly, said nothing.

"We haven't had this conversation yet, but we will," I assured him. "I can't be in your world, and perhaps you can't be fully in mine, but remember we can meet on a bridge."

"There's no bridge here," he said, but I could see that he was looking for one.

We met up the next day. For two people to have the same dream is no ordinary thing. I'm used to such occurrences, of course, but as I described what I had dreamed, I saw the colour drain from Shay's face before me. His dream, he told me, was not identical, but too similar for comfort. There had been a garden and a conversation, but he couldn't remember what about, only that it had made him feel strange. When I heard this, I was excited and pleased. It meant our experiment was working. He had stepped upon the Path and it had welcomed him. This should be the beginning of wonders.

I was too enthusiastic. "This is it!" I cried. "Shay, it's wonderful. There is so much we can do, so much we can try."

"It's difficult for me," he said, troubled, but at the time I was too elated to take any notice of that doubt.

I took his hands in mine, shook them. "Can't you see?" I pleaded. "Please see, Shay. Think about how you can be great. You can make your mark upon history. You don't just have to live a cipher of a life. I can really feel it. Stand up! Own your power. Together, we can achieve anything. Don't you realise what we have achieved? But it's only the first step."

He pulled his hands from my grasp roughly. "My life means so little to you, doesn't it?" he raged. "You despise it. You think you're better than I am. But I want my life. I don't want to change it."

I was confused. "But Shay," I said gently, "you said you wanted to see what I did, and I showed you. You did it willingly. Everyone wants to better themselves, don't they? I have great faith in you. You're not supposed to have a little life doing exactly what your parents did. There is more to life, much more."

But for Shay this was not the same as it was for me. He hadn't expected our dream experiment to work. I couldn't see this at first. I thought I had allayed his doubts, assured him I only had his greater good in mind. Yes, I did despise his life and was convinced that he could achieve so much more than what his mother had planned for him. What I didn't account for was the strength of blood.

He didn't say anything further on the subject to me but, from that moment on, things changed. A few days later he informed me that he was very busy with family commitments and our meetings would have to be less frequent from now on. I took this badly, even though he assured me it wasn't personal. We still met, but whenever I suggested carefully that we do some more work, he would change the subject, deftly start talking about something else I was passionate about – a new picture, a destitute girl I'd seen dying on the street, the colour of the sky. I sensed a distance in him, sensed he was slipping away from me, even though at the same time we were drawing closer. We hardly ever touched, but when we were together an energy fizzed between us that could have illuminated the grandest summer fair. It was like the building of a sea storm, rolling inexorably to land. I could feel his moods even when we were apart, and thought that perhaps he experienced the same. If only we could direct this power towards a particular goal, I was sure we would achieve amazing results. But I suppose I was a relentless cudgel, crashing into the walls of his sanctuary, smashing and destroying, when I should have been a slow moving river, slowly eroding the bricks away. If only I could have communicated my feelings, mind to mind. But we were not that much in tune and words were not enough. To follow my way of life, to whatever small degree, would mean he'd have to disobey his mother, change his future. Cenaggara had challenged him, perhaps. There was a fork in the road. One way was certain; the other, while more exciting, was fraught with danger.

One day, the owls lifted from the towers of the city where they had roosted for so long and, to the astonishment of onlookers in the area, threw themselves as one into the river. They made no sound and did not struggle with the water. They merely floated as a sad sodden mass towards the sea.

Shay did not come to our meeting that night. I waited alone at a toddy booth on the Swan's Neck Bridge, watching a scum of feathers bobbing about the bridge supports where they met the water. I knew he would not come. I felt it in my heart. I was surprised by the pain and realised, too late, that I loved him. I took from my throat the cheap necklace he had bought me. The metal had dyed my skin black and now the swans themselves were blackened and tarnished. Without thinking, I threw the necklace into the river, far out.

Shay sent me a note some days later. "I'm sorry," it read. "I'm not the person you thought I was. Don't try to contact me. It's best this way. Goodbye."

I held the note in my hands, absorbing the essence of Shay that lingered in it. I felt his confusion, his desire to take up the challenge, and also his fear and conditioning, which were iron bars that broke his limbs so he could not run. I realised that all this time, as we had drawn closer, bound by what I had thought was magic, he had felt uncomfortable but had not said so. It had not been the magic that had kept him coming, but me, our friendship. And now all that I was had come between us. There was no bridge.

Our parting tortured me. I felt as if some vital organ had been wrenched from my body. I hope never to feel that agony again. It's been over a year now, yet still the wounds will prick me sometimes; scars from a battle I did not win. I wondered how he felt, convinced the wrenching must be similar for him, but he had clung to what was safe. This had made him strong enough not to give in, to contact me. I waited for so long, stood on that bridge so many times at sunset. But he did not come.

Dwine, as ever my comforter, told me, "Yes, you and Shay were a destiny. That's why you feel you are being pulled apart. But Shay wasn't ready for it. There is plenty of time, many lifetimes." He paused, touched my face. "Just not this one. I'm sorry."

Someone called me in my sleep last night. It was a call over space and time, a scream into darkness. This was his voice: I was certain. It woke me up and I sat panting in the bed. There were no echoes in the room around me, but an echo in my head rebounded through eternal abysses. When you step upon the path there is no going back, and to walk that path alone with no guidance or experience is a terrible thing. Cenaggara had given Shay a destiny; we were meant to meet. I think now it was only that, and the magic had been secondary. He and I ourselves were magical. But he'd been afraid. What he'd felt and experienced had compromised his heartfelt beliefs, his whole being. Where did I fit into the world of what his mother desired for him, and the faceless girl who already had her mark upon him? I wish he'd spoken of this. Instead, he had remained silent and thought he could retreat back into his narrow life to lick the wounds an inconvenient love had inflicted upon him, but now he was discovering that he couldn't. He would never speak of it, but there would be Needles upon his path, for ever. As his life closed over him, that tiny box, he would lock a madness in there with him. Owls into the river. Drowned wings.

I still have a copy of the symbol we created, in a drawer of the small cupboard next to my bed. Now, with cold fingers, I take it out and look upon it. Did we weave pain into that design? I don't know. I light a candle with a dull ember from the grate. "Cenaggara, be merciful." My words are a steam upon the air.

I hold the scrap of paper as it burns in the candle flame, hold it until my fingers hurt, as I would the hands of someone dying, someone holding me too fast, but inexorably fading away.

Storm Constantine is one of the most respected figures in fantasy fiction. Her career as a writer began in the 1980s with the acclaimed Wraeththu trilogy, a series about a mystical post-human race of androgynous hermaphrodites coming to terms with themselves and their new world. Storm has now written more than thirty books in various genres, including several volumes of non-fiction. In 2003 she established Immanion Press, initially to publish her own back-catalogue, but the venture has rapidly expanded and now boasts an impressive catalogue containing both new work and old, by established authors and exciting new arrivals.

Seaborne

Kari Sperring

Sometimes, the tide left dead men for her on the strand. It was her sole companion, the tide, sealing off her point from the curious, dropping broken gifts for her on the shore. The wolves might have found her long ago without the treacherous, daring tide. There was no friendship between them, exactly, but there *was* something. She needed the tide.

The new man arrived one dusk. She came dancing heedless and trackless across the sand, so that her feet were the first to find him. He lay caught up heavy amidst the sea-wrack and tumble, hair dirty with grit, clothes torn, one hand flung out before him. His skin was no colour she had seen before. His eyes were closed. She liked that. It made her afraid when drowned men looked at her. Their minds were too open, eager to tangle her down to fill their own empty insides.

This man was different. His mind was full of the sea. A still greenness enveloped him, shadowed by the memory of wave-sound. It washed over her, taking nothing away, tickling a little, like the sand between her toes.

She squatted beside him to watch the water trickling from his hair. Soaked as it was, she could not be sure of its colour. Perhaps he would still be here when the sun rose and it would have a chance to dry. Perhaps the tide, having displayed him, would tug him back to itself. She didn't know. She just liked to look. She had not known that skin might be the colour of tree-bark. Her own skin was moonlight and cobweb. All the dead men before this had worn the sea under their skins: white turned to green and liable to darken at a touch. When she laid a light finger on this man's palm, his colour did not change.

His hand was cold and firm. She touched it again, and his dead fingers moved. She recoiled, crab-bitten. There was a pause. His fingers moved again. She waited. The man's head rolled a little to one side and he coughed. Water bubbled between his lips. A strange clawing sound came from his throat. His head jerked once as if he would lift it, then fell back. The sound increased. Her feet wanted to run away. But her eyes and her mind held her. And her rash wild hands reached out to the man and pushed him, hard. He rolled under them onto his side and the water escaped from his mouth. He coughed and heaved and lay still again. Then his eyes opened. They were dark, like his drenched hair and they were not the eyes of a dead man.

They looked at her, square.

The tide had left her a living man. She had reason to fear the living. The living should in no wise be able to set eyes upon her. Yet this tide-driven man could see her. She turned to run. Soon or late, the tide would return and take him back. The man coughed again and said a word she did not know. His vagabond hand raised a scant inch from the sand. He said, still echoing the sea, "Please..."

His voice was as strange to her as the colour of his skin. It hooked onto her, holding her from flight. She trembled. His hand fell back, limp and dirty. His mouth twitched faintly as if he tried to smile. He did not look like a wolf.

She might leave him here to take his chances with the tide. She had no use for the living, out here on her point.

The tide had never left her anything remotely this troublesome before. His eyes closed again. Sand clung to him: there were stains on his wrecked garments. He did not look as though he might become a threat. She was not used to having to decide. It had been long and long since she had had any dealings with any creature save herself and the winds and the tide. The water from his hair made narrow braids in the sand. He was still.

She chose. Her hands had moved him once: they might do so again. Besides, she liked to look at him. Her hands rolled and tugged him up the beach, to a place where the tide would not reach high enough to pull him away. He did not move himself again. He made no sounds.

She sat beside his still form all through the night.

Sunrise drove her from the beach. When dusk drew her back, the man was no longer where she had left him. She looked at the dry sand. No sign there that the sea had exerted itself to steal him back. The sand was mussed and marred where his body had lain. An irregular pattern of tracks trailed away, bordering the beach. She followed them edgewise, aware of the gravelling tide. She did not often wander so far from the point and its guardian shelves. The man had been looking for something. Her nervous feet felt that, a vague warm questioning. They drew her into the rock-tumbled, wire-grass bounds, where the sand lay thick and dirty out along the curving rim of the bay. The grass did not know her, whispering to itself of her passing. The sand was sluggish and dull. It told her no tales. The sky above was overcast, no stars, no hint of either moon. It left her thin, skittish, world-shy. She gathered shadow about her to bring fear upon this man who had come to litter her point, her shore, with his living bones.

He had made his way along almost two-thirds of the bay to where water slipped and curved from the land to be absorbed in the sea. It made no sense to her. He had escaped water. Why choose to seek it out again? The living defied all rules. Her shadows clung tighter. She could see that the man had come to rest alongside the little water, limbs drawn up, back to a fallen boulder. Her feet halted, holding her just outside his range of sight. The last of the sea had been driven out of his hair by the day. It had dried lighter than his skin, hung clumped and salt-dusted to his shoulders. Like his skin, his hair held a colour she had not known that the living attained.

The shadows wanted to move. Her eyes counselled caution. Caught between impulses, she swayed, alarmed. His head lifted from his knees, turned itself toward her. She gathered her comforting shadows tight, ready to defend. The living had no place here. The living should flee from her and her shadows. The man peered carefully into the gloom, eyes a little narrowed. He said something which she could not shape. Then he shook his head, and said, in his voice which was unlike her voice, unlike the voices of the sand and the tide and the dead, "Hello. Please don't be frightened." The words were clumsy, as though their form eluded him. Her feet trembled on the sand. He straightened up and continued, "I saw you before. Thank you for helping me." And his lips made the form of a smile.

29

Long and long since anything had smiled at her. The shadows slipped from her shoulders. He was not afraid. Some darting thing behind her eyes drew her forward, wanting to know more. Two steps, five, then a halt. She crouched down a few paces away from him, and watched. He was calm and still. His thoughts eluded her, smooth and slippery as small fish. He was not afraid. The living were always afraid.

His voice was gentle. "I remembered a child... I'm not quite right, am I? I think you belong here." She was filling with silence. One of her hands pressed to her mouth, holding the silence inside. The man said "I don't want to disturb you. But I don't think I'm strong enough to leave."

The silence was too big. Her lips parted as it escaped. No thoughts to steal. She had the words only of the drowned. One rose up inside her. "Who?" Such a little sound. It hurt her, breaking free.

He made the smile again. "Thierry," he said. "I was travelling on a ship, but there was a storm. As if the sea wanted to board us... I was caught by it and pulled overboard." The smile died. "I suppose the others think me drowned." A shadow floated over the shape of him. She shivered. "I'm sorry," he said. "I don't belong in your place."

She did not understand. He had no business seeing her and knowing no fear. The wolves... The wolves would rend her apart. His name was no help to her. She used it on her tongue, to discover if taste might provide meaning. "Thierry."

"That's right," he said, nodding. And then, "Do you have a name?"

The wolves would take made names and use them to attack. She would vanish into their mouths. Her feet gathered her to run. Her body bundled her backwards.

The man's eyes widened. He said, "No, I'm sorry. Don't go. I won't hurt you. I was wrong to ask."

Her feet did not trust him, aching to flee. Her mind counselled more study. She hesitated. He said, "I should have known better. My friend Gracielis says that names have power. I knew someone else like you, long ago."

Another? She had not known that there could be another like her. She could not hold the notion: another point, another her. There was this beach, this point, this sand, the tide, and herself. This living man. The sea and the sand had never spoken to her of another her. She was afraid. She did not feel big enough for there to be two of her.

The man uncurled. His long limbs looked clumsy. She drew back. The dead had always lain down. She was unaccustomed to the idea of height, of living men like trees. "I thought", he said, "I'd look for driftwood." His mouth twisted in a way that was not a smile. "I'm not sure if I know how to start a fire, but it's a bit too early to give up."

Driftwood belonged to the sea. The sea had caught him once, and might again. The sea was a miser. She came to her feet. Her hands had control, pulling her forward, pushing at the man, away from the sea. He stepped back obediently, but his brows came down. He said, "I'm cold and I'm hungry. Don't you remember that?"

She knew cold. Cold came from the sky, on the air across the sea, lashing waves into anger, driving out birds, uprooting grasses. Cold whistled through her, under her borders, tugging and testing. She did not like to be cold. She did not know 'remember'. She was cold or she was not cold. She did not know 'hunger'. The sound had claws, like the claws with which the tide stole things. Sometimes the sea lay calm and still, hiding its claws. She looked at the man. There was a stillness in him which might hide anything. The sea took what it would and devoured it. The wolves swallowed everything they found. Fear formed between her eyes and trickled down her spine towards her feet. When it reached them, she turned and ran.

For a night and another night she did not go near the man. If the living felt cold and hunger, then perhaps they might be destroyed by them. The man might be easier to encounter dead. She held to her point, to the strand and the black shale. The tide brought her wood and weed and fragments of cloth. The beach was wiped clear each day of change. The two waters, salt and sweet, swept it clean. For a night and another night, she was dancing feet and moonlight.

On the night after those, the sea came in high over the edges of the point, teasing the dunes and their grasses, holding her back to the place which was less beach than land. In the dry sand of the dunes,

31

the wind brought her intimations of flame. Long and long since she had last known fire. The thing behind her eyes remembered heat, searing bright light from the sky and the sad grasses burning. Fire did not belong. She tracked it, careful, along the curve of the beach into the deep dunes. The fire had made its home in a hollow, well out of reach of the tide, sheltered from the wind. It was a small fire, constricted by a collar of stones and given more to smoke than flame. The man crouched beside it, feeding it driftwood. She halted on the rim of the hollow. He made the smile at her. "The wood is rather damp," he said, "that makes it smoke." She liked his tone. It told her he recognised her right to explanation. He said "Are you cold? Come and join me."

She was not cold. There was not enough anger in the sea and the wind to chill her. Her head shook itself, once, twice, but her feet led her down anyway into the hollow.

"The problem is," he said, "that I have to stay awake to feed the fire or it goes out. And it's a terrible trouble to re-light." He made a hunching gesture with his shoulders. "I don't think I'm making a very good job of being a castaway. I don't know how to fish or set snares and I don't know what's safe to eat and what isn't." He shivered. "The seaweed tastes bad, but I don't think it's killing me." He looked at her. "I don't suppose you know anything about that?"

His skin was changing its colour; his eyes seemed duller. An air clung to him, reminiscent of the dead. He was cold still, despite his fire: she could hear the murmur of it in his bones. And there was another thing, set deeper, a growling need like the tide's demand, which grew and grew. This, perhaps, was hunger. The sea took indiscriminately to feed itself. She knew nothing about the feeding needs of the living.

He was not a wolf. He had no interest in her. His surface thoughts were open to her, supplying images she did not understand. Bread and meat and wine. Perhaps the sea would bring these things, leave them awhile in the wake of its rage.

She watched him. He did not seem to mind although he spoke little. In a while, the driftwood fell from his hands and he passed into a state of unwakefulness. She rose and tracked out of the dunes. The sea had drawn back down to the rocks. The beach was littered with prizes, wood and weed and the broken pieces of creatures. She gathered without selection and left her gleanings in the dunes. The man did not wake. His fire had died. A little before sunrise, she dropped some of the new wood into the ashes and told it to ignite.

When the sun rose, the man woke and found her gifts. She watched him use them before approaching. He raised his head. "Thank you." He looked rather better than the night before. "The fish were good. And the wood..." He gave her another smile. "Perhaps there's something I can do for you?" That made no sense. She had no use for the living. He said, "No? I'm sorry. Well, perhaps we'll think of something." She was puzzled. She did not know 'we'. It shaped to mean the man and her, but that could not be so. She was herself. She did not belong with anything aside from her point. She did not belong with the living. The man said, "Did you know there are rock pools at low tide?" Her head assented. "They're pretty," he said. "I almost caught a fish. I thought I'd try again tomorrow." She had changed something, giving him what the tide had left her: she had given him energy. She did not know if she had ever given to anything before. She had put a change in her point, in herself. Perhaps that was this 'we'. She had put a hand to wet wood, and told it to burn. She had put a hand to the sea's leavings, and turned them to food.

She had made the man continue living. When she rose to walk with him along the beach, she stood a little taller than before.

A night, and a night, and more beyond those. One moon reached full and turned the sea wild and silver. The other dwindled into blackness. She touched what the tide left and made it change. The man – her man – grew strong. He talked to her about places which were not the point, not the beach, not the sea; about fields of trees, mounds of rock and earth higher than the dunes and coated in grass denser and tougher than any she knew. He told her of great stone places thronged with the living, shaped into houses and streets and halls, huge words she could not hold inside. And as she changed things and heard things, she grew. A dim flush of colour crept through her, starting in her bold feet. Something inside her began to stretch, to explore beyond itself, beyond the confines of the point. She was learning to be bigger. She had grown too big to be able, any more, to feel finely everything within her old world of sea and rock and sand. Her ears filled up with the man and his words. She no longer listened so hard to her point.

On a night of two crescent moons, a wolf came down to the sea. The sand thrilled under her feet as she danced along the strand. The wind tugged and twisted at her, snarling in hair now grown heavy and glossy and brown. The sea cursed and threatened, filling her footsteps. She paused to heed none of them. She danced along the shore, across the rocks, on to the edge of the dunes, to her warm living man and his fire. The sand weighed her down and she flashed anger to it. The wind threw dust in her eyes. The sea growled, too distant to do more. From beside his fire, the man waved. She ran forward, into the dull sand of the dunes.

She ran into the wolf.

He was a young wolf, still very akin to a living man. He had no very great height. His skin was as pale as hers had been. His long hair was dark in the darkness. He had eyes like stone. Passing overhead, the wind called alarm. But the underfoot sand was silent. The wolf looked at her. She grew still.

The man, her man, rose from his place by the fire. He said, "What are you doing? Don't hurt her, Gracielis."

The wolf did not take his gaze from her. His voice hurt, going under the layers and layers of change. Such a soft voice, to have such teeth. The wolf said, "Do you know what this creature is, Thierry?"

"She helped me," the man said, building walls with his tone. "She pulled me from the sea. She brought me driftwood and food."

"Doubtless," said the wolf. "But I asked what she is, not what she has done."

"I don't know," the man said. "I suppose she's a ghost of some kind."

"Ghosts," said the wolf, "don't grow up." His eyes held her motionless. He continued, "Look at it, Thierry. It looks like you. Don't tell me it had this shape when you first saw it." The man was silent. The wolf said, "It isn't human."

"Neither are you," said the man.

"No," said the wolf. His stone eyes gripped her. His voice turned attention wholly upon her. Despite the hard grasp of his eyes, she trembled. "What makes a wolf?" he asked her. "Do you know?" The man took a step forward; the wolf held up a hand. The wolf said to her, "I am born of your kind. When your kind grow too closely akin to a human, learn love, learn desire..." He pointed to the man. "Lie with him, and you make my kind. Would you like that? Are you big enough, yet, to understand?"

She did not understand. She could not hear the sea or reach the wind. Under her feet, the sand admitted more of the wolf than of her. She felt fear, sharp bursts of it along her new long limbs, constricting her. If the wolf looked at her for long enough, she would shrink back to nothing.

She did not know desire. She knew that she wanted to go to the man for shelter.

The man stepped round the fire. His shadow fell across her. She shivered. The man said, carefully, "Gracielis, don't. She hasn't hurt me."

"Yet," said the wolf.

"I would be dead," the man said, "if she hadn't helped me. Do you understand that?"

"I understand death," said the wolf.

The man said "She's done no harm."

"I know." The wolf smiled. His smile was unlike all the smiles of the man. It was full of knowing, full of the things which ran through the land, which held together rock and sand, which held her together. His smile knew her, all of her, and made her less than she had been. Her skin was cold. The wolf said, "You're the one that's done the harm. Look at it, Thierry."

The man's gaze turned to her. The wolf said, "It's not meant to be human. It has a place. It has a role; it exists and that's all it should do. You've confused it. You've pulled it out of shape." The soft, wounding voice turned gentle, so that the pain grew all the sweeter. "What is it now? Not what it should be. Not human, either. It's power, only power, and it'll give you anything you want, if you can only teach it to understand. You're the danger, my heart."

"If I am," said the man, "why hurt her?" The wolf was silent. "Let her go," said the man.

"I can't," the wolf said. Under her feet, the dull sand shivered. The fear ran through her, leeching strength from fingers and eyes and hands. She shook. She could not hold onto herself. She could call no shadows. She was bleeding away through the sand.

"Don't," said the man. "Please don't. I can leave. We can both just go. What harm does that do?" She shaped 'leave', felt herself shrivel, felt the first breath of emptiness. Spaces opened up inside her, black and clawing like the tide. There was nothing to fill them. The man said, "I'm begging you. Don't hurt her."

The wolf turned his head. The stone eyes released her, boneless and shivering, onto the sand. It made no sound, receiving her. It was not hers. The wolf said, "Don't you understand? You've changed it. You'll leave it with nothing." His voice cut slivers from her, buried them under the sand. She curled about herself, bold hands hiding eyes, legs drawn up, body awash with fear.

The man said, "Can't you put her back to what she was?"

The wolf laughed. Her hands filled with the sand, seeking denied comfort. The wolf said, "You know I can't. I can't heal. I only destroy."

"Don't," said the man.

There was a silence. In her dry fingers, the sand lay heavy. The sea whispered. The man said, softly, "Just take me away from here. Don't hurt her."

"Thierry," the wolf said, and the word tripped his voice. "Thierry, I'm not causing the pain."

"I don't understand," said the man, and the words lifted her head, brushing it with a pain outside herself. Water streaked the man's face, water with the same salt shape as the sea.

She had drawn him from the sea and the sea was still within him. The sea was everywhere, stripping everything away. Soft and soft, she filled her hands with the sand. The wolf stepped away from her and held out his hands to the man.

"Hush," he said, and his words excluded her utterly. "Hush, then, love. We'll leave."

His hands took the man, drew him close, hid his face, hid the murmur of his thoughts. The sand trickled behind them, wiping away their footprints, out of the dunes, onto the strand. She could not stand. On sore palms and knees, she pulled herself after them, hampered by the sand. They outstripped her with ease. On the edge of the sea was a sound wooden boat. They stepped into it and the tide drew them away. She could not follow. The waves moved in and became a barrier.

The tide had brought the man. The tide had taken him back. She lay down on the sand for the tide to take her also.

Kari Sperring grew up dreaming of joining the musketeers and saving France, only to discover that the company had been disbanded in 1776. Disappointed, she became a historian instead and has published several books on mediaeval Britain (as Kari Maund) as well as one on the musketeers (with Phil Nanson). She is mostly Welsh, but lives in Cambridge, England, where she writes fiction and non-fiction, works for a very exciting tax specialist and fends off cats. 'Seabourne' is her third published short story, while her first novel, *Living with Ghosts*, is due to be published shortly by DAW books.

And Their Blood Will be Prescient to Fire

Freda Warrington

Violette: she is the Death Lily. Her eyes blaze violet, drawing you in with the light of forbidden wisdom. Her midnight hair and glacial skin leave you wrecked upon the rocks. I love her. I would give my life to meet her. Off-stage she wears silver and lilac and black diamonds and that is her: soft as silk, hard as gemstones.

She is the mysterious celebrity in the shadows. Fêted, celebrated, unknown. The latest in a family tree of prima ballerinas called Violette, Juliette or Mistanguette Lenoir; when one fades, another young protégée steps into the white satin shoes. For seventy years this has continued. No one realises, since it's impossible, that they're all the same woman. But I worked it out. I know her secret.

I've loved her all my life. I have collected every old book, every press cutting, taped all the arts programmes. I've travelled to every performance I could afford – and those I couldn't. Violette is an expensive obsession. From the audience I watch her create her bright world of enchantment and I fantasize that she is dancing just for me.

In reality she would never notice me: a small, skinny nobody. In our family, the looks, height and charisma passed me by. Not in her immortal life would she ever look at someone like me.

And yet, I heard she fell. It burns me even to say this. She fell for my sister.

"It's a dessert wine," said Charlotte. "Try it."

She slid a dewed glass across the darkly varnished table. Within, liquid shimmered straw-gold. Violette stared suspiciously.

"What the hell is this?" She looked ragged tonight, Charlotte thought; black hair a bird's nest, toned body airbrushed into black jeans and purple tie-dyed cotton. Around them stretched the anonymous semi-darkness of a bar in the basement of a large hotel.

Freda Warrington

Low music, murmuring voices, Tiffany shades glowing in the dark.

"Muscat with a twist," said Charlotte.

"We don't drink wine." Her smile was sardonic, dangerous.

"A little something created by our good friend Stefan. He thinks it's a bore to sit in a bar and not drink along with humans. Think of it as protective colouration."

"Blood tastes like the finest wine," said Violette. "Actual liquor, however, tastes like bleach with a dash of battery acid. If you think I'm putting that to my lips, you're out of your mind."

"That's what I said, but…" Charlotte took a mouthful, to show it was safe. A burst of familiar nectar, laced with spice and a fiery afterglow. Violette took the smallest, hesitant taste, held it in her mouth, swallowed with the shudder of a human sampling his first raw oyster. Her compelling eyes opened wide.

"It's wonderful. What is it?"

"Plasma, fermented with herbs and other ingredients according to Stefan's secret recipe. He's been working on it for a while."

"Why?"

Charlotte shrugged. "For the pleasure of immortals." She felt heat swimming in her head. A pleasant feeling, but strange; alcohol from human veins only induced a flat headache.

"It tastes…" Violette frowned, turning the glass between elegant fingertips. "Intoxicating."

"I believe that is the idea." Charlotte smiled.

"Stefan is the devil."

"He really is," said Charlotte, amused. "He loves to put humans in thrall, often using more than his own charm. Opium was a favourite, in the old days. Perhaps he's found an addiction for us, too. I wouldn't put anything past him."

"So, are you trying to get me drunk?" Violette was sweet and sharp at the same time. In these unpredictable moods she could tip into playfulness or fury.

"No. To relax."

"Only, the last time you got me drunk, I passed out human and woke up crazed vampire goddess. What was it you used?" Violette tipped her face sweetly towards Charlotte. "Laudanum?"

"That was years ago." Shocked, Charlotte drew back. She ran her fingers up and down the stem of her glass. "Surely you've forgiven

40

me by now."

"Forgiven, yes, but not forgotten." The teasing edge to Violette's voice sounded dangerous. "I never forget anything."

"All right, what's wrong? Whenever you're upset, you play games."

"Nothing, sweetheart." Violette reached out and stroked the tender skin of Charlotte's forearm, where it lay relaxed on the table. Her hand strayed upwards, over the silk and lace of Charlotte's old-fashioned dress, caressing the bronze and gold fabrics. These days, if Charlotte wanted to be pre-Raphaelite and Violette a Goth chick, no one noticed any more. "Boston gets to me."

"Yes. Sorry. I know."

"I'm restless," the dancer went on. "Danced my feet off for weeks, one city after another. Endless receptions, after-show parties, press calls. Always on my best behaviour." She smiled, suddenly looking endearingly tired and human. "I can't be the great Lenoir all the time. The demon-goddess part really ticks me off as well. I needed to be in a different world, where no one knows or cares who I am."

Charlotte flicked a glance at the ceiling. "Hence we leave a perfectly good hotel and end up in another with a huge business conference upstairs?"

"Different world." Violette sipped her wine. "They wouldn't know the ballet from their arses. I want to be among strangers who are not fascinated by my every move. It makes for better hunting."

Charlotte glanced around at other tables and became aware of guarded but intense male attention.

"You can't escape. There are drink-sodden businessmen ogling us."

"Eugh," said Violette. "I've lost my appetite."

"Perhaps they think we're lovers," said Charlotte.

Violette leaned in and kissed her on the mouth. Charlotte tasted Stefan's wicked nectar on her lips. "Are we?" Violette whispered.

The unanswerable question. "I worship you. You know that."

"I know the love that made you turn me, Charlotte. I raged and hated you for it, until I understood that you only made me become myself. Don't keep fishing for absolution. You love someone else, and my nature is solitary." The dancer sat back, her dark tone lightening. "They're looking at you, not me, dear. The voluptuous one, hair shining all shades of gold. Sometimes it's fun to have sex with your supper. Is there nothing to tempt you?"

Charlotte surveyed the bar. Amid an ocean of trolls, she saw one tempting blond young man in a fall of light. He caught her eye in startled fascination. She looked away.

"Nothing."

"Liar, liar."

Then the woman walked past. A conference delegate, neat in a grey tight-waisted suit, name badge on the lapel, leather folder under her arm. Passing their table, she bumped into an empty chair and dropped the folder. The table shook, spilling wine. Papers fanned out on the carpet. Swearing, she bent down to collect them up. As she did so, the mass of her long chestnut-brown hair fell forward across her face.

Quick as a snake, Violette was down there helping her. And as the woman rose, pushing back the glorious hair, Charlotte saw her face, heard the precise upper-class-Boston accent.

"I'm sorry… thanks so much… that was really clumsy of me… oh no, did I spill your drinks? I'm so sorry."

"That's all right," Violette said softly. "Only a drop, it's fine."

Her hands, giving back stray papers, brushed the woman's.

"Oh, you're British, right?" said the stranger. Violette inclined her head. "Well, have a nice evening."

She went on her way, her step quick and business-like in high heels, luscious hair swinging against her back. Violette's face was frozen, her lips parted. All her languid teasing sarcasm had vanished. She looked nakedly shocked.

"That was Robyn," she said.

"No, it wasn't," Charlotte gasped. She'd seen the resemblance, but Violette's reaction alarmed her. "I know it looked like her, but… Violette, it wasn't."

"Yes," the dancer whispered. "It's her, it's Robyn."

Robyn. Seventy years dead. Violette, who thought she couldn't love, had loved her. Perhaps she'd come close with others since, but Robyn was the ruby set in her heart. A glorious courtesan defying

Boston's high society; a wounded soul, beautiful, warm and funny. The miracle was that Robyn had wanted her too. But Violette had turned her away. *Robyn, if I let you come with me... I will destroy you.*

It had seemed the right decision at the time. Even with the prescience of a goddess, how could she have known that Robyn would die at the hands of another vampire? The joke was that he'd loved too. He'd been trying to transform her. But Robyn hadn't wanted to become a cold crystalline shell feeding on the living. The transformation failed because Robyn chose to stay human. She chose death.

Violette was hardly aware of her surroundings. She could only see Robyn's face, smell her hair. Charlotte's voice startled her.

"Where are you going?"

"To speak to her."

Charlotte's hand shot out and circled her upper arm. "Don't."

"Do you think a day goes by that I haven't longed to find her again?" Violette hissed. "Let me go."

Too much liquid swam in Charlotte's eyes. Fear, jealousy. "Violette, it isn't Robyn."

The dancer plucked Charlotte's hand off her arm and pushed it away. "Let me go. Whoever she is, at least let me look at her face again for a few minutes."

The main lobby of the hotel was bright, sparkling with huge chandeliers. From the marshmallow comfort of a sofa, Violette watched the woman pacing, talking into a mobile phone, high heels clicking on the marble floor. At last she ended the conversation, turned and saw Violette.

"Hi again," she said, about to walk straight past. Violette sat forward and made brazen eye contact, her posture demanding conversation. With those brilliant kohl-ringed eyes she could convey emotion to the back of the stalls. The effect on the woman was virtually physical. She halted, bemused as if Violette had tripped her.

"Hi," said Violette. "Is your evening going as well as mine?"

"Oh, my dinner date stood me up. Migraine, sure; too many brandies at lunch is more like it."

"Same here," said Violette. "That is, my friend was called away. Ordered this bottle, and now no one to drink it with." She indicated

Stefan's demon-brew, which she'd seized and brought with her. The thick green glass of the bottle glistened. There were two fresh glasses beside it. "I'd love it if you'd help me out."

Despite the cool poise of her exterior, Violette was trembling inwardly like a teenager. Her approach felt inane and desperate. The desire to keep this gorgeous, distracted stranger beside her was turning her into a fool.

"Oh, sure, why not." The woman flopped down, stretching stockinged calves. She took out a palmtop computer and began tapping at it, at the same time trying to keep the folder from sliding off her knee. Violette, hypnotised, watched Robyn's warm face with its mischievous dark eyes, Robyn's unruly thick hair falling forward and being pushed back. "It's such a damn nuisance… hope the guy's okay for a working breakfast… Oh, and my sister's picking me up at nine… Damn, I need to email Mark; that's my husband…"

Violette had a vision of breaking into a strange house and sucking the life from a faceless man. No more husband. She poured syrupy straw-gold plasma into the woman's glass.

"What do you do?" she asked softly.

"What? Oh, pharmaceutical company. Really dull." The woman flipped the palmtop shut and into her purse. "Sorry, I'm not normally this rude. You so don't look part of the convention, and you'll turn out to be head of some huge corporation and I'll have blown a billion-dollar deal."

"Relax. I'm not."

"I'm Ruth Sarandon." She reached out and shook hands, her fingers warm in Violette's cold ones.

"I read the name tag."

"You're not wearing one," said Ruth. She took the glass. There was no sign of Robyn's calm, sensual personality beneath the brittle energy.

"I'm Violette." She didn't think to offer a false name.

"Well, cheers, Violette." The dancer watched as Ruth-Robyn took a mouthful of blood plasma. She swallowed hard, eyes watering. "Wow, that's different. Kind of bitter, like an aperitif. Not bad." She turned the bottle, holding it by the neck. "No label. That's scary."

"It peeled off. Condensation." Usually Violette dealt in the truth. Tonight it felt all too easy to spill one lie after another. The spiked blood made her unguarded and she was floating in a dream where all that mattered was what she wanted.

"So, what brings you to Boston?" Ruth asked. She took large mouthfuls of her drink, shuddering a little with each one. Violette looked at the chestnut hair lying against her throat.

"Oh... working trip," she began, but Ruth sat forward, speaking over her.

"You know, you look incredibly familiar. Did you say your name was Violette? Are you a ballet dancer?"

Violette bit her lip, cursing inwardly. She felt the magic bleeding away. The chatter of people in the lobby became deafening. She shrugged, gave a self-effacing smile. "I'm off-duty."

"You're *the* Violette Lenoir, right?" Ruth put down her drink and clapped her hands. "Oh, my God, my little sister worships you. She will *die* if she knows I met you."

Violette's eyes widened. She had an image of a small girl, like a child in an Edward Gorey cartoon, literally expiring in the face of her big sister's news. Meanwhile Ruth's chatter went on: "I say little; Sarah's twenty-three. Oh, her room's a shrine, she has every one of your ballets on DVD, she truly spends every cent of her wages on you..." and Violette sat transfixed by dismay. This was the last thing she wanted. She wanted Robyn, the wordless bliss of finding each other again. Not the inane flutter of a stranger. She wanted Robyn so badly the feeling pushed tears into her eyes.

She drank down the herb-fragrant blood. It gelled inside her like disappointment. She let the words wash over her until she couldn't hear them any more. The world was buzzing madly around her, speeded up in time while she sat utterly still. No longer seeing the babbling woman there, only seeing Robyn.

She became aware that Ruth had stopped and was staring uneasily at her. "So – I guess an autograph's out of the question? For Sarah, not me."

"Forgive me." Violette's attempt at graciousness sounded wooden. "It's wonderful that your sister... To know my work's not in vain."

"I'm sorry," said Ruth. "You must get this all the time. Another gushing idiot, and here you are trying to relax. I'll stop."

Her voice had an edge suggesting disapproval of stars who

weren't meltingly grateful to their fans. Violette didn't care. She leaned into the sofa, her body turned towards Ruth's, one hand supporting her head and the other resting lightly on her hip.

"Actually, I'm trying to pick you up," Violette said coolly, not blinking. "Can we please go to your room before everyone in this bloody hotel recognises me?"

The narcotic wine dissolved boundaries. It blurred the room into a cocoon of gold, softened edges, intensified feelings, elongated time. They were falling in through the door, kissing. Violette twirled away, peeling the t-shirt over her head; her small breasts were bare beneath. How wonderfully strong and arched her feet were, stepping out of jeans and a tiny violet thong. Ruth followed, mesmerised by the slender body, lily-white as if the sun had never touched it. The sable triangle, black as her hair. Now Violette was kneeling in the centre of the bed with Ruth perched on the edge, languorous but uncertain; the dancer leaning forward, turning her so their mouths met.

Ivory fingertips worked at Ruth's buttons. Her skirt and jacket with their satin linings slid easily to the floor. Cool hands moved onto her naked flesh, sliding beneath her underwear, impatient to remove it. Dancer's hands, smooth yet unbelievably strong. Their lips folded together, moist and hot. Violette's tongue, parting her teeth, seemed to send a snake of heat all through Ruth's body, a hot stiff column of aching fire. Pulling each other down, they lay alongside each other; nipples touching, Violette's thigh loosely bent and raised to cover Ruth's darker limb. Ivory on amber.

When Violette rose above her, she was everywhere, a soft bell tolling. Her hair was a black waterfall. Eyes two violet moons, arousing werewolf madness. She filled the world. Her face almost touched Ruth's, so close the eyelashes brushed her cheek. Her scent... hardly there at all. Lily of the valley, faint and pure. It was Ruth's own musk that perfumed Violette's body.

Her tongue tasted Ruth's breasts, trailed all the way into the centre of fire, explored exquisitely until Ruth cried out. The goddess rose again. They devoured each other's mouths.

In this fever no inhibition remained and Ruth caressed the dancer everywhere; felt strong sweet notes of pleasure where

Violette's thigh pressed hard between her own... felt the muscular contractions of the dancer's climax against the hot wet palm of her hand...

Ruth's head fell back, eyes closed. The piercing convulsion of orgasm lit another sensation, a burning pin-prick in her throat. Violette's head was heavy in her shoulder, silken hair spilling over them both. Strangest pain, like something pulling, pinioning her. She was drowning in hair. Spinning in the darkening honey light, Ruth looked down at her own body and saw that it was covered in bruises; each a black flower with a red centre.

I have never tried to meet her.

This may seem unbelievable, but I never dared. 'Giving my life to meet her' is a dream; dull prosaic reality is that I'm afraid. If I met her, everything would change. Perhaps she'd be enchanted and take me under her wing as some kind of fledgeling assistant; yeah, right. She might turn viciously on me, one adoring fan too many. But her indifference would kill me.

So I am listening as Ruth spills out this incredible story.

She is pale but too animated; hardly able to talk at first, then stumbling on the words. "You'll never guess who I met... oh my God...I know she's your idol but..." almost in pieces. I'm not even clear what she's trying to tell me – until I take her hand. Then I see everything.

Images of black and bronze hair tangling, small rounded buttocks rising and falling. Violette must have made comparisons with her hands... the texture of the breasts softer perhaps, the hips narrower, scent and taste subtly different from that of the long-dead lover. Did she like the differences or hate them? How could the two women be the same? I know nothing about Robyn, but I know there is only one Ruth.

Who now veers from shock to amazed laughter to sudden gentle horrified apology. "God, Sarah, I know she's your hero and I'm so sorry to destroy your illusions, but you had to know. She's not what you think."

But how the hell does Ruth know what I think?

I grip her hand so hard that she jumps and says, "Ow, what was that for?"

"You touched Violette," I explain.

Ruth woke from a heavy sleep, her mouth dry, pain hammering delicately behind her eyes. She pushed her hair out of her face and remembered...

Not shame or guilt, but disbelief. Before Mark she'd had affairs she'd regretted, but never in her life had she succumbed to a stranger, a celebrity, a woman. Her skin felt burnished smooth like leather, beautiful. She remembered sensuality, heat, orgasm, all laced with a nightmare of being pinioned and drowning. Her neck throbbed. As she tried to move it began to hurt, really hurt, shooting pain deep into her shoulder. She reached across the crumpled landscape of sheets but the space beside her was empty.

The ballerina sat on the end corner of the bed, staring at her. Violette's knees were drawn up, arms wrapped around them, ankles crossed. Under the shower of raven hair, she was a white statue. She gazed at Ruth like some lavender-eyed cat, unblinking. There was blood on her mouth.

Pushing herself up on her elbows, Ruth asked, "You okay?"

No answer. The ballerina appeared catatonic.

"Violette? What's wrong with you?"

The blood gleamed freshly on the parted lips. Ruth put her hand to the sore place above her collarbone and her fingers came away red. A recent nerve-memory of pain lanced her, of being pulled down into a red-black whirlpool where pleasure and horror congealed together.

"What did you do to me?" Fear made Ruth angry. "You have to be some kind of..." The word *maniac* didn't touch the slow, oppressive heartbeat of fear, the wrongness of an atmosphere tainted with the bitter honey of opiates. "For God's sake, say something!"

Still no response from the thing on the bed. Ruth panicked. She was on her feet, struggling to dress, stuffing her belongings into her designer holdall, muttering, "Oh God, oh Jesus." She couldn't breathe properly. Couldn't make her limbs move fast enough. As she floundered to escape, the only parts of the ice sculpture that moved were the eyes, watching her.

At daybreak, Charlotte wandered the hotel looking for Violette and in a corridor she found the woman who looked like Robyn. She was emerging from a room, struggling to heft a bag, fasten strappy shoes and talk into her mobile, all at once.

"No, I'm done with the conference... Something happened and I'm kinda freaked out... I sound weird? Babe, wait 'til I tell you...

Yeah, come pick me up like *now*. Yeah, you can park in front of reception like we said... okay, 'bye."

"Anything wrong?" Charlotte asked.

Ruth Sarandon jumped so hard she nearly dropped her phone. Pushing uncombed hair out of her face, she looked at Charlotte wild-eyed. "Your friend is out of her mind. I don't give a rat's ass how famous she is." She pointed at the half-open door. "She's just sitting there. And who the hell is Robyn?"

Charlotte let her face betray nothing. She probably looked as strange to Ruth now as Violette did, all porcelain and glass. "I'm sorry," said Charlotte. "I tried to warn you."

"Warned me – what?"

"You reminded her of someone else."

"No kidding." Ruth's face was beautifully flushed with anger. She rubbed at faint bruises on her throat. "She used to bite them too? That's assault. She put something in my drink. I should call the police!"

"I'm sorry you were hurt." Charlotte meant it; her low tone seemed to calm the woman. She pushed her hair back again, sighed shakily.

"It's okay. Consenting adults, and all that. But she is seriously disturbed. I have to go meet my sister."

Ruth went striding away, shoulders back, as fast as she could without actually running. Charlotte watched her from a distance, stabbing at an elevator button. Then she entered the room.

The dancer sat folded on the end of the bed, a dark elf.

"Violette?" Charlotte said softly. "What are you doing?"

"Wondering if I can love her or not."

Charlotte gave a short sigh. "It's academic, since she's bolted."

"She wasn't Robyn."

"I tried to tell you that."

"But I had to touch her and taste her before I could believe it." Violette relaxed, turning to drop her feet to the carpet. Her hands rested loosely on the bed cover and she sat forlorn. "The question is, would I hate her for being so like Robyn but not actually her, never her? Or could I accept her as a different person and love her anyway?"

"The thing is," Charlotte said, folding her arms, "that while you were having this debate with yourself, you freaked the living daylights out of Ruth, and didn't even notice."

Violette's eyes flashed up at Charlotte through a winter lattice of hair. 'Did you try to warn her away from me?"

"No. I wish I had!" Charlotte put up her hands but Violette came at her and seized her arms.

"Yes, you still think you have a right to interfere with my life. Still want to control me, all out of guilt for having unleashed me on the world."

They stood face to face, glaring. Violette's words hurt, but they were true.

"I'm only pointing out the obvious, since you can't see it," Charlotte snapped. "You're only thinking about what *you* want. You don't even know her! You're in a dream, wondering can you or can't you? Meanwhile, she's too terrified out of her brain to know or care what's going on in yours. You drugged her, drank her blood and called her Robyn all night. From her point of view, this is not the start of a promising relationship."

Violette released her. "It was Stefan's wine. What a sad excuse." Outlined by the glow through the curtains she was a creamy silhouette like Venus rising. "It was a dream, a lovely, depraved dream."

"Come on," said Charlotte. "It's time to leave."

Violette's bloodied mouth twisted in a smile. "I can't."

"Why not?"

"I think Ruth, in her haste, took my top. I'm not asking for it back. Best we never meet again."

Charlotte half-smiled. "She's in no mood for an apology. Take this." She took off her cardigan, a lacy thing crocheted of gold silk.

"Poor Ruth," said Violette. "That's it: I've forgotten how even to pretend to be human. I'm designed to be alone. I know that. I bring light to others, but I'm damned if I can find it for myself. I feel as if I'm made of bone." She came forward again, slim hips swaying; so beautiful, Charlotte could only stare. "That sounded wonderfully self-pitying, didn't it? I should be beyond all that. But it still hurts."

"You've always got me," said Charlotte.

Violette shook her head sadly. "No, I haven't."

Charlotte leaned in and kissed her on the mouth, tasting Ruth's blood, lapping the red sweetness from Violette's tongue and lips until the stain was gone. They stood looking at each other, hands soft on each other's arms, as they had a thousand times in the past.

"Ruth tasted nice," said Charlotte.

She touched Violette.

Safe in my parked car, Ruth spills it all out. "You have to know the truth, Sarah," so apologetic – as if she's doing me a favour, while plainly relishing every moment of the scandal. Calm at last, she even starts making little jokes about it. "What a night! (Oh, Mark must never know, right?) Wow, what a kick."

She doesn't notice my silence, my knuckles turning white on the steering wheel. Ruth of all people – with her perfect career, perfect marriage – Ruth has had what I've only dreamed of. Violette's attention, her desire, her yearning, her body, her pleasure and anguish. And it meant nothing to her. Just as she didn't truly see Violette, she doesn't see me either.

I feel like telling my sister the simple truth. When she bit you, it was me who felt it. When she realised she couldn't love you, those were my tears that fell.

But I can't speak and suddenly she's getting out of the car again. "I'm acting crazy," says Ruth, fishing in her bag. "I can handle this. I'm going to go right back in there and give Violette her shirt back."

Daylight couldn't burn Violette's skin any more than it could burn limestone. In morning splendour the lobby was palatial, so bright it hurt the eyes. Fresh white lilies on plinths filled the air with fragrance. Violette walked dazed through the brightness; paused by a sofa and watched a housekeeper clearing last night's wreckage; the unlabelled bottle of thick green glass and the empty glasses. For the pleasure of immortals, indeed.

Looking up, she started. Ruth was standing in front of her. Ruth, not Robyn.

"Oh, you started blinking again," said Ruth. "That's good, right? I realised I…"

She held out a purple scrap. Violette took it and whispered, "Thank you."

Ruth ducked her head nervously. "I'm sorry I ran out. I panicked."

Violette tried to smile. She knew her smiles looked cold,

however warmly she meant them. "Your sister will have to tear down her shrine."

"Oh, god." Ruth lowered her eyes.

"This is all my fault. I should have warned you, I'm quite mad."

"Just a little drunk, both of us." The woman sighed. Their eyes met briefly, awkwardly. "I wanted to say… it was weird and wonderful, and no hard feelings?"

Violette nodded. Turning to go, Ruth added, "I hope you find her. Whoever it is you're looking for."

Light dawns. It didn't happen to make me jealous. No, Ruth was there to become my bridge. My only chance.

As I said, I've never tried to meet Violette. I know I could never be anything to her. Just another obsessed fan. I know that.

But in my own mind I'm something special. I'm her archivist. I'm the one who knows what she really is: Lilith, the immortal Death Lily. Perhaps this knowledge makes me dangerous.

I climb out of the car. Sunlight cascades down the tall glass doors of the hotel. There are two veils of glass between me and Violette and I can't see her, can only see my own small reflection, sliding off the door as it hisses open for me like stage curtains. Then the last veil parts and I'm breathing the same air as her. The foyer is a softly shining theatre centred around its star and she's there, in all her magnificence. Snowy skin, raven hair; a poised figure, exotic even in jeans; more petite than I expected. My fate.

My sister is stepping away from her. I hardly notice. I am thinking, Violette fell. She's not perfect after all. Her wings caught fire and she fell. Do I love her more for that, or is she tainted – no longer above me? I have to know.

The air is white with fire. I walk steadily towards her. Violette glances up and, with those brilliant uncompromising magisterial eyes, she watches me coming.

Freda Warrington grew up in the beautiful Charnwood Forest area of Leicestershire and attended Loughborough College of Art and Design. Since the 1980s, she has been the author of twenty-odd epic fantasy, vampire and supernatural novels, including the critically acclaimed *Blackbird in Silver* (1991). Her eagerly anticipated next novel, provisionally entitled "All About Elfland" is due out soon.

Do You See?

Sarah Pinborough

We didn't speak. Not at first. Not for a long time. But then, London's like that sometimes, isn't it? Thousands of people occupying the same few miles, sitting on the same buses day in and day out on their way to wherever, recognizing the faces but never giving more than perhaps a nod and a grunt of recognition. It just isn't done, talking to strangers. Not when you're a grown up.

So that's how it was. At first the bench was solely my own, as it had been for years. I had probably become almost invisible to the regular visitors to the children's play area in Paddington Street Gardens, as if I were maybe a statue that they saw so often it faded out of their immediate vision, creating space for newer and more exciting colours and shapes.

I remained constant and it was they that changed; a rotation of children who toddled and then grew and then grew too big for the pleasures of swings and slides and cold hands in mittens. I didn't mind. It was good to see new chubby faces, flushed red in the cold and screaming for five minutes more when their frozen mothers and nannies and occasionally fathers told them it was time to leave, stamping their feet into the hard concrete path, trying to batter warmth back into them before starting the walk back to their various homes with numb toes.

Paddington Street Gardens is beautiful in the summer. I can see it from the window of my flat above All Bar One. It wasn't All Bar One when I bought the thousand year lease to the small maisonette, but like the children, the businesses below me come and go, and at the moment it's the sleek bar filled with grown-ups who rush in against the cold and have forgotten that they too once shrieked for five more minutes of sliding down cold metal with the burn of frost on their tongues. Funny how times change. Or how time changes.

Yes, the gardens are lovely in bloom, but I don't sit there much after late April. The sun attracts ice-creams and picnics, and then the rubbish bins attract flies no matter how often they're emptied, and there is nothing tranquil about sitting on a park bench with flies buzzing around and tickling at your nose. Flies like me but I don't like them. Neither do I like to sweat under my best polyester underskirts, and so a long time ago I decided it was best to save my park days for the cool crisp winter and damp autumn afternoons.

Anyway, I didn't go every day back then when the bench was my own. Sometimes the arthritis in my knuckles was just too much to handle, especially on the wet afternoons when the chill seeps right into your bones, and so on those days I'd take a seat by the window instead and sip tea and eat bourbon biscuits while watching the children play from a distance. I still thought of the bench as mine though. Occasionally someone might sit there for a while, but never frequently as I had done for so many years. It was my bench.

And then one November day, she was there. And again the next day. And the one after that. After a few weeks I think she was becoming as invisible to the rest of the park inhabitants as I was. Not to me though. Every time I saw her she became a little clearer. More interesting.

But of course, we didn't speak. Not at first. We were grown ups. And strangers. And more than that, we were very different creatures indeed. Perhaps if she'd been more like me, an elderly woman, well turned out in a winter coat and hat, handbag on her knee, tan tights above sensible brogue shoes, then perhaps we would have spoken sooner. When it would have been politeness rather than curiosity that forced me to break the comfortable, expected silence.

She was *not* like me, though. She was fat for a start; her pale face doughy as if she'd spent her thirty years or so eating far too many chips and burgers and not nearly enough brussel sprouts, and her dark hair was pulled into a greasy, untidy pony tail, hanging lank down her broad back.

She often wore an anorak that almost covered her shiny tracksuit, the sort with stripes down the legs that come cheap at any market or discount store. I never recognized the labels and logos that adorned her thick legs nor those on her trainers, and although I may be old, I still have eyes. In London, labels are everything and even a dried up invisible woman like me knows their Nike and their Puma. And even if I hadn't, I'd have known from the shine and the poor stitching that her clothes were cheap. She wore a heavy signet-ring on the middle finger of her right hand and it would flash garishly in the bright afternoon sunlight as she smoked, staring intently at the playing children. She didn't have any of her own, I realized after her first visit. Like me, she just came to watch.

I decided that she must come from one of the tower blocks half a mile away or so, near Paddington Station. London was sometimes like that. Wealth and poverty placed side by side. Different worlds existing within the space of a few streets. I wasn't wealthy, not when compared to some London residents, but it would be safe to say that we came from different classes, if it were still politically correct to use such a term.

I came from steely middle-class stock, my grandfather returning from India with jewels and secrets that would create a life of comfort and good education for my father and then for me, but the woman beside me on the bench reeked of the gutter, all working class aspirations coated in cheap perfume and stale smoke. That didn't bother me. In fact, it made her more interesting.

I've often thought that my heart belonged in the gutter. There is honesty to be found there. No pent-up emotions hidden behind a tight-lipped smile. In the gutter, rage is allowed to rage, hate spits foul words in the street, and drunken lustful fumbles make a whole new generation. When working class children go missing their parents wail and shriek their honest grief at the cameras. No stiff upper lip for them. You have to admire that ability for emotional release, don't you?

So there we were, sitting on the same bench, a polite foot or so between us, the same cold biting at our different noses in the watery sunshine of a November afternoon when a ball rolled across the path, bounced off the edge and landed by my shoe. Ignoring the ache that flared into a sharp stiff pain down my back as I leaned forward, I picked the ball up. There was a cartoon character on the side that I didn't recognize, bright and garish with wide eyes and big teeth. I didn't see the appeal. But then it had been a long time since I'd played with childhood things.

A small boy, perhaps six years old, trotted over. I'd watched him playing with his little brother on the slides for maybe a year or so now on and off, but as he smiled shyly I do believe it was the first time he'd really seen me at all. He wiped his nose on his padded sleeve. I despaired of the coat. Why did parents seek to wrap their offspring up in cotton wool, as if by adding layer after layer they could somehow save them from the world? I remembered the blitz and the boys out in the cold in their short trousers and thin jerseys rummaging through the wreckage of houses looking for shrapnel. Times changed. Children couldn't be saved from the world. Better to prepare them for it. Better to make them just a little bit afraid. I looked at the boy. Harry. His name was Harry and his little bother was Tom.

"Could I have my ball, please?" His voice was small and shy, not the brash yell I'd heard from him so many times as he charged through the rope netting bridge to the slide and frame beyond.

"Of course you can," I said, but I kept it in my lap. Instead of handing the ball back, I rummaged in my handbag and pulled out some pick n mix. "Have one of these. You'll need the energy for all that playing." Looking up, I peered over to where his mother watched carefully from the sidelines. I nodded towards the sweets. After a moment she smiled back. Harry was hesitating. *Don't take things from strangers.* He'd been brought up safely, but then I'd known that from the coat that was more like a quilt than a jacket.

"Go on. Your mum says it's all right." He glanced over to double check and then with a grin began to rummage in the paper folds for the brightest or the biggest or the tastiest.

"Are you scared of the dark?" The words were so quiet they slipped straight out of me and into him, barely touching the air in between. He looked up and right into me with wide, innocent eyes. He wasn't smiling anymore. He nodded.

I leaned forward and whispered in his ear. Soft words that went on for no more than twenty seconds. For a moment his hand froze, before it latched onto the nearest sweet and absently put it in his mouth. I smiled.

"Well, run along then."

He chewed and stared at me for a second before taking his ball and running back across the path and in through the gate in the railings. He didn't look back. Looking down into the crumpled bag I pulled out a licorice comfit. Those were my favourite after strawberry bonbons. I've always had good strong teeth and I could still chew on the hard toffee centres without any problems. Sometimes God smiles.

I looked over to the stranger sharing my bench and found she was looking back at me. She had dark rings under her puffy eyes. I held the bag out. "Pick and mix?"

She smiled a little and shook her head. "I'm on a diet. And sugar's not good for me."

"Not a lot *is* these days if you believe the papers." I chewed on the licorice and wondered if she saw the irony as she pulled a pack of Marlboro lights from her anorak pocket. Lighting one, she inhaled deeply. I watched the smoke drift off to go and play with the pollution on the Marylebone Road

"Children from this park go missing," she said, eventually.

I felt a little shiver prickle on the base of my spine. We both stared ahead, me chewing on my sweet and her smoking. "Unfortunately, children seem to go missing everywhere these days." I sighed. "Apparently nowhere is safe."

"They don't go from here. They're not taken." She emphasized the last word, the t and the k cutting into the air between us. "Something…else…happens to them. At home. Later." She paused. I took another sweet from the bag. Sugar was good for me and the afternoon was becoming more interesting.

"It happened to my nephew," she said.

"What happened, dear?" On the other side of the path that separated the observers from those in the midst of the action, I watched Harry's mother strapping his little baby brother into the pushchair, wheeling it awkwardly round while trying to hold her older son's hand at the same time. She was flustered in the cold and they hadn't even left the park yet. I kept my eyes carefully on the boy as he walked away. Eventually, just as they reached the gate, it happened. He looked back, directly at me. I smiled secretly. The words weren't lost on that one. He'd remember.

"They don't believe me, but I know what happened."

I watched the boys until they'd disappeared before turning to look at her. "And what was that?"

She sniffed, and just like Harry had done, wiped her nose on the sleeve of her anorak before staring down at her shoes. The signet-ring flashed as her hand flicked ash on the pavement.

"It was almost two years ago now. I was babysitting Courtney because Jodie wanted to go out. She hadn't been out, not properly, not in ages and she was only a kid herself really. She was sixteen when he was born and when..." she faltered a little, "when it happened, he was five. Everyone needs to go out and let off steam at twenty-one, don't they? Especially when they've been doing their best to raise a kiddie on their own."

I nodded sympathetically, although I'm not sure she really saw me. She was lost somewhere in her own story. Trapped in a place and time where it all went wrong.

"And it wasn't as if our mum was much good for anything. Not anymore. All Jodie had was me and Courtney." She threw the cigarette butt down and ground it out under her trainer. "I think maybe that's why she used to like bringing him down here to play. Because our mum brought us here when we were kids. Before the booze really got her. I think Jodie had happy memories of this park."

She frowned. "I never came with her when she brought Courtney though, as much as I loved him. I used to avoid it. Find other things to do. Something about this place, it... it gave me the shivers. Because of that thing with Jason Arnold's little brother."

"Jason Arnold?" I asked.

"Yeah. Jason Arnold used to play with us here when we was kids, and his little brother used to tag along. He was even younger than Jodie, a real toddler. After a while, they moved out of the flats and to somewhere up by Baker Street and didn't come here to play anymore, but we still all went to the same school. About a year after they moved, Jason Arnold's little brother disappeared. He was taken out of their house in the middle of the night. There was a lot of the usual talk but no one ever really figured out what had happened.

"When Jason came back to school he was different. Once I asked him if he was okay and he got all shaky and whispered that it was what we'd heard in the park that did it. And I don't know why because it made no sense but something about that totally freaked me out. I was only nine. I didn't understand then." She lit another cigarette. "I never spoke to Jason Arnold again after that the whole time we were in that school."

More children were leaving and but I didn't pay them, or the encroaching twilight, any attention. This was far more interesting, even if my brogues weren't doing much to keep the cold away from my still feet. "And what does this have to do with little Courtney?" I asked, pulling a couple of milk bottles out of the bag.

"Courtney was manic," she continued. "Like me, sugar wasn't good for him. Sent him hyper. But that didn't stop Jodie letting him have sweets and coke. She found it hard to say no to him. And he was a good kid, not mean or angry like some, but he wasn't the kind of kid that would sit still for long. Not even in front of the telly. He needed to be running around, chasing things, playing loudly right up until he'd collapse into sleep.

"But that night, two years ago, he was quiet. Really, really quiet. I didn't notice until Jodie had gone, 'cause we'd been giggling and having a glass of wine and picking her outfit and laughing about the men she was going to pull, all that kind of stuff. But once she'd gone, I realized that all that time he'd been sitting on the sofa, totally still like a little statue, just staring at the telly. And it was Eastenders or something else grown up, not cartoons.

"I asked him if he was feeling sick or anything but he said no and eventually it was time for his bed. He wanted the small light left on. I remember that. But I said no. I said he was a big boy and he shouldn't be afraid of the dark, but that I'd leave the hall light on for him in case he needed to go to the loo. I thought I was doing the right thing. I'd forgotten what it was like being a kid. I was at the door when he called my name. His voice was soft, I remember that. And I remember how small he looked in the bed, his wide eyes peering over the top of the duvet.

"'Monsters have shadows,' he said and the words stopped me. I hadn't realised that his stillness, his quiet, was because he was terrified. But I knew it then. I could hear it in the terrible sadness of his little voice.

"'Sometimes the shadows are more dangerous than the monsters. That's what they say.' He didn't sound like a five year old. Not like our Jodie's little Courtney.

"I remember staring at him, one foot in the brightness of the hall, and one in his small dark tatty bedroom covered with Buzz Lightyear wallpaper left over from whoever'd had the flat before Jodie.

"'Don't be silly.' I said to him. 'There's no such thing as monsters.' I remember that my throat was tight, even under the wine buzz I had. I remember he was scaring me and I wasn't sure why but I knew I wanted him to shut up. I wanted him to be Courtney again. Not this scared kid that was making *me* feel like a scared kid. But he didn't shut up.

"'Shadows are real though.' He said. 'If you say words at them they'll show you the monster.'

"I told him that was enough. I told him to go to sleep."

She let out a long sigh.

"And those were the last words I ever said to him. I didn't tell him I loved him or anything. Just 'Go to sleep'.

"I was closing the door when he spoke again, and the volume gone from his voice, as if he'd already given up. 'I wish I didn't know them. Those words.' That's what he said."

She paused, taking a long pull on her cigarette, which I found slightly over-dramatic. Sometimes there was something to be said for stiff upper lip. "Children are so fanciful," I said.

She looked over at me and smiled and for a moment I could almost see the pretty person she would have been had her life run along a different route. The edges of her eyes twinkled brightly and I wondered if she ever slept or just survived on nicotine and coffee. I stared right back at her.

"I don't think he made it up. Because later that night the monster got him." She sighed again. "I drank the rest of the bottle of wine dead fast once Courtney was in bed. I'm not much of a drinker really, because of Mum, so it wasn't long before my eyes were closing and my head spinning a little. I was glad about that. I just wanted to go to sleep or pass out. I didn't check on Courtney. I didn't want to go into his bedroom. I kept thinking about Jason Arnold's little brother James, you see. I kept thinking about him and something kept niggling me, something that I knew deep inside, something that I'd once heard and worked so hard to forget, and I kept thinking about how all those things were linked, but how the most important thing was for me not to remember. Not remembering would keep me safe.

"I fell asleep on the sofa. I think I woke up once when he screamed. I think I did. I remember seeing a huge shadow out in the hall and then squeezing my drunken eyes shut again. I definitely woke up when Jodie came home and started screaming. She must have seen me sleeping in the lounge and gone to check on him before waking me up.

"He was gone, you see. There was just a bloody mess left in his bed. His sheets were ripped and the mattress was soaked in red, but all the damage was contained there. No trail on the carpet or out in the hall, but only one smeared handprint on the wall as if maybe he'd been grabbing at something there when the monster took him. And that was it. Nothing left of the little boy at all.

"Of course the police never caught anyone for it. They questioned me for a long time but in the end they had to let me go. I hadn't done anything to Courtney. There was no trace of blood on me, or in fact anywhere else other than that bed and the wall. Still, that didn't stop people looking at me sideways, my own family amongst them, and I haven't seen Jodie in over a year now.

"I tried to tell her about what Courtney had said before he went to sleep, about the monsters and their shadows, but she wasn't having any of it. She hated me. I could tell and I couldn't blame her. I hated myself."

Around us, the park lights were slowly coming alive as the gloom turned to a deep blue, grabbing each corner and slowly possessing it. As the bulbs glowed, shadows appeared and hovered in the bushes. The cold was becoming bitter and I thought it was probably time I got home and had a nice cup of tea. It didn't do for a woman of my age to sit out too late.

"So what brings you back here now, Melanie?" I asked her, scrunching up what was left of the sweets and putting them back in my handbag.

"Jason Arnold," she replied, without a second's hesitation. "You see, after what happened, I kept thinking about him and his little brother and Courtney and I tracked him down. It took a couple of months, but I eventually found him in a flat over at Willesden Green. He had a job working the night shift at Tesco and then used to go home and smoke weed until he passed out. He said he was scared of the dark.

"I told him about Courtney and what had happened. I told him I thought there was something in my head that would make it clearer. He laughed a lot then. And then cried. And then pulled a massive folder out of the cupboard under the sink. We shared a joint as he talked me through all the children that he'd researched that had gone missing in London like Courtney and James. Lots of them had spent time here, in these gardens. And lots of them had talked about shadows and monsters and special words.

"I asked him if he knew what the words that brought the monster were because, I said, high on skunk, if we could bring the monster, maybe we could kill it. He cried some more then and said he couldn't remember. He'd known the words once. He said we'd been together when we were told them, right here in the park when we were little. But when he shared them with James, just to scare him a little, just to dare him to use them, it was like they went out of his head. And then little James used the words. Just like Courtney did, and the monster's shadow came for him.

"I let myself in to Jason's flat yesterday 'cause his phone was just ringing out. He wasn't there. There was just a huge red sprawl on his sofa." She paused. "I guess he remember the words in the end. I just wish he'd waited for me before he used them."

"Did you call the police?" I asked. The evening wind bent the trees as if they were leaning in to listen with me, their thin worn branches jostling for position in the thin light.

"No," she said, her husky voice empty. "I just took his folder of children and left. They wouldn't have believed me anyway. Or they'd have arrested me again. Either way wouldn't help."

As the lamp above us slowly brightened, I pushed myself to my feet. My hips roared with stiffness, my joints clicking angrily straight. I slid my handbag up to my elbow and clasped my hands across my waist. "Well thank you for such an interesting story." I smiled at her. She didn't look as if she was planning to move. I wondered what she thought she could gain by sitting on that cold bench all night. Other than a nasty chill. "I hope you find whatever it is you're looking for, dear." I almost added, *Before it finds you*, but managed to resist the melodrama. I was, at the end of the day, far too middle class for that.

Leaving her there, I turned and headed back to the lights of Paddington Street and All Bar One. I was at the exit when she called after me.

"Wait! Wait!"

I turned. Her huge shape was black in the darkness, her face a blur.

"How did you know my name? I didn't tell you my name?"

I smiled, even though she probably couldn't see it. "It was nice seeing you again, Melanie. It's been a long time."

I crossed the road and didn't look back.

Back in the warmth of my flat, I put the kettle on before taking my overcoat off and hanging it on the old-fashioned coat stand in the small hallway. I rested my hands on the radiator for a moment, enjoying the heat in my old bones. Back in the lounge, a shadow slipped away from the wall and out under the windowsill and into the night. I wondered where it would go tonight. I could feel the monster purring inside me, its excitement rising. I thought of Harry and his brother, the Arnold boys, and Melanie and Courtney. Children never really changed. Not deep down inside, in the places where fear and superstition lived.

I'd have a nice cup of tea by the fire to warm up, and then I'd file my teeth, just in case.

Because they all remembered the words in the end, no matter how long it had been since I whispered to them.

Sarah Pinborough spent much of her childhood travelling in the Middle East due to her father's job as a diplomat, but now lives in the Buckinghamshire village where she was born. With four novels published and a fifth imminent, Sarah has quickly established an enviable reputation as a horror writer, particularly in the US. Recently, she has begun to branch out, working on crime and thriller novels as well as a non-supernatural YA piece.

Queen of the Sunlit Shore

Liz Williams

I first set eyes on her at dusk as she walked along the strand, carrying strangeness with her like a shadow. She was unchaperoned, and in any case, entirely unlike the fashionable young women who thronged the streets of Lyme Regis under flower-petal parasols. Her clothes were not up-to-the-minute, but had an oddly antique air, their soft draperies reminding me of the classical statues of Greece, and they were the colour of twilight: soft grey and lavender and hazy blue over a white underskirt. Her face, too, was not artful or coquettish under a fall of blonde hair. She had a long, strong nose, a firm mouth, unfathomable dark eyes filled with melancholy, and her hair was dark, too.

She captured my imagination immediately. I longed to paint her, could hardly wait to get back to my watercolours and pencils – for she was suited to watercolour and its subtle shades. I nearly forgot myself and approached her to ask if I might take the liberty of drawing her, but she was clearly a respectable woman and I told myself sharply to hold back. Young men in Bohemian dress do not accost solitary women, even in fashionable watering holes, and demand artistic license.

Instead, I wandered down to the shingle-and-sand that ran along the side of the Cobb. I looked back once, but the woman had gone. There was charm in the scene before me, however – the boats drawn up on shore between coils of tarry rope, the fishermen mending their nets before heading out for the night's fishing. I sat down by the side of one old man, already forming a composition in my mind, and asked if he would mind if I made a sketch.

"No, no, I don't mind 'ee." The Devon accent was very strong. "A painter, are you? Plenty of society ladies here for you to draw."

I laughed. "I'm not interested in society ladies, sir. It might be good money, but it's art that interests me." I was young enough still to be a little pompous. He looked amused.

"Art, is it? Harmless enough, but don't 'ee make us too pretty. Fishing's not an easy trade."

"That I know, sir. I spent school holidays with my uncle – he was a Dartmouth man. A ship's captain, once. He sailed the Horn. I used to watch the fishermen going out."

"Going out, and of a time not coming back. There was a ship wrecked here but a few days ago, the *Bridport Maid*. A storm blew up, a spring gale – you'll have seen those as a boy."

I nodded. "Were many lost?"

It was his turn to nod. "All but one man. He's staying with the doctor now, waiting passage when his wounds heal. The boat was driven onto the rocks." He pointed to a distant cliff, all stripes and striations. "Smashed to pieces."

"I'm sorry to hear that."

We lapsed into silence, he with his nets, me with my sketchbook. I had made a few small drawings, but it was the woman who filled my mind.

So when the old fisherman collected his nets and rose to go, I hastened back through the mild summer air to my lodgings, to set about capturing her image. Imagine, if you will, my disappointment when I found that someone else had already done so.

The painting was hanging in the hallway of the guesthouse, in a dark corner. Nonetheless, I could not understand how I had come to miss it. And now, of course, I wonder whether it had initially been there, or had appeared only after I had set eyes on the woman.

The print was called *Queen of the Sunlit Shore*, and it showed someone very like the woman I had seen, though dressed in more starkly classical garments, with her arms bared. The shore, too, was recognisably not Lyme, the cold southern coast of England, but somewhere washed with golden light and warmth, lying beneath a small white temple on a cliff. There was an azure sliver of sea to the far left of the picture and the woman was at the centre; crouching on the sand and surrounded by gulls.

She must be an artist's model, then. This would explain her rather unconventional appearance, and for a moment, I berated myself for my foolish hesitation. But would I have wanted to use her, when someone else had already done so? I had no good answer for that. This painting was curiously perfect, all the elements hanging together in the way that the muse will sometimes bring disparities into a harmonious whole. For the painting should have looked wrong. Despite her Grecian appearance, the woman's colouring was too cold for Homer's wine-dark coasts, and the gulls looked like none that I had seen in either Britain or the Mediterranean, being white dappled with grey, with long pale beaks like slips of bone. And still the painting sang to me, lodged itself in my head. I peered to see the signature, but it was black and spidery, impossible to read, more as though it had been scratched rather than signed.

I asked the landlady if she knew who the artist was.

"Why no, Mr Bryce," she said. "The painting belonged to my grandfather. I don't know where he bought it, but it always stood above the mantel until the day he died. I remember it when I was a child. I loved it, but it's too big for my little parlour."

So the woman I had seen could not have been the model. But – I found when I queried further – my landlady's grandfather had been a local man. Perhaps the lady of the strand was from a local family. Country folk – for although Lyme is a sailing town, the red earth of the fields that rise above it shows where many folks' toil must lie.

That night, I dreamed of gulls.

They clustered on the roofs that surrounded the boarding house, shrieking and squalling, a sound that, to me, always conjures the memory of storms. In my dream, I went to the window and drew aside the curtain. The whole town was filled with the gulls, not just the tiles below my window, but every roof, every sill. There was a bright light in the west, like the sun rising, the turning of the world reversed. It grew until the wings of the gulls glowed white-gold and their eyes were sparks of gold, too, gleaming until the whole flock rose up and flew in a spiral towards the light. The light was so bright now that it hurt my eyes and I squinted away from it, wincing. As I did so, I thought I saw a ship, black against the west, then blood red as it sailed up and over the town and broke into pieces, spars and rigging and fiery fragments of sail floating down onto the cobbles.

I woke. Images roared through my head, still fresh from my dream, but although I recollected their strange beauty, I was disappointed nonetheless. I would rather have dreamed of the Queen of the Sunlit Shore.

Perhaps the artist had dreamed, too, of a woman and a temple and seagulls, and perhaps this accounted for the odd juxtaposition of elements in the painting. I thought I might use aspects of my own dream, too, but not the gulls. I thought I knew where the sailing ship had come from – the wreck of which the sailor had spoken. The *Bridport Maid*, or what remained of her, had sailed into my dreams.

The dream left me with an odd, clammy feeling, a wrongness. To shake off this miasma I went downstairs and out, heading down the steep streets of the town towards the harbour and the Cobb. It was a mild morning, with a pearly sea and a milky sky. If I had not seen how swiftly calm and sparkling water could change to a hammering torrent of wild wave, or how the cloudless heavens could boil into storm like a kettle left too long on the stove, I might have found it hard to believe in the recent wreck. But my uncle the sea captain had told me too many stories and I'd seen too much of how the weather can change.

There was no sign of the fishermen themselves, but far out by the striped and rumpled cliffs I saw the little fleet. I passed an orange cat, a woman carrying a bucket, and a small ragged child. I walked out onto the long line of the Cobb, admiring the peaceful scene before me: as an artist, it was harmonious enough but lacked drama, as a man, I was thankful only that the weather had held.

Upon nearing the end of the Cobb, I saw that I was not, after all, alone. A man was standing at the edge of the wall, gazing out to sea. I greeted him as I approached.

"Good morning."

"Morning." He turned. I saw a bearded face, lined with a series of red marks like the cliffs themselves. The grey pallor of his skin made him look older. One arm was in a sling.

"You have been in the wars," I said, ruefully.

"True enough." His voice was hoarse and husky. "The war of the sea."

I realised who he must be: the only survivor of the *Bridport Maid*, the sailor who had been saved and who was now staying at the local doctor's. His next words confirmed my suspicions.

"I survived a wreck. Maybe you heard about it?"

"The *Bridport Maid?* Yes, I did. A nasty business. You're a lucky man."

He gave a harsh laugh. "Luckier than some."

"I heard about the crew, too. I'm very sorry."

He shrugged, but I could tell that it was with an effort, and not merely a physical one. "The sea takes what she takes. As soon as we saw the bird, I knew we were in trouble."

"The bird?"

"A big white gull. Huge. You wouldn't know about something like that." He gave me a disdainful glance, perhaps without realising it, the look of the sailor for the landlubber. I felt a sudden need to prove myself.

"I've never been to sea, that's true. At least, not in the way that you have. But my uncle was a retired sea captain. He told me a few things."

"Ah. Then did he tell you of the white bird, the death sign?"

"I don't recall. I think I would have remembered if he had."

"If he was retired," the sailor said, "perhaps he never saw it. I must be getting back. Doctor's expecting me and there's a skipper coming to town from Cornwall, may have a berth for me."

"I wish you luck," I said.

"If it's better luck than I've had," he said, "it'll be enough."

I watched him walk back along the Cobb and up the hill. He moved slowly, like someone old. I wondered how serious his injuries had been, whether he would indeed be well enough to take up that berth. I turned back, and saw the woman standing on the shore.

She was staring after the sailor. She wore no hat, and her tall figure was covered in a cloak the colour of violets. A shadow passed over me and I glanced up to see a white speck, high in the milky air. It was falling fast and in doing so, it resolved into a gull, a small bird, perhaps a tern. The bird did not hesitate but shot straight towards the woman on the shore. I stood breathless, as if the painting had come to life before me. I felt certain that the bird was about to strike the woman in the face and I think I cried out, but at the last moment her hand glided out from beneath the violet folds of the cloak and she caught the gull from the air like a hunter calling home a hawk. The woman turned away. I could no longer see the gull, imagined it perching on her wrist, and then she was gone into the shimmering air.

Half-believing myself still within my dream, I followed her. Curiosity won over a growing fear. But although I thought I saw her figure disappearing along the shore, she moved too fast for me and I could not catch her up. At last I reached the edges of the red cliff and the end of the shore. No one was there. Cold and shaken, I returned to the guest-house and an ordinary breakfast.

I looked at the sketches that I had done on the previous evening, of the old sailor mending his nets, and they seemed lifeless and flat. Annoyed, I took up a pencil and let my hand drift over a clean sheet of paper with my eyes half-closed, a technique taught to me by one of my teachers at the art college. A staunch Christian, he likened it to listening to God. Perhaps he was right, perhaps not, but the technique itself had taught me a great deal and I employed it now. Half an hour passed, maybe a little more. When I next glanced down at the paper, I expected to see that I had drawn the woman, but instead the wounded fisherman's face stared back at me from the page, haggard, appearing on the edges of death. Above him hovered a bird, a gull, with the sharp beak lowered towards the crown of his head.

This drawing was not lifeless. It was filled with menace. Disturbed, I put it to one side and went down to the hallway.

In a shaft of afternoon sunlight, the painting of the woman looked innocuous, a seaside idyll. The woman's face was serene as she gazed about at her avian charges, the scene behind her filled with warmth, unlike this cold English coast. I felt that the painter had not understood her as I was beginning to understand her, that she was a harbinger of some sort, an omen of death. I told myself not to be so foolish, that she was just some local woman, nothing more, but the memory of that tern plunging out of the heavens to alight on her hand was still fresh in my mind.

My suspicions were granted greater weight later on that afternoon, when, restless and unable to work or read, I walked back down the hill to the shore. But instead of heading along the Cobb, now filled with those parasolled promenaders, I walked up the hill to the handsome house overlooking the harbour, which my landlady had told me belonged to the doctor.

A maid answered the door, a pale girl, with a froth of brown hair beneath a cap.

"My name is James Bryce. I came to see someone," I told her. "I'm afraid I don't know his name. He was injured in the wreck, the *Bridport Maid?* I was given to understand that he is staying here –"

"Oh, Mr Bryce," the maid interrupted. I saw now the reason for her pallor. "Then you have not heard? He died, in the night. They have taken him for burial now."

"Dead?" I stared stupidly at her, while all the time a small voice told me that this was something I already knew, had known from the moment of a white bird falling from the sky and the swirl of a violet cloak.

"I'm sorry," the maid said now. "Doctor did not think his injuries were so serious, but they must have been. He took a turn for the worse yesterday evening. It was very quick."

I offered my condolences and walked slowly down to the shore. The old sailor was there, tarring the sides of his boat, and I greeted him.

"Sad news," I said next. "The last survivor of the *Bridport Maid* has gone." I told him what the maid had told me.

"I'm sorry to hear that," he said. "Sorry to hear of any death at sea. And there'll be more, mark me. See that?"

He pointed out to sea, to where a long, ragged line of cloud was building. "Know what that is? Those streamers?"

"Rain," I said.

"That's right. And no drizzle, either. There's a storm coming up from the south-east. Due to reach this coast later this evening. I'll not be putting out tonight, and neither will anyone else." I nodded. "A wise decision."

But as it happened, not a choice that was open to everyone.

The gale hit Lyme around seven. I was sitting in an inn on the harbour, nursing a pint of ale, and I saw it strike. One minute, the distant cliffs were livid in the last red light, the next, they were blotted out behind a wall of mist and rain. The windows of the inn were struck by a hammering shower of water and spray as the wind hit and whipped the waves up over the harbour wall.

Storms are an artist's gift. At once, my unease and sorrow were wiped clean, gone with the exhilaration of watching the sudden force of nature. I felt an instant longing to be outside, so I finished what was left of my pint and stepped through the door.

This was a real summer squall. As I got through the door, thunder pealed overhead and the clouds were split by a bolt of rose-coloured lightning. It would be foolish, with this churning mill-race sea, to stand on the Cobb itself, and yet I wanted to get closer to those waves. I crossed the cobbles and came onto the shingle.

The sun had completely gone now, and the sky that showed through the gaps in the racing clouds was dark, with only a glimmer from the crescent moon that rode low over the water. The air itself was not cold, but the spray that hit my face was icy, as chill as a winter sea. I looked up and down for the gull woman, but although somehow I expected her, she was nowhere to be seen. Then there was a shout from behind me.

"There she is!"

For a moment I had the oddest impression that the fishermen knew all about her, and in this time of tempest had sent out a hunting party. All this flashed through my mind in a briefest instant and then I realised that what they were next shouting was "The ship, the ship!"

The clouds parted, the moonlight streamed through, and I saw a small sailing ship riding close to the harbour. One sail was torn and trailing across the deck, and she was listing heavily to one side. Turning, I saw the old fisherman at my side.

"You were right!" I shouted above the wind. "I wish you had not been!"

"The *Jenny Lee*, out of Plymouth," he shouted back. "Came across from France today, didn't make it in time. The boat's going out." He pointed and I saw a group of men running a boat down the slipway.

"Do you think they have a chance?" I called.

"In this storm? They'll be lucky. She's already halfway down."

The *Jenny Lee* was even further over now, tilting at a dangerous angle above the waves. The old man hobbled towards the slipway and I was going to join him, although there was nothing I could do, when I saw her.

She was standing at the very end of the Cobb, directly above the lashing sea. One arm was upraised and I thought I saw something white hovering above it, but perhaps that was only her sleeve. I stumbled over the wet shingle and onto the flags of the Cobb. I half-expected her to disappear, but she remained standing, facing the sea. It seemed to take an age to reach her. When I did so, I looked back and the land appeared much further away than it should have done, the lights of Lyme lost in a mist of sea. The Cobb itself looked endless: a causeway into nothing.

I could see the ship, too, the *Jenny Lee*, or what was left of her. She was listing so hard that her port side touched the sea; another few moments and she would be over, rolling down into the green deep. Water sluiced across her deck and there were a few desperate figures clinging to ropes. I caught a fleeting glimpse of the lifeboat, bobbing up on a wave before hurtling downwards.

I looked back towards the woman. There were gulls around her head, and they shone as if lit from below. And suddenly I saw them not as gulls, but as the spirits of men, sucked out of the lifeless bodies that now floated amidst the waves.

"Stop!" I shouted. "You must stop! Leave those poor souls alone!"

She turned, slowly; her face was not a woman's face, but was for an instant the predatory visage of a great white bird, the long sharp beak, the yellow eyes. I could not let her take more men. I threw myself at her, finding myself clutching something bony and long, my face buried in the softness of feathers. We went over the side of the Cobb and down, falling into the roil of cold-and-black. The shock of freezing water smacked the breath out of my lungs and I swallowed salt. The woman, or whatever she was, twisted in my arms and lunged upwards. I struggled to hold her, thinking of those men on the *Jenny Lee*, sinking even as I was sinking, but the tide tore her from my grip. I saw her sail upwards in a flutter of skirts, or feathers. I kicked out, trying to swim to the surface, but the tide had me in its grip, too. Then my vision went dark. The last thing I saw before the tide picked me up and slammed me against the wall of the Cobb was a white bird, spiralling up as if flying through summer air. I followed.

Sunlight, and the taste of salt in my mouth. I ached all over and the breath was raw in my throat. I blinked against the light and sat up. I was lying on the shore, but soft sand lay beneath me rather than shingle, and the sea was a pure, calm blue. I turned. A small white temple stood on the hillside, yet along with it lay Lyme, shadowy and spectral, the ghost of a town.

She stood a short distance away, a white gull on her wrist. She looked like a woman again, her hair falling down her back. She spoke a single word to the gull and threw it high into the air. It fluttered once, then veered off over the sea.

She came to kneel by my side. The touch of her hand on my face was feather soft. She smelled of the sea, of weed and salt and open ocean.

"What are you?" I whispered.

"I am the White Ghost."

"You lure sailors to their deaths?" I frowned. That wasn't right. I thought I had seen the truth, but I had not.

"I guide home the souls of those who have already died at sea. I am the steerswoman."

"Is this – death?"

"This is the in-between, the sunlit shore, the waystation for souls. You cannot stay here, Mr Bryce. You must move on."

I swallowed. "I am dead, then?"

She smiled. "You are lucky that you are not. You did a brave thing, Mr Bryce, a thing you believed to be right, no matter the cost to your own life. You are to live."

"Wait," I said. That painter had not done this place justice. It glowed with a light of its own, as though every stone and wave possessed its own sparkling spirit. But she shook her head and the sunlit shore began to fade. The last sight I had of her was of the violet and grey gown changing to feathers, whitening as she transformed into albatross and was gone into the air, skimming over the waves like a thrown stone. And I was back on the shingle of Lyme, a grey day above me and the sea frothing down to sullen lace.

Liz Williams possesses the rare ability to write either science fiction or fantasy with equal skill, but then her SF is wonderfully surreal while her fantasy is as well-constructed and plausible as the best of SF. A prolific writer of short fiction, Liz has also published more than a dozen novels, with the latest, *The Shadow Pavilion*, due this May.

Heart Song

Kim Lakin-Smith

Perched on the lichened rim of an old forest well, devouring the last rosy apple of the bygone summer, Juho Pyörni felt his heart strings come undone. Eeva Uosukainen, first-born of Urho, master of the midsummer dance, maestro and miller, was in love with another, and that beautiful green day when she wore a circlet of lily-of-the-valley, when sunlight played across her face, her attendants danced rings around a pole of stripped birch, and he first lay her down amidst the foaming underbrush, was long over. Juho sighed through a mouthful of fruit. It hurt his heart to think of it but hurt his pride more.

Easing a last piece of apple between his lips, Juho twisted at the waist and dropped the core into the well. He listened for its muffled splash. So that was love disposed of, he mused sourly. From that moment on, he would live only through his music.

The kantele rested alongside him on the wall of the well. Grazes to the sides of the chordaphone lent the instrument an earthy quality. Otherwise, it was a metaphysical box of tricks shined with a life's worth of elbow grease.

Juho swept up the instrument by the scruff of its neck, urged it onto his lap, anchored his boots on the iron earth and lengthened his spine. His eyelids felt heavy; he allowed them to close then started to play.

Pirjo worked her fingertips into the crevices between the mouldered stone and eased her body up. The murky water above her head was beginning to clear. She made out a smattering of stars, a great grey owl on the wing, northern lights streaking the sky like oiled rainbows... Her stomach flipped. Had it really been so long since that beautiful green day when she gored her finger on a spindle? She could still see it now, slipping from her fingers and falling into the depths of the well. Fearing her mother's reproval, she had been left with little choice but to follow after it.

Tears formed in Pirjo's eyes; the element through which she climbed washed them away. She was part of a new world now. Part of Vanaheim. Her heart belonged to Mother Reija, and literally so, since the crone had eased it from her chest, dipped it, soaped it, buffed it free of grime, and stored it neatly away. If she missed the homeland then, such a feeling was only a ghost of emotion, Pirjo reminded herself. But that didn't stop the hole where her heart once hung from aching.

She surfaced unexpectedly. The air hurt her lungs like a blast of spice and she floundered, slipping back below. Suspended in the cool water, she imagined herself a babe tucked in amongst the vitalising fluid of the womb. It occurred to her just how sheltered her life had become in Vanaheim. She longed to sink back down to that world between worlds, twilit, meadowed, and in the shade of death. At the same time, she was struck by a snatch of kantele song gleaned from the arid air. How pure the instrument had sounded for that second or two when she was broke free of the water! How free of lethargy and barren sentiment. No wonder Mother Reija had dispatched her to distil a measure of its sterilising quality, and with instructions to convey that prize to Vanaheim with the same care she might show 'her own heart'.

The girl felt for the purse floating near her hip. Mother Reija was a task mistress but she outshone Pirjo's biological mother, that wizen old shrew with the beating broom, day or night. Moreover, she had transformed Pirjo from a green girl with soft, maiden hands into a devotee of the household arts, unable to abide the dull or the tarnished but who took pleasure only in the swept, the scrubbed, the woven and the crystalline. Acknowledging her debt to Mother Reija was one incentive to resurface. Assuring the eventual safe return of her heart was another.

Emerging from the water with spidery bursts of movement, Pirjo ascended towards the circle of starlit sky. Water sluiced from her head and naked shoulders like jewels scattering. Blue-black locks suckered her face.

Set against the native chorus of the woodland, Juho's was a sophisticated lament. Notes bled off the strings, innocent at first then rising in mournful waves – and it was a song of aloneness, spooling from fingers that trembled in their pluck or press of strings. The sound fed under the boughs of great dark oaks, whispered through the needles of spruce and pine, ascended on an updraft to ruffle the breast of a cresting white-tailed eagle, and said to the ancient rocks, 'Love is caustic. Love is kind. Love is the unifying thread.'

Juho's eyes remained shut. So intent was he on the sanguine notes patterning his inner eyelids that he failed to notice a pair of hands crane up from inside the well, claw the mouldered stone and gain purchase. A slim leg crooked over the rim. Seconds later, a waif in a soaked, off-the-shoulder gown spilled over. She sat alongside Juho, one hand resting on the crook of the well's iron spit, the other cupping a purse at her hip.

Unnerved by the whoos of the owl or some subtle intuition, Juho left off playing. He opened his eyes and almost fell backwards into the well. Boots dancing like a hanging man's, he used the kantele as a counterweight, swung back onto his feet, swiped a sleeve across his brow and blinked stupidly at the stranger.

Stifling the urge to curse, he stuck out his hand. "Terve. Hi!"

Grey-gold lips pulled back from tiny stabbing teeth. Juho shuffled to put an arse's breadth between them; his uncle hooked perch with not dissimilar mouths through a hole in the ice in Kempeleenlahti bay.

The girl neither spoke nor shook his hand, a snub that made Juho hug the neck of his good, solid, dependable kantele and secretly berate the spitefulness of women.

"Forgive me if I disturbed your walk but I didn't expect anyone else to be out in the forest at this hour. It's late. Does your mother know you're out?" Juho waited. When the girl still refused to speak, his gaze hardened. "It's rude to sneak up, even ruder not to answer when spoken to."

She nodded, tendrils of inky hair washing her face like pond weed.

"You know it's rude to sneak up? No. Your mother knows you are out."

An incline of the head.

"Are you mute?" Juho heard the brusqueness in his tone but every part of him felt weary. He had been abandoned by Eeva with her yolk-yellow hair and snowy, plump thighs. More importantly, his musical lament had been interrupted.

The girl parted her lips – those pincer teeth! Pity the poor mother who had tried to put that babe to the breast – and a vile squawk issued from her mouth. Eyes, infinite and sable like those of a seal cub, flicked up to meet his as if amused by the joke. Juho felt a fresh sting of resentment. He was not amused. Maybe the girl was simple.

His fingers twitched. He was eager to get back to his exorcism of love.

"Run along home, girl," he growled, adding nastily, "There are wolves out here and bears that would eat you up."

The girl maintained her daggered grin. She gestured lightly to the instrument, crooked against his chest like the body of a lover.

"You want me to play? This music is not meant for virgin ears."

Again, the girl indicated the rosed belly of the instrument. Juho noticed the state of her hands, the callused knuckles and welts at the nail beds. He cringed inwardly. His fingers had also been toughened over time but by art not labour.

"The notes I conjure are not for farm girls. They are symphonies of retribution. They are the tears of kings." His chest swelled and his eyes glazed agreeably.

A dark look crossed the girl's piscine features. Had he hit a nerve? Juho felt elated then quickly ashamed. Taking pleasure in confusing a simpleton? Abandonment *had* left him jaded!

He parted his lips to try a softer tact, but was freshly perplexed when the girl sucked in her cheeks then curtly raised her chin. Dipping a hoary hand into a purse at her hip, she produced a small metal pot, similar in shape to the one Juho and his father used to steam the filth from their nakedness at home. She offered it.

"A saunanpata? No thanks. I've a larger one at home."

She poked a finger at the pot.

"Inside?" He edged his nose to the rim, sniffed and threw the pot down. A black treacle oozed out of the mouth of the pot onto the ground. "What is *that*? Sugar syrup? Tar?" The girl's helpful nod grated. Her feeblemindedness was confirmed when she retrieved more hidden treasure in the form of a goose feather.

Snatching the feather from her grip, Juho inspected it by the light of the swollen moon. Then he fattened his lips and blew the feather out over the maw of the well. "Pretty, but my father's yard is littered with them. Like a ryijy rug worked from dung and down."

Pirjo watched the feather melt into the shadows of the well, her brow knitted. She was relieved to see the thing swallowed up by the depths that had fashioned it, especially since Mother Reija had bequeathed it to her all of those moons ago as a sign of 'slovenliness on unworn bones'. But the musician had plucked it from her hand like a cook tearing fistfuls from a fowl's breast, disposed of it just as clinically, and so her relief was tinged with an element of regret. Like the round paljinsolki brooch securing the neck of her calico dress, it had pinioned her to both the world above and below. And now it was gone.

Pirjo pressed her tongue against her teeth. She refused to dwell on something as bucolic as sentimental attachment to a feather. Instead, she reached back inside the purse. Her fingers knocked against a glass vial that Mother Reija had placed in her possession and then closed around the shapely wooden rod of the spindle.

"More treats?"

The musician eyed her, a corner of his mouth knotted up. Somewhere in the blackness, the owl whooed; it was a mocking call, reminiscent of a favoured sister's taunts or a mother despairing. Pirjo clasped at the underside of her ribcage. She could not give up the spindle, reclaimed from Mother Reija in exchange for her heart, and with it, her need to spin words.

"Got something sinful in there?" The man's pupils glinted like struck flints.

On instinct, Pirjo hooked the purse onto her opposite side.

The musician let his head fall forward, shook it and snorted. He glanced across at her. "Go away." Readjusting the kantele on his knees, he let his hand hover above the strings. "Please go away," he muttered.

What else could she coax him with? Pirjo counted off the few possessions that she owned: the slop of tar, the feather, the vial, the spindle, the coin… She lit up on the inside. Retrieving the coin, she offered it to man and moonlight. Its coruscations mirrored the grey-gold facets of her skin.

"Gold?" The musician reverted to a greedy-faced child. "That's a fine thing for a farm girl to carry on her person. Did you steal it?"

Pirjo shook her head vehemently. She had earned it in return for six months honest servitude to Mother Reija.

Nipping the coin from her hand with scissoring fingers, the musician bit it daintily then slipped it into a pocket of his short woollen jacket. He pursed his lips. "So what would you have me play?" Readjusting the kantele on his lap, he peered down his nose at her. "A lullaby? The devil's polska?" The rolling movement of her hands made him grimace, but he soon caught on. "Continue from where I left off. Okay, you can share my anguish. But I warn you, I hope it gives you nightmares because then I will have torn the thing out by the root and set it free into the world. Then I can sleep easy."

Anguish? Nightmares? Pirjo cocked her head. Wasn't love the cleansing note in any opus?

Her befuddlement seemed to move the man at last. Head lolling as if to better observe the skilful interplay of his fingers, he plucked a bell-like toll from one of the strings. The air was instantly aquiver.

Pirjo joined her hands in prayer and pressed them to her breastbone, working them into the crook beneath the join. The music was breathtaking, even if she lacked the organ of emotion – and in all of the time she had spent in the dusky flaxen fields beneath the well, she had never thought to question her loss. But here in the woods, under a sky as broad, black and colourful as a child's chalk scrawl, she wondered if it was right that Mother Reija should hold her heart to ransom? Hadn't she worked her fingers to the quick to appease the sacred crone?

For the first time since her ascent, Pirjo noticed the voice of the forest. Animals shuffled. Birds evacuated mid-slumber in lofty nests and pitted tree trunks. The great oaks creaked like tired old men. Wind moaned. Insects chittered amid the grasses or scuttled inside hollows. The owl called softly, a kiss of breath.

Pirjo's instinct was to repel the cacophony since it was unordered. But she also recognised a weird if symbiotic harmony, the din of the forest acting as the chords to the purifying ache of the kantele. Half-distracted by the fact, she drew the vial from the purse and pressed a thumb to the cork, about to lever it open. But then she paused. Why should she follow orders and distil the elixir that was the musician's song into the vial, only to convey it to Mother Reija and Vanaheim, which was, after all, just a half-world between the land of the living and Helheim, realm of the dead? If a heartless man could endure the mess of Life and still weave music that was luminous as aprons dashed against a scrubbing stone and pegged in the trees to dry, maybe she could stitch herself back in amongst it.

Resting the vial on the rim of the well, Pirjo wondered how best to communicate her empathy to the ignorant musician. In the absence of words, she was restricted to an abstract ballet of the hands, or the feeble contents of her purse. But it occurred to her that he might appreciate some small offering of sustenance, and while it was part-gnawed, she had discovered just the thing in the well water.

She reached into the purse a last time, drew out the browning apple core and offered it. The musician's eyes stayed closed. She held the core under his nose and tried to speak to him in her non-voice.

The cider scent would not have been enough to rouse Juho from his depth of poignant sorrow. Far more offensive to mind and ear alike was the guttural squawk that pierced the night. He snapped his eyes open and felt his jaw go slack at the sight of the apple core. The next instant, he threw aside the blood-hued kantele to scramble to a spot several paces away, where he doubled over, hands cupping his knees, choking on his breath.

"What the hell are you doing with that?" He glared at her, eyes red-rimmed and fear-soaked. "I threw it into the well just five minutes past and now you wave it up under my nose like a wizened witch levitating chickens for a crowd." His exasperation cooked up to a white hot rage and he powered forward to stand, hands on hips, towering over her. Before she had struck him as mind-addled, but now he saw her as an embittered shrew.

"What are you going to conjure up next? Something that turns my abdominals into fat white worming meat for you to suckle?"

The girl clawed at the powdered brickwork in an effort to back away. But he would not have it. These succubae with their pricked noses, mouths like springs, and salty effervescence, what right had they to feast on his fine, talented nature then leave him hollow like a sack of bones? Shunting hard against her, dashing a small vial off the rim into the well in the process, he gripped her chin, forcing her eyes from the bottle's swift descent.

She was weaker then, her face flowing over and not just with tears. Cleansed with emotion, he saw such openness in the green-gold girl as if, with his words, he had forced his hands past the tiny razored teeth and ravelled out whatever it was that choked her. He faltered in his tirade. She was not the muse to his grief; that honour lay with Eeva. Yet she had seemingly materialised out of thin air and taunted him to play. Did it really make a difference if a mother had bled her womb in a sauna to produce Eeva or this gilded Fae with her mouthful of knives?

"Do you think the notes I tear and charm from the strings are trifles for silly girls? They are precious to me as all the years I gave to their perfection. Just as whatever it is you've kept hidden in that purse is dear as life itself."

Her eyes ran wild, but before she could snatch for it, he had ripped the purse from her waist. Dancing away, he opened the drawstring and forced a hand inside.

"*This* is your cherished possession?" He held up the crude wooden spindle, wove it in and out of a gleam of moonlight. She darted at him, skirts sloshing at her ankles. Juho stretched higher on tiptoe, a hand pressed to his breastbone to control the pain of laughing. He reeled back his arm like a whaler readying his harpoon for the kill before launching his prize out into the air above the well. It dropped like a dead thing. Seconds later, it could be heard to hit the water with a soft splash.

"Who's going to fetch your spindle now, girl?" Juho crowed.

Pirjo stared at the brambled fairy gate of the well. So it was gone, the one treasure that had mattered enough to her to give up her heart. As the spindle was returned to the cavernous halls of Vanaheim so she abandoned the idiotic fancy that she could ever belong above ground again. The vial which had been her siphon to drain the sparkling music was also lost.

Her chest concaved. She drove her fingernails up into the hard pads of her palms.

Hands on hips, the musician threw back his head, laughing. "Why so glum? It's never good to attach yourself to any one singular possession. Trust me, fish girl, they'll always turn around and bite you." He shrugged, a dead smile stitched into his lips. "My mother has more spindles, poking out from the woven reeds of her largest parekori basket. So forget that sour look. I'll get you a better one. You should kiss me by way of thanks."

Pirjo took a bite from the remnants of the apple. Before the musician had the chance to reel in his words, she leapt up onto the rim of the well, crouched down, grasped his hard head and put her mouth to his. Her tongue broke past his lips like a bobbin interlacing the weft and she fed on the vital essence of his song. Then she crammed the apple in and broke away, sated by the roughness of the gesture if uncertain of its motive.

The musician stared at her. A bead of blood welled at a corner of his mouth where she must have nipped him. He choked on the pith of the fruit she had deposited, hacked in an effort to dislodge it from his throat and finally forced it down. Putting a finger to his lips, he traced the blood into a stain of a kiss. Hunger flickered in his pupils.

Standing, she balanced awkwardly on the rim of the well and edged away. The aged brick gave under one of her bare feet and she leapt back from the inner perimeter as a dislodged hunk fell away into the well. With her gaze darting between the advancing man and the secret depths just a pace away, Pirjo listened for a splash. Nothing reached her ears. Face draining to the colour of sage moss, she arched back as the brick came flying out from inside the well to land a few feet away.

The musician halted in his tracks. Two pools of viscous black, his eyes alone reacted to the numerous pairs of hands that thrust up and out from the well to claw the mouldered wall. Skittishly the horrors emerged, nine, ten of them, to sit clustered about the rim of the well, legs dangling over its unseen depths. They wore Tykkimyssy caps, the lace trims all dusty tatters poking out from beneath shaped silk domes prettied up with gone-off daisies. Their skin was gilt-flecked and mildewed. Their mouths and eyes were darned with crisscrossed black thread. In faded kirtle or darned smock, Mother Reija's handmaidens were between life and death like the strange, gold-green world they inhabited.

Pirjo stood rigid. Brittle fingers caressed her ankles then wormed towards her calves, waist and outstretched arms. She found herself buoyed up over the handmaidens' heads like a slain warrior. At the same time, her chest swelled of its own accord, as if ballooning with some purified quantity of air, her mouth craned open and she threw her useless voice towards the sky. The noise was ear-splitting. But almost as if the godless squawk were being dethorned by the muscles in her throat, a softer note broke through. It deepened sweetly to a bell-like tone and then soared, voice of love's labour, voice of the kantele.

Mother Reija's handmaidens clawed her into the watery dark. Pirjo did not stop singing the whole way down.

Juho staggered back from the old forest well, abandoned anew. He waited for the water sprites to return, bundle up his young supple bones and drag him forcibly below. But he found himself disappointed and somewhat irked when the abduction did not take place.

His mind felt oddly hazy, or was that lazy? He was not entirely sure, but he was struck by just how cold it seemed now he was standing all alone in the depths of the forest at night time. There had been a wound, he remembered quite incidentally, a heart break or was it a nip to the mouth? He put his tongue to his lips and tasted blood there. Yes, that was it. The girl had bitten him in the throes of desire. He was pleased by the fact, if drained of any inclination to dwell on it.

When his gaze wandered to the scuffed kantele at his feet, he squatted down and plucked a string. The note was coarse and he huffed. Why did he keep the useless unbeautiful old thing? He could do worse than heave it into the crooked well a couple of feet away. In fact that was exactly what he would do, he decided, dragging the instrument off the hard ground and propping it on the mouldered stone wall. He paused and caressed the kantele's womanly curves with a hand, conscious of their jagged edges. Careless to all but the instrument's spoilt nature and the biting cold, he tipped it in.

Juho pulled his kairalakki cap low. The black knit fitted snug about his ears as if the top of his skull had been dipped in tar. He did not feel inspired to do anything except sleep and he strode away, piped home to the bleak tune of an owl who-whooing.

Kim Lakin-Smith is currently working on the sequel to her debut novel, *Tourniquet: Tales from the Renegade City* (Immanion Press, 2007). Themes such as rock music, cyber-culture, motorbikes, hotrods, twisted fairytales, dark desires and lurid living suffuse her writing. Kim, who also has a story in NewCon Press's other recent release, *Celebration*, is one of the up-and-coming stars of British speculative fiction.

The Grass Princess

Gwyneth Jones

It was April, and down in the orchard the first flashing blades of the new year's growth were pushing aside the old, worn, winter stuff. The sky was blue and very clear, but the wind was cold. So the nursemaids put the little princess down under an apple tree, wrapped in her shawls, and ran away to play tag under the twisted apple branches, to keep themselves warm. And that was when the grass took her. Why did it happen? Was it the magic-making of a distant sorcerer, offended by some slight the royal family had forgotten? If that was, nobody ever found out. Or did the grasses embrace her because they had found a sister, as new and fresh and innocent as they? Perhaps, as some authorities later claimed, it was the baby herself who made the magic.

"But never mind who did it!" stormed the king, pacing up and down beside the tree while the nursemaids wept in a huddle. "How do we get her free again? That's the question."

The green tendrils that were wound around her little body seemed as soft and fragile to the touch as grass blades should. But they held the child in a grip stronger than steel wire. Every cutting edge that the royal household could think of was brought down to the orchard. They tried steel, stone, bronze, and even a knife of sharpened shell: a ritual object, relic of the old days when a king succeeded not by inheritance but by the sacred murder of his predecessor. They tried fire, they tried weed-killer... But when the king sent for his enchanted, diamond-bladed broadsword and started to saw away, dangerously near to the child's throat; and the baby started to scream, the queen called a halt. She protested that if all they wanted was to get the baby loose from the grass, a couple of pounds of high explosive, strategically placed, would probably do the trick. At last they decided to dig up the whole patch of grass on which she was lying, and carry it back to the nursery; roots, dirt and all. "Look at it this way," said the court magician. His spells had been helpless, and his nerves were all on edge. "You're not so much losing a daughter, as gaining a window box."

The infant had a little peace then, while messages were sent out, chasing up magical practitioners from all the lands around. She slept, and woke and slept again. She did not cry. She did not want to be fed. She smiled and slept and woke, and the grass blades twined ever closer and thicker around her tiny limbs, until only her face and one hand remained visible. A day and a night passed. On the third day the princess, who till then had kept up her usual baby cooing and babbling, grew very quiet. Her mother, who was watching, saw a change come over that small familiar face. "She looks so sad," thought the queen, and leaned closer, so that the grass blades fluttered in her breath. She put out a finger to touch the baby's hand... Was it possible? Was the grip of those determined tendrils getting weaker? Yes, it was true. The springy green coils were relaxing; the brilliant sheen of life was fading from them... The queen got slowly to her feet. She said aloud, as if the grass was a human enemy and could be deceived. "I think I will call the maid, and go downstairs. Baby is so quiet." She crept out of the room, and rushed down the stairs in a swirl of skirts, biting her fists in excitement. But before she could call for the servants or the king, something stopped her. *I will tell no one*, she decided. *I will not hope, I will not be excited. I will wait...*

It was terrible to wait, because the grass might be growing weaker just to grow stronger again in a little while. Perhaps she was missing her last chance to free the child. But the queen thought of how you might lift and tug and tear – and have in your arms a baby bleeding from ten thousand wounds. The queen did not believe in the 'malign sorcerer' for whom all the king's men were hunting. She was afraid of the grass itself. It was alive, it had if not a mind then at least a will of its own. The grass had taken her baby, for its own inscrutable reasons: and it would not willingly let her go.

She said nothing. No one else noticed that the grass was fading. In the middle of the night she came into the nursery very quietly. The nurse was drowsing in her chair. What of the child? From the cradle came the very faintest of sounds, a breath of a sigh. The queen looked down at her baby. Uprooted, shut away from the sunlight and the air, in spite of the earth that had been carried with it, the grass was withering. Already the blades were turning yellow and wan, like something grown in darkness under a stone. The princess lay still. Her eyes were open. She looked up at her mother, patiently: quietly accepting the suffering that was marked on her face, with no more outcry than the grass itself... which was also dying.

The queen saw that it was too late. Whatever made the baby a separate being, separate from the tendrils that bound her, was lost. She *was* the grass. Uprooted, she would wilt and fail and die. The queen stooped and picked up the whole bundle in her arms. She was so blinded by tears that she stumbled and several times almost fell as she hurried down the stairs, through the great still, dark rooms of the palace and across the gardens; to the apple orchard. There, standing out dark in the moonlight, was the small ragged trench where the turf had been cut away. The queen knelt beside it. She looked down into the pale dreaming face of her lost daughter. There was no longer the faintest hint of recognition in the princess's open eyes; nor of any human expression. She put the bundle into the hole, and scratched and worked the soil until she had done all she could to make the plot whole again. Then she went to the gardener's potting shed and came back with a can of water. It was as she sprinkled water indiscriminately over baby and grass and earth, that she understood the full strength of the enchantment. For the baby stirred, and started to laugh. Looking up through the moonlit drops, she smiled as if she was greeting her mother. But it was obvious that she did not see the queen at all. As surely as Persephone, overtaken in the flowery fields of Sicily by the king of the dead, this child had been kidnapped by the powers of the earth. She was gone, she had been stolen out of the human world... maybe forever.

It was a tough fight, but in the end they let the queen have her way. The king thought the whole thing made him look a fool. Within hours, the conjurors and the alchemists and the amateur heroes would be pouring into the palace grounds, eager to do battle against this wicked spell. Now the queen wanted him to cancel everything, and *let well alone*. The king said he couldn't see anything 'well' about this. He had a six month old daughter staked out like a cucumber vine in his backyard, and how could it possibly make sense to leave a situation like that undisturbed? Luckily for the queen, the bulk of magical opinion soon came over onto her side. The professionals felt that the kind of power that would be needed to break the bond between grass and baby would certainly break the baby too. The theory that *the baby herself had done this* appeared, and quickly gained ground. They decided it must be necessary for the princess to be enchanted like this, so that some prince (whose identity would emerge in time) could fulfil his destiny by freeing her. "Wait until she's older –" was the general run of advice. "Let Nature take its course." The queen found that these wise counsellors were reluctant to look her in the eye, as they took their fees. She felt that she understood their message only too well. But the king was satisfied.

The first thing he did, when he had been forced to wind up his rescue operation, was to assemble a team of architects, and get them designing the daintiest little summer-house, an orchard palace to be built around the enchanted apple tree... The queen was very sorry to do so, but she had to stop him again. She knew the poor man was doing his best, and that his rather inarticulate nature found relief in action, even the most futile action. But she also knew that his dainty arbour would kill her daughter. The baby's nature was one with the grass, and neither wind nor rain nor snow nor frost must be taken from her. She must live the life of the earth to which she was bound, or no life at all.

"What do you want me to do?" cried the king. "Go down there and tramp on her?"

"Of course not," replied the queen. "It would upset you horribly to do that. But *she* wouldn't mind, not if you trampled her into mud. She'd be back, as soon as you gave her a chance. That's what you must understand. *She is the grass.* Oh, I hope you'll be ready –"

"Ready for what?"

"When winter comes."

Winter came, and under the apple tree the child sickened and faded, as the queen knew she must. The king bore this very well, except for one frosty day when he was caught creeping down to the orchard, unrolling an extension lead behind him; an old one-bar electric fire hidden under his robe. But the queen's persistence was rewarded in the spring, when the child bloomed like the loveliest of April days. All through the summer she was well and strong, all through the winter she faded: and so it went on, through many winters and many springs. As well as thriving and failing with the changes of the season, the princess grew with real human growth, from a baby into a girl. The grass grew with her, so that her lengthening limbs made a green girl-shaped mound under the tree – a kind of horizontal topiary. Though she never spoke, and grew entirely silent before she was a year old, her eyes were alive. They opened to the daylight, closed at night; and seemed to smile at sun and rain. Some people said she was lovely - as far as you could see. Then, just as the girl in the orchard reached 'marriageable age', the queen died. She was still young. But she had spent so many hours sitting out under that apple tree, in all weathers – and perhaps she wasn't very strong to begin with: anyway, she died. This happened suddenly. A cold turned in a day or two into fever and inflammation of the lungs. The queen hardly knew she was ill before she found herself on her death bed, comforting her weeping husband.

"Don't be sad. My daughter has taught me. I am not afraid to lie down in the earth. I believe she is happy, maybe happier than any of us. But my dear..."

Afterwards, the king had a sneaking conviction that if she had managed to talk any more, she would have forced him to promise to leave their daughter in peace. But luckily she didn't. So, after a decent interval, he began his preparations.

The court physician was called to a consultation in the orchard, with the king, the court magician and a crowd of other functionaries. He gave the grass princess as thorough an examination as was possible, and told her father, looking very grave, that even if she was released there was little chance that his daughter could ever 'live a normal life'.

"And if one of these heroes of yours *could* somehow free her," said the great man. "Would he want her? Have you considered that she must be horribly scarred?"

"But this is *magic*," protested the king. "When the spell is broken, everything will be fine."

"There are some enchantments," declared the physician, "that aren't worth breaking."

But the court magician supported the king. Years of doing nothing about a bad magical situation on his own patch had galled his pride. He had always secretly resented the queen's triumph, and he and the physician were old rivals. He saw the grass princess problem as opportunity – not for himself, of course, but for the prestige of his discipline.

He sighed – a wise and reluctant sigh that put the blame for anything that went wrong firmly on his master's shoulders. "I don't think it is possible," he declared, "for us to accept the advice of medical science. Though we take these considerations seriously, we have here to do with a matter of destiny – a concept that 'medical science' cannot, with all due respect, fully understand. By my art I have learned that the princess must and will be freed... by one bound as she is bound, and scarred as she is scarred..."

"*What?*" spluttered the king. He stared at the magician accusingly. He had thought the two of them were agreed. There was nothing really wrong with the princess, no reason why she should not make a complete recovery –

"Ah –" The sage blinked. He had not meant to say that. Sometimes these things happened to him. That was one of the disadvantages of his profession. Just occasionally, one was not altogether in control. He corrected himself hurriedly. "Metaphorically speaking, that is. Bound and scarred as – er – a metaphor for the heroic experience."

The physician snorted. "I thought we were concerned about the girl, not the 'destiny' of some unknown youth. Well, I wash my hands of the whole affair." He stalked off, and the consultation was over. Magic had won the day.

Alas, it seemed that the doctor's pessimistic estimate was shared by the eligible young princes and nobles around about. There were ten or twenty young men who should have been the princess's suitors – some rich and handsome, some not so rich or not so handsome, all of them eager to make a good marriage. But they were not interested in the mound of grass in the king's orchard. The king was uncomfortably aware that his daughter had become a joke amongst his neighbours' sons. If you suggested to anyone that he should try his hand at 'the grass princess job', it meant you considered his prospects to be in very poor shape indeed.

There came a grey cold day in November, two years after the death of the queen. Under the old apple tree, the princess lay wan and haggard and worn. The shape of her in the grass didn't change with the seasons now that she was grown: but in winter her face, what you could see of it, looked like that of a sick little old woman. It was her birthday, she was eighteen years old. A young man rode into the gardens, garbed for hunting. His name was Damien. He was the same age as the princess – a rather dishevelled young man, with a look of angry unconcern. He had come dressed up for this quest, his manner seemed to say, but that didn't mean he took it seriously. He left his horse and came down between the trees. He had been sent here from the palace office, but he surveyed the scene in bewilderment. There was something distinctly macabre going on. Two middle-aged noblemen and a pack of servants were cavorting around the dead body of an old woman... who appeared to have been long buried, except that her face and one withered hand had been dug up. Somebody was tying *balloons* in the branches above this half-exhumed corpse –

"Excuse me. Can you direct me to –"

They didn't hear him. The whole crew had suddenly burst out singing: "Happy Birthday to you! Happy Birthday to you!" Suddenly the prince realised where he was and what he was seeing. He had not imagined it would be like this. *Evil enchantment* had a distant, romantic sound... He decided to leave, quietly.

"Hey!" yelled one of the middle-aged men. "Hey – you there, wait!"

He recognised the king. The other gentleman must be the court magician. The king was a friend of the prince's family. He couldn't escape now. He bowed, awkwardly.

"Hail, sire. I have come, if you will permit me, to attempt to free your daughter from foul enchantment, and thereby win her hand in marriage."

No one spoke. A manservant who was holding a pink iced cake on a tray, coughed. The princess's nursemaids gaped at the prince, making him feel extremely self-conscious. Damien, who had few friends and was oblivious to gossip, did not know that he was the only suitor who had taken up the king's well-publicised offer. He was unnerved by this reaction.

"So, what do I do? Do I kiss her, or what?"

He saw that there was something else showing besides a withered face. The princess's hand lay by her grass-grown side. The fingers were bare, they looked like thin and sallow grass roots. He guessed he must take her hand. The king and the magician were still staring, as if affronted by his presence. He stepped forward and went on one knee...

"No, no, no –"

One of the servants was pulling him to his feet. The two older men moved, making a barrier between the grass princess and her suitor. They were dressed identically, in sober suits under dark court robes. Their eyes were smug and old. He didn't even want the princess: but there they stood, age and authority incarnate, between Damien and all the world's prizes...

"I see," he said angrily. "I'm not good enough. Fine. I'll be on my way."

"Ah –" The king suddenly produced a smile. "Not so, ah, not so fast, young man. You see there are certain – ahem – requirements. You can't expect to win the hand of an enchanted princess just like that!" He laughed lightly. "You'd better come to my magician's office."

The magician had devised a list of tasks. He had spent time on this, and performed several magical operations, in his dark tower away in the remote fastness of the West Wing. He was proud of his list. He felt that it reflected the importance of the grass princess affair in the annals of magic: and that the success of the hero would also, and rightly, be the crowning achievement of his own career. Prince Damien studied the list of magical treasures that he had to secure – beg, borrow or steal – while the king and the magician explained to him how he would be welcomed when he'd completed his tasks. There would be a newly devised and very impressive ceremony. He would be escorted in state to the orchard, where he would take the princess by the hand – and she would rise from the grass, a beautiful maiden, ready to be his bride. He must, of course, agree to complete confidentiality. No interviews, no publications except with the express permission of the palace Office of Magic.

Damien wasn't paying attention. The first item he had to deliver was *the silver sword of the Divine Huntress*. His spirits rose. He signed everything they put in front of him. There were handshakes all round. The king and the magician returned to the birthday party and Damien rode away, full of hope and determination.

"Unfortunate case," said the king, when the boy was gone. "Young Damien. The mother ran off, you know, back to her own people under the hill. But the son's completely human. One of those things, genetics, they call it, I believe: it can play tricks. So he ended up with his father, who married again. There's a pack of new kiddies, new wife can't stand the boy of course, and his father is doing his best to fix the succession. It would be a funny thing if he – well, you know. I had a soft spot for his mother... but that was long ago."

The magician nodded thoughtfully, but his eyes gleamed. "Fairy blood!" he remarked. "Things are falling out very well for me... Ah, for the princess, I meant, of course."

Damien knew exactly what to do. The Divine Huntress is another name for the goddess of the moon. The silver sword would have to be a moonbeam. For any other young prince or sprig of the nobility, the first task might have been impossible. Moonbeams tend to slip through one's fingers; and it was clear that the 'sword' had to be a functional weapon. For once his mixed race was going to be an advantage. His mother had lost interest in him, the way those people tend to lose interest in fleeting human affairs. But he still had friends (as far as those people can be called friends) under the hill. He rode straight away to Wild Swan Lake, where his mother and father had first met, one midsummer dusk long ago. There, on a night of the full moon, he tapped on a certain door (invisible to wholly-human eyes) in the hillside that rises from that lake shore. He was not allowed beyond the threshold. He would never be allowed beyond, unless he consented to give up his humanity; but he spoke to someone there. The first price demanded was a strip of skin the whole length of him, but he beat the fairy haggler down. He gave up a strip of skin from around his wrist, and didn't ask – he thought he'd rather *not* ask – what it was for. In return he was given a black, polished tree root shaped like the hilt of a sword; and a long sheath of birch bark, sewn with spider thread. Then he knelt at the water margin and touched the hilt to one glimmering silver ripple, which slipped into the bark sheath as if they'd been made for each other.

He returned to the palace a month after he'd set out. His wrist was painful, and there'd be a scar there for life, but he was feeling confident. The king and the magician received him in strict privacy. In the West Wing, in the magician's comfortable study on the floor below his magical laboratory, they dimmed the lights. The magician took the fairy sheath and, slowly, drew out the sword of the Divine Huntress. The bright scalloped blade shone like silver. He laughed in delight. "Excellent! A triumph of my art!"

"Well done!" said the king.

Damien noted that somehow his achievement had become the old conjuror's 'triumph'. But it didn't matter. He had questing-fever now. He set out at once for the uttermost ocean, where he was to mine the yellow foam for a bushel of mer-gold. This transaction was not so simple. The Smith of the Uttermost Ocean lived in the galleries of a great cavern of green serpentine, which was half-filled by the tide twice a day and only visited by one questing hero or so in a generation. He was a lonely and embittered minor divinity, and he insisted that Damien had to work for his gold, as well as pay for it. The Smith knew how to distil many precious and useful ores from the sea. He was an exacting taskmaster and he treated Damien like an apprentice. Damien spent two years in the damp, snakestone gloom, the roar of the waves a constant booming in his ears, learning more than he had ever desired to know about the trade of smithying and the inner nature of metals. Time and again, he thought he'd completed his task: and then the Smith, who complained that the terms of the engagement were vague, changed his mind as to what quantity of gold constituted 'a bushel'. But at last, Damien managed to escape with his prize.

When the magician's security guards escorted him once more to the sage's study, he could see that the king and the magician didn't recognise him. He himself didn't recognise the room. It seemed larger, and everything looked shiny. He limped across to the magician's huge desk, and dumped his burden. "That's a bushel," he said. "The equivalent of eight gallons of sea-foam gold, dry measure. It may seem like less, but I got the Smith to sign for it."

They were looking at him strangely. "Are you hurt?" asked the king.

"Not exactly. It was the price of the gold. One hamstring tendon: the Smith needed it to mend his bellows, he's lost both his own hamstrings, as you know."

The magician opened the seaweed sack. A greenish glow oozed out. He dipped in his hand. The magic gold dust slithered over his palm. "Beautiful," he murmured. "And all mine!"

Damien could still hear the sea rushing and roaring in his ears. It was as if an endless earthquake had taken up residence in his head.

"Very good," declared the king. "Very good... You are doing a good quest, my fine fellow. And now, I believe it's the Lost Helmet of Invisibility."

So Damien set off in search of the Helm. He thought of going home to visit his family first, but decided against it. His oldest step-brother was now crown prince, and Damien's presence would only open old wounds. Besides, he had questing-fever.

It took years, this time. The Helm had been lost for over five centuries. Before he even began to look for it he had to learn *how* to search: in old libraries and record offices, in museums and monasteries. He had to work to support himself as well. Since the crisis over the succession had been weathered, getting money out of his father was a lot more difficult. Sometimes he thought of the princess. He saw in his mind's eye that pallid hand, and wondered what it would feel like to touch it. He wondered what they would talk about, when he was king and she was queen. But the achievement was more important than the reward. When he finally returned to that orchard and freed the famous 'grass princess' from her bondage, (she was famous now. The court magician had made sure of that) he would had *done something* with his life, and nobody would be able to deny it.

Damien discovered that around the time when the Helm disappeared, a certain giant called Lamerish of the Crags, had been a prominent social figure. He had been much more socialized than the average giant: in fact he was a noted art collector. There had been rumours. But no one could prove - or dared to try - that he had a secret collection of stolen treasures, besides those that he kept on open display. The Helm of Invisibility had disappeared from the treasury of a royal family that was now extinct. Lamerish the giant, Damien learned, seemed to have vanished from history at about the same time. The first part of the search ended when Damien established that a small craggy piece of a neighbouring kingdom's highest mountain range had also vanished from modern maps.

He knew that the only way to reach a place made invisible by magic was to travel there through fairyland. So he went again to the door in the hillside – a different hillside from the one above Wild Swan Lake; but the same entrance, to the same forbidden realm. The guardian of the threshold could have been the same as the person with whom he'd bargained for a moonbeam swordblade. Damien couldn't tell. One doesn't *see* those people clearly. In this world, they are a trick of the light. He saw the shadow of leaves moving, a glint of sunlight eyes; a hint of dappled animal limbs... He was told that the price of his journey to the Invisible Crag would be that he would not be able to find the door in the hill again. He would be earthbound, forever. Damien accepted the bargain. Something touched his eyes lightly. He saw and felt nothing until he found himself standing knee-deep in alpine snow, a terrifying desolation of rock and ice and snow rearing up around him.

He climbed to the giant's castle. No one challenged him. He passed through the fallen gates, through snowdrifts to the great doors of the keep, where human and giant-sized men-at-arms were still standing, frozen and mummified; upright in their corroded armour. The giant must have stolen the Helm, or had it stolen; used it to hide his castle, and then discovered too late that he could not undo what he had done. Obviously he wasn't a student of magic, or he would have known that the Helm was protected. Any thief who used it would find he couldn't take it off again, and couldn't return himself or anything he had rendered invisible to the visible world. Damien walked into the great hall, through ranks of priceless, mouldering artworks. The giant Lamerish was sitting there alone, in a huge bronze chair that had once belonged to an Emperor, facing the doorway, with dark, unseeing eyes. He must have died, along with all his people, of hunger and thirst. The Helm was like a closed crown, the bands of magic metal set with dim grey jewels. Damien lifted it from the giant's yellowed skull, being careful not to touch it with his bare hands. He wrapped it in his spare shirt.

The crag returned to the real world as soon as Damien took the Helm from the skull. He set off to make the long descent. He'd been prepared, but conditions above the snowline were worse that season than he had imagined possible. By the time he reached safety, his hands and face and feet were ravaged by frostbite. It was months before he was fit to travel back to the palace.

The magician was ecstatic. He positively drooled over the Helm. The king was excited too. He kept repeating: "Well done, well done, very good work! --" and patting his hands over his plump belly, as he sat in comfort in the magician's splendid audience chamber. They were both looking extremely prosperous, as was the whole palace.

Damien just felt terribly tired. But some profound emotion began to stir as he watched the two self-satisfied old men.

"I'd like to see the princess again now."

"Eh? See the princess?" The king, bemused by this suggestion, looked to the sage for guidance. The magician discreetly pursed his lips and frowned. "I'm afraid that's impossible." declared the king. "You see, my boy, you haven't completed the tasks –"

Damien set his teeth, and clenched his scarred fists. *"I'd like to see the princess."*

To avoid a scene, they took him to the orchard, accompanied by the minimum security escort. Nothing had changed much there. The rest of the palace was full of people these days, bustling about the business of the 'grass princess affair'. But the magician had wisely realised that the enchanted princess was not, in herself, an impressive object. It was better that she remained a mystery, unvisited and secret.

It was September and the grass had been allowed to grow rich and long. It had gone to seed in plumes of russet and gold. There was a humming of insects in the sultry afternoon air. A few red apples glowed between the leaves of the old tree. A single ageing nursemaid jumped up from her chair and curtsied.

The king and the magician had to wait for Damien to catch up. He limped towards them, flanked by guards, and stared down at that blurred hummock in the long grass: the weather-browned leaf-shape of her face, the sallow root-fingers of her uncovered hand. He remembered the scene he'd imagined: the delicate hand waiting for his touch, the sweet face looking up like a fallen star... A rush of bitterness overwhelmed him. He saw what the grass princess was.

She was bait in a trap. She was the bait those two gloating, fatherly *monsters* had used, to lure Damien into their service. They had taken the treasures. They had taken his strength, his youth, his time, his birthright... And for nothing. Because suddenly he knew that he would never win. That hump in the grass would never stand up, a human girl. He'd been so naive! It was obvious to him now that the magician hadn't the slightest idea how the 'enchantment' could be broken. The list of tasks was pure greedy invention.

"Damn you!" he yelled. "You old bloodsuckers! Liars! Thieves!"

The guards reacted quickly. But they didn't know how much force they should use. After all, Damien was supposed to be the hero of the story that was keeping everyone in business. The prince, lame and weary as he was, shook off their restraining hands. He flung himself on the grass. He got hold of the hand. It didn't respond: it was inanimate as earth. He dropped it and started tugging and tearing, sobbing furiously.

"Cheats! I gave you my life! For this *thing,* this scrap of dirt –"

The guards dragged him off, prising loose his twisted fingers. The king was shaking his head sadly, the magician looked wise and pained.

"That won't do, you know," said the king mildly. "You can't force her."

Damien stared at them. The grass cuts on his hands were stinging. "I've finished." he said heavily. "You can keep your quest." He kept on looking back, staring with the same dull anger, as he stumbled away.

The magician made a sign that the guards were to let him go.

"Most regrettable," he remarked. "Very shocking."

"What a shame. And he had only one task left to perform. What was it, by the way?"

"Bring peace to the House of Ayi," supplied the magician. He shrugged. "Something for the good of the community. A social service, you might say. There's no treasure involved. I put it in –" he added, in a lapse of unusual candour, "because I felt otherwise our requirements might seem a little, well, acquisitive – to ignorant opinion."

"Any chance that he might perform it? And come back?"

The two prosperous gentlemen glanced at each other, with almost a sly look. Secretly, the king was well aware that the quest was bogus, and that if a hero managed to fulfil their conditions, they'd have to start thinking of new excuses for why the enchantment remained unbroken... The magician knew that the king understood this.

"Very little," he assured his master. "No chance at all, I'd say." With a nod to the nursemaid, they turned to leave the orchard. "Well, Damien has failed," went on the magician. "We must seek a new champion. There will be plenty of candidates, there's been a great deal of interest building up." He rubbed his hands in anticipation. "I must compose a new list."

Damien left the orchard where the grass princess lay dreaming far behind him. He decided to take up the usual career of a disinherited prince, and become a mercenary soldier. Despite the exigencies of his quest he was strong, from the years at the smithy, and he still had the remains of his early training in his father's castle. But he was lame and scarred, and he couldn't raise his own troop or even equip himself well. He wandered for months through the neighbouring kingdoms, without finding employment. At last he came to a country where warfare had become a way of life. The farmlands were devastated, the people were starving. The cities were battered fortresses, struggling along from one siege-and-burning to the next... Damien rode into this blighted land at the beginning of winter. He couldn't locate the armies, but one day, as he was riding through the desolate fields, a woman stepped out in the road in front of him, and took hold of his horse's bridle. She was dark-skinned, like many of the people of this country. She was dressed in ragged leather, unarmed as far as he could see, and had a bloodstained rag tied round one shoulder. She wore gold braided in her wiry hair, and gold rings on her fingers. It was dusk: the gold and her eyes and teeth shone like life in the gloom.

"That's a fine horse," she said.

The mare was not a fine horse. But Damien looked at the woman – brigand, beggar or soldier, it was all the same in this country: and he loved her. He knew from the way she looked up at him that she felt the same sudden flame. "Who are you?" he said.

"I am a queen, but at this moment a beggar-queen. Will you help me?"

"And I'm a general," laughed Damien. "Get up behind, I can give you a lift."

The beggar queen thanked him, got up behind and directed him across the fields, past the gibbets where the dead hung in chains, through a burned village: to an armed camp. When she slipped to the ground at the first guard post: uproar burst out. Damien learned that he had met a genuine queen: Nenya the Black, who had been captured by the Duke, her brother, and had escaped as he found her -alone and unarmed.

So the prince joined Nenya's army. He never became a general, but before long he became her lover. The other officers, a desperate crew of cut-throats, called him Hob because of his limp, and they didn't resent his privileges. Nenya the Black was a tigress, too hot for any but this brave fool of a stranger. Damien heard her story, partly from Nenya herself and partly from one of her real generals, a grizzled old soldier called Camiero Goodwill. There had been war for generations, between the Black Ayi and the White. The Black Ayi were indeed often black-skinned, but that wasn't how they got their name. They were devils, declared Camiero with pride. Nenya and Ester of Ayi, when they were very young, had ruthlessly destroyed the Whites and briefly pulled the whole country together. They were brother and sister, and lovers too, as was the custom. Then the Emperor – a foreigner, explained Camiero, who for some unfathomable reason imagined he owned Ayi – interfered. He made Ester a Duke, with legal title to the whole domain, on condition that he marry his 'White' cousin, a child who had been taken off and reared abroad (which was how she came to be still alive). The Emperor didn't know or care about local customs.

"Nenya bided her time," explained Camiero. "Until the White arrived. She nearly cut the little girl's throat, and then we'd have had peace. But we were betrayed. That traitor Ester turned the army against us and threw us out, Nenya and her whole train – I was with the queen then already, you see. So she raised her own army, and the war began again."

The story was told differently in the countries where Damien had been a prince and a questing-hero. But he accepted the new version, in which a blood-feud made sense and Black Nenya was in the right. He forgot his old life almost entirely. Sometimes on the edge of sleep, he would remember the grass princess, and wonder if she would ever find a hero... *scarred as she was scarred, bound as she was bound.* He knew the famous words now, though he hadn't heard them before he started the quest. The magician hadn't been able to prevent them from passing into popular mythology. But it was not his problem any more.

One day – it was the end of another winter – Nenya took him out onto a tawny, snow-stained mountainside, to a ridge that overlooked a wide view of rolling hills. Things had been going well for the queen. She was about to begin her great attack on Ayi itself. It was a fine morning; they were on horseback.

"Do you see those towers?" she said. "The four great towers against the sky? That's the castle of Ayi, where I was born. I will never rest until I am back within those walls."

She did not look at Damien. But he looked at her, and he was consumed with jealousy, and hatred for the Duke of Ayi. After that day the lovers began to quarrel. Camiero and the other officers – men and women both, because in Ayi Nenya was not the only tigress – looked on and shrugged and didn't try to intervene. They'd seen this happen before. Damien was jealous, and Nenya scornful. Damien demanded proof of her love, Nenya told him he was a common soldier, and she owed him nothing. He still shared her bed. Her passion there grew savage, as her forces closed in on Ayi. But Damien knew that it was the Duke's face she saw in the dark, her traitor brother's body she embraced.

They were preparing to attack an armed supply train. It was a minor part of Nenya's plan, this ambush in a pass called the Scartaran Defile, but she was leading it herself. Damien had been sent off, with jeers from the queen, to guard the spare horses. He decided that this was his chance to tackle Nenya alone. He left the horses and sneaked around the lines of ragged soldiers, hidden in the boulders and the long brown thickets of winter grass, to where Nenya was sitting by herself a little way off from her officers; as always before a fight.

"Nenya," he whispered, "we have to talk."

"No." She jumped up and turned on him, a long knife in each hand. "I have made up my mind. I'm going to kill you. It will be your release, poor fool."

So they fought. But it was Nenya the Black who fell, her life choking out of her.

Without Nenya, the ambush became a rout. And it was that day, after the battle, that the Duke Ester killed himself, on learning of his sister's death. It was that same day, as Nenya lay in the castle courtyard on a wooden trestle, at rest within the walls of Ayi, that the Duke's young wife came down – looking like a child before the crowd of war-hardened savages – with her baby in her arms: and spoke to the people, saying that the lovers should be buried in one grave; and from now on there would be peace. Damien was there through these great events. He found that he was somehow counted responsible for ending the feud. He said all he wanted was to go home. So the Duke's wife gave him money and a fine horse, and set him on his way. Some time later, maybe days or maybe hours, he found himself on a road somewhere, got down from the horse and ran into a wood. He was looking for the door into fairyland. He could not find it. He ran wildly into a thicket of thorns, and struggled there until he fell, bleeding from ten thousand wounds.

When he woke up, he couldn't see. He heard the pad of bare feet, and felt that someone was bending over him. "You're awake," said an old, kindly voice. "That's good. I am the Hermit of the Borderland. I found you hurt in the wood and brought you to my home. Don't be afraid, you will not be blinded for long."

Damien touched his own face with his scarred fingertips. "What's this?"

"A compress of bruised herbs. It's a kind of wild grass. It will speed the healing."

The prince lay and thought about that. "Grass," he repeated. "It smells of earth." He sighed. "I have to make a journey. One more journey."

"In a few days."

"No. At once."

So they set out.

In the apple orchard it was April again, with a wind like ice and the sun like honey. The princess who lay bound in the grass was blossoming like the trees. The nursemaid, who had once been a blossoming girl herself, playing tag in the chilly sunshine, talked to the princess quietly, while she did her knitting. She liked to talk, and no one could prove that the grass princess didn't hear you, even if she never answered.

The Hermit led Damien, his eyes still bound. The prince heard a comfortable murmuring voice, which broke off suddenly.

"Am I in the orchard?"

"Yes, sir," said the nurse.

"The king? Is he here? The magician?"

"Oh no, they've all gone, I'm sorry sir. The king is on his holidays, in the Fortunate Isles. And the magician... if you mean the old one, he left us a while ago. You see, we didn't attract the right kind of hero, after prince Damien failed. And our sage had a very good offer from a big, 'multinational' I think they call them. So we're very quiet here now. The palace is mostly shut up. Should I show you to the reception office?"

"No thank you."

Damien sat down. His hands brushed the young grass. He could not tell if it was warmer where it covered what had once been the body of a girl; he could feel no pulse of separate life. He groped, and found her hand. It lay in his for a moment, like a twist of dry grass. Then the world shivered, and changed. Warm fingers grasped his. The princess stirred, sat up, and stood; drawing Damien to his feet.

"Who are you?"

Damien let go her hand and pulled the grass from his eyes. The princess was standing there, clothed in the rags of a baby shawl and her tumbling dark hair: a strong, shapely young woman, with no visible scar from her long imprisonment.

"A friend," he said. "Just a friend."

The nursemaid ran and fetched the clothes, the set of clothes that was traditionally kept ready. The Hermit told the new young woman what she must do to give thanks for her deliverance. Soon she was dressed. She returned to the stranger, looking shy and solemn.

"They tell me you broke the enchantment. And that means... I belong to you?"

He shook his head. He thought of his bitter experience, his long trials, his guilt and shame. He was stricken, scarred and bound. He had nothing to say to this stainless creature. How could she possibly understand?

"No. You don't belong to anyone. Walk away, princess. Forget what happened here. Be your own woman."

So the princess walked away. But when she came to the orchard gate she stopped. She turned, and came back. Damien saw that the scars were there, after all. He saw the misery and frustration of her bondage, the silent courage and endurance, all the voiceless suffering of the years, looking out of eyes that mirrored his own.

"This isn't the end of the story," she said. "It is the beginning. Be my friend."

Gwyneth Jones was born in Manchester and graduated from the University of Sussex. While still a teenager, she won a Manchester Evening News writing competition – her first literary-related prize. Many more were to follow, notably the James Tiptree Jr. Award (1991) for *White Queen*, the BSFA Award (1999) for "La Cenerentola", the Arthur C. Clarke Award (2002) for *Bold as Love*, and the Philip K. Dick Award (2005) for *Life*. A resident of Brighton, on England's east coast, Gwyneth has published twenty-odd books under her own name and a similar number of YA novels under the pseudonym Ann Halam. "The Grass Princess" and the collection it appeared in, *Seven Tales And A Fable*, earned Gwyneth a brace of World Fantasy Awards in 1996.

Understandings

Accurate interpretations and comprehension of meaning through the use of intelligence.

Tales From the Big Dark: Found in the Translation

Pat Cadigan

Nothing was normal after Jean-Christophe found me in the Terrarium.

He materialized in front of me on the footpath, a thousand-watt smile splitting his neat beard. His salt-and-pepper hair was long again, just past his shoulders, and there was more green in his eyes. He seemed to get better-looking every time I saw him. Not that I tried to see him a lot – he's bad for me. Of course, that was never a consideration for him. He drives me crazy.

He held up a picnic basket and said, "I hoped so much that I would find you here!" And it wasn't those good looks or the picnic basket – of all things, God help me – that took me by surprise but the buzz that came from my translator. It was a very mild buzz, barely more than a hum, but a definite indication that there was some discrepancy between what he had said and what I'd heard. This was unprecedented with Jean-Christophe. He's one of the very few other people out here in the Big Dark who hails from the same world I Do – i.e., he's not merely from the same planet but also from the same general time period – and although he always speaks French, my translator has never so much as quivered even on the idioms.

I was so taken aback that I let him kiss me on both cheeks without protest. When he homed in on my mouth, however, I came to my senses and pushed him away.

"What are you doing here?" I demanded. "You know you're bad for me."

He looked around. This area was nearing the peak of the summer cycle – the trees were in full leaf, the grass was as thick and soft as a carpet, and the flowers lining either side of the footpath made a bees' buffet. "I remember how much you love it here in this season. I thought we could have lunch."

"Thanks but I'm too old to roll around on the ground while I'm eating."

The thousand-watt smile again. "Then we shall eat first and roll around after."

"No, we shall *not*," I told him firmly. "Even if you weren't bad for me – I did mention that, didn't I? – I have to get back to work soon. So if you'll *pardonnez-moi*, I'd like to finish my green time in peace. Happy trails." I tried to walk past him and he moved to block me. "No fooling, Jean-Christophe." I tried to give him a blistering glare. "I'm walking a timed circuit here."

He patted the picnic basket. "But I promised your assistant I would feed you."

"*Charlie* told you where to find me?" How could he do that to me, I wondered. Now I'd have to kill him.

"No, no, he refused to tell me anything," Jean-Christophe said quickly. "I just guessed right. Knowing you as well as I have – as I still do – it wasn't so hard. I told Charlie that when I did find you, I would be good for you. And I am." He hefted the picnic basket again. "I have here a very nutritious lunch."

I shook my head. "The food is good for me. You're not."

"But if I bring the food, then I must be good for you, too, yes?"

"What, are you a lawyer now?" I drew back from him.

The smile fell away from his handsome face like a mask. "Please, Hannah," he said, openly begging, which was also unprecedented. "I need someone to talk to and it can only be you because we come from the same world. We may be bad for each other but we share an understanding."

"We're not bad for each other. *You're* bad for *me*. Big difference."

"Please. I need to tell you something: I'm leaving."

I gave him a look. "Leaving how? Moving to live among the chlorine breathers? You won't like having to wear a protective suit all the time."

"No, I'm *leaving*. I'm *going away*."

"Uh-huh. As if you could. Don't bullshit me, Jean-Christophe."

I thought I sounded stern but somehow he'd already taken hold of my arm and was leading me toward a grassy spot under a big old maple. Maple trees are the most common large woody botanicals in the known universe, or at least that part known to me personally. If and when people from Earth achieve interstellar travel, one of the biggest surprises awaiting them besides the number of sentient races will be the ready availability of maple syrup for their pancakes.

Fortunately, Charlie called me just in the nick of time to tell me we had a new arrival at the shelter. Relieved, I ran for the nearest service exit and took a high-wall express transport back to the shelter.

"Of course it's a real pick-up." Charlie gave me a funny look as we headed for the intake pen with the folded stretcher trundling along behind us. "You know I would *never* call you and say we had one when we didn't."

I did know; it was a cultural thing. Charlie's people weren't above telling white lies now and then but crying wolf was a serious transgression with them, in the order of a taboo. "It's just that your timing was so perfect," I said. "If you hadn't called right then, I don't know what would have happened."

"*Oh.*" Charlie's gaunt, cave-man-esque features took on a sour cast. "Jean-Christophe found you, did he?"

"Yeah. Apparently I'm predictable if you know me well enough."

"But that's true of anyone, isn't it?"

My translator buzzed through the last part of that exchange in a way to let me know Charlie's was also buzzing, signifying that neither of us grasped the exact meaning of what we were saying to each other.

"I find that really hard to believe," he said, tapping the area above his left ear where the translator was implanted. Mine was behind my right ear, lower down.

"You do? Why?" I asked, honestly curious.

"All this time we've spent working together, you must have noticed how things have changed between us with the buzzing. I have. At first, we had at least a few mutual buzzes in every conversation. Then it went down to a few every day. Now it's just every so often. The understanding we've come to share, it's better even than the one I have with Agnes or Sarah or Japheth."

Two mentions of shared understanding with two different people in the space of a few minutes? A small alarm bell went off in my mind. On Earth that would have been a coincidence; out here in the Big Dark, however, it's a symptom. "Well, to be fair, Agnes is a recent arrival and there's no temporal overlap between you two," I said, hoping I didn't sound as uneasy as I felt. "And Sarah and Japheth have been here for so long they've pretty much forgotten any other life." Those weren't their actual names, just how I heard them. Whether the translator based its renditions on meaning or phonetics was one of many things I didn't know. It probably didn't make any difference either way but some names, like Japheth, were just odd enough to make me wonder if there was some other, more esoteric element involved.

"I know all that," Charlie was saying as we reached the end of the hallway and merged with the traffic in the wider thoroughfare leading to the intake pens. "But there are times when I think that even if I did have more in common with them, you and I have worked together for so long that we would still understand each other better. Or you would understand me better, anyway. Like just now – I can't believe that you didn't understand exactly what I was saying." Pause. "Or that I didn't say exactly what I meant to, in a way you could hear correctly." He made a pained face. "Translators – as soon as you start talking about them, it gets confusing."

I tapped the spot where my translator was implanted. "Either that or I've got a loose wire."

Charlie laughed like I'd tickled him, although his particular branch of humanity isn't at all ticklish and is thus unacquainted with the concept. I'd have thought that would make them seem more alien to me but, oddly, it doesn't. Maybe it's because, being extremely ticklish myself, I like people who can't even think of tormenting someone that way.

"*Wait*, please." A traffic warden stuck a feathered hand in our faces and then, to make sure we got the point, stood in front of us with her arms out to either side. I barely managed not to laugh out loud – it's the sort of position no feathered but flightless lifeform can take without looking silly. "We have a cargo chain coming through …"

I sidestepped into the centre lane, pulling Charlie along with me, and kept going.

"Just a moment!" the warden called after us, feathers ruffling sharply.

"Sorry, medics en route to intake pens," I called back over my shoulder. "Can't wait."

She yelled something about reporting us.

"Can she do that?" Charlie asked, sounding anxious. He's so law-abiding.

"She can, but they'll only tell her the same thing I did just now. We're entitled to use the centre express lane for travel."

"Then shouldn't we have been there all along?"

I shrugged. "If we had been, she'd have found some reason to stop us there and it would have been harder to get away. You know what feathered bipeds are like."

Charlie gave me a disapproving look.

"Hey, feathered bipeds themselves say the same thing, and proudly. They don't just drive me crazy – they drive everyone crazy. It's what they do."

Another team of medics were coming out of the intake pen just as we arrived. "It's two for the price of one today," said the senior member. His name came to me as Tiller; he was mottle-skinned and hairless and cycled between air and water. His partner, Ophelia, was also cyclical; she was a hibernator. Judging from her slightly hung-over look, she had only recently woken up.

"Two from the same ship?" I asked, looking at the man on their stretcher. His face was almost familiar. "That's got to be the Dacz.va."

"None other," Ophelia said through a yawn.

"But not from the same planet," Tiller added. "This one's from your locale." He nodded at me.

I gave a short laugh. "Funny, I was just thinking that he reminded me of someone I knew."

Tiller and Ophelia angled the stretcher to give me a better look at him. "You think you might have breathed the same air?" Tiller asked, his mottled face hopeful. "Wouldn't that be lovely for both of you."

I shook my head sadly. "Would but won't. In the words of the prophet, certain things are likely, but probably not today."

Tiller cocked his head to one side; he probably hadn't heard anything except a buzz on prophet. Another odd cultural variance –

odd to me, anyway. Truth to tell, Tiller's people didn't seem to be any poorer for the absence of prophets than Charlie's were for not being ticklish. "We have that saying, too. I heard it from my first father."

I smiled apologetically. "Actually, I think I originally heard it from you."

"Oh." He looked at me sideways. "So would your people think I was a *par-fay*?"

I resisted an ice cream sundae joke – there was no way to tell whether I was hearing Tiller's phonetic approximation or a translation of a phonetic approximation. "If they did, they wouldn't pay you as much as you're worth."

His laughter was a bubbly gargling noise much more pleasant than that description makes it seem. "Last chance – you sure you don't know this guy?" he asked.

I shook my head again. "At this point, I'm not expecting to meet anyone else with even a small temporal overlap."

"Now, now," Tiller said. "You know it doesn't always work that way. Time gets slippery out here in the Big Dark. One guy's before is another guy's after, it's sooner than you think, and you're only as old as anyone else your age…"

Ophelia broke in with a loud yawn. "I've got an idea – maybe we oughta move before I'm asleep again and he's awake."

Charlie looked after them longingly as they moved off, which was both amusing and surprising. He wasn't often given to showing his feelings, or at least not those feelings.

"Is it him or her?" I asked.

"Both," he sighed. "I want to reproduce with her and raise the kids with him."

"Better throw yourself into your work instead." I ushered him into the pen with the stretcher bumping at my heels.

The nude woman lying unconscious in the fetal position on the floor had smooth white hair that started at the very top of her head and stopped at the base of her neck, with a narrow spread, a bit like a horse's mane. There was a faint radiance to her dark brown skin, as if the tissue itself contained some luminescent element. The radiance was strongest in her face, which looked Japanese.

The Dacz.va always drop off their abductees nude. It's a thing with them – strip the memory, strip the body. While that saves us the trouble of having to remove and dispose of any garments, it bothers me that they don't even so much as cover any of these people with a sheet or something. Of course, we'd have to dispose of it in the recycler if they did but that's not the point. This just seems so disrespectful. But then, I come at this from <u>my</u> point of view, which, considering the Dacz.va aren't mammals, is all wrong. Still, they drive me crazy.

We covered the woman, eased her onto the lowered stretcher, and waited for it to access the data in the bracelet around her left wrist.

"Hey, her CV says she's from Neep's world," Charlie said, looking at the readout. "Funny, she doesn't look dually-sexed."

"You can't always tell just at a glance," I said, knowing Charlie would barely have given our new arrival that much. Nudity embarrasses him. Exactly how he ended up in this job is a minor mystery but he managed to be good at it in spite of his hang-ups. I checked the bracelet and the stretcher memory but neither had any defects or malfunctions. "Maybe the Dacz.va, in an unprecedented fit of incompetence, put the wrong bracelet on the wrong abductee."

Charlie frowned. "Nothing like that's ever happened before."

"That's what *unprecedented* means."

"I mean nothing like that has ever happened with *any* race or civilization, for as long as the shelter's been operating," Charlie said. "You were speaking only of the Dacz.va."

I stared at him for a moment, unable to decide if this was sharply perceptive, kind of creepy, or highly unsettling. "You're right, I was." I replayed my original statement in my mind. Maybe it was just logical, given the fact that Charlie knew how I felt about the Dacz.va and their abduction habits.

"If they did leave us the wrong information," Charlie continued, sliding the readout back into the stretcher frame, "it is definitely something to be quickly and severely discouraged."

The words clanged – I hadn't heard anything that stilted come out of Charlie in a long time – but there was no buzz. "I'll get right on it," I told him as we wheeled the stretcher out of the intake pen and down the corridor.

"The same way you got them to stop leaving their abductees here without a CV?"

I chuckled. "It worked, didn't it? We haven't had anyone arrive here without a data bracelet in ages. I don't see why my threat to abduct a whole crew and dump them without memory or pertinent data couldn't be extended to include erroneous information. We don't want them thinking that they can get away with that, even just by accident."

"Sure," Charlie said. "I was just thinking you might up the threat a little."

I looked over my shoulder at him in surprise. "How? Should I threaten to hurt them, too?" Charlie may look like my world's idea of a gaunt caveman but he's the gentlest person I've ever met, human or otherwise.

"More like suspend their license to travel and ground their spacecraft."

"Good idea but I don't think I could get away with that one. Yanking licenses and grounding spacecraft is too official. The Dacz.va would never buy it. They aren't stupid enough to believe I have that kind of power." *Almost, but not quite*, I added silently. "And if they complained to Maintenance, who knows how those guys might discipline me? I might wake up in an intake pen myself."

"I can't believe Maintenance would do that to one of us," Charlie said with the conviction that comes out of the purest naïveté. "If the Dacz.va did put the wrong bracelet on someone, that's a very serious mistake. We could suggest Maintenance take some kind of serious action."

"Sure we could. And they might do it." I chuckled. "Right after they fix the orientational anomalies. Like this one."

Charlie looked at me with dismay, mainly because I was walking on the ceiling now. Every time we picked up a dump job, one of us spent part of the time upside down, usually but not always on the way to the hospital. Anomalies could appear anywhere at any time in the Big Box. The only place I've never heard of them happening is in the Terrarium.

Neep didn't even bother looking at the preliminary readout before we transferred the abductee to a waiting bed. "There's no mistake," the doctor said cheerfully. "This one's definitely from my world."

"Okay," I said. Charlie and I traded a quick glance, which wasn't lost on Neep.

"Oh, come on," s/he said, laughing. "Does everyone on your worlds look just like you? Are you all the same colour, the same height, the same weight?"

"Okay, you got me there," I said, thinking that with her red-gold skin and short fuzzy cap of yellow hair, Neep couldn't have looked more different without growing another limb. There was something else as well. "But isn't everyone on your world dually-sexed?"

"We certainly are." Neep was busy at the nearby console, coordinating information coming from the bed.

"Pardon me for saying so, but this person looks monosexual," Charlie said. "Like us."

Neep gave us a quick smile. "That's because he's pregnant. You can tell by his skin – he has a glow. The gestational parent is temporarily monosexual until after the birth. So we'll be calling our new arrival here 'he' and 'him' for a while. Of course, that's just a social designation. All the basic biology is still intact and he remains dually-sexed."

I had been waiting for my translator to buzz but I didn't get even a twitch.

"Oh, I know how confusing this is for you monosexuals," Neep went on, chuckling a little.

"It's just the grammar," I said. "It's backwards from what I'm used to. On my planet, we'd be calling him 'she', both for his appearance and because of his role as the, uh, gestational parent."

"I know," Neep said, his/her tone deeply sympathetic. "If I hadn't been a doctor for so long here in the Big Box, I'm not sure I'd ever be able to get my mind around the idea of such rigid designations. He, him, her, she – you know, our ancestors had to invent new sex-specific pronouns to…" Her/his voice trailed off. "Oh, dear."

"What's the matter?" I asked.

Neep straightened up from the console and turned on the holographic display. A three-dimensional, high-resolution image of

117

the new arrival's innards appeared over his unconscious form on the bed. The fetus was larger and more developed than I'd thought; Neep's people were designed to make more room internally for child-bearing.

"What we have here," s/he said, "is a case of cross-pollination. That other abductee that came in with him is the fertilizing parent."

For a moment, I wasn't sure I'd actually heard her/him right. "I didn't think there was enough commonality for that."

"There isn't. This isn't something they did – it was done to them."

My jaw dropped. "By the *Dacz.va*? They can barely *cook*. How the hell did they learn to splice?"

"They probably picked up a kit somewhere," Neep said distractedly. "Whoever gave it to them ought to be abducted."

"Why would they do something like that?" Charlie asked.

"Because they thought they could keep the puppies," I said. "So to speak."

"Then it's lucky for everyone concerned that they changed their minds and dumped them here," Charlie said. I got a buzz on <u>lucky</u>; Charlie's people don't have <u>luck</u> the way we did on Earth. Not many races do.

"That depends on how well we can clean up the mess they left us." The unhappiness on Neep's red-gold features deepened. "This isn't just a matter of breaking the news to a couple of innocent victims that they were kidnapped by a crew of thoughtless aliens and then abandoned out in the Big Dark with no memory of the event and no way to go home. These two will have no memory of each other, let alone that they're going to be parents. I'm going to have to call Maintenance in before I do anything."

"Can't you just remove the fetus and freeze it? Then after he's been in rehab…"

"The law says I can't do that without his consent. I can only offer him the option."

"I imagine he'll probably go for that," I said. "That's what I'd do in the same situation."

"Very sensible." Neep gave a look that might have been amused under other circumstances. "Of course, that's skipping over the hard part – breaking the news about impending parenthood to someone who may have never intended to reproduce, at least not as the gestating parent. Or if he has, to tell him that the fertilizing parent is not merely a stranger but an alien whose biology is so different that this could never have occurred naturally." Neep looked down at the abductee. "I doubt he's ever encountered monosexuals and here he is pregnant by one." S/he gave a deep sigh. "Then there's the matter of notifying the other parent. It's the law."

"Does the other parent have to give permission for anything?" I asked with a sense of *déjà-vu*.

"What do you mean?" Neep asked, looking puzzled.

"Like, if he wanted to have the fetus removed and frozen, or brought to term externally."

"Of course not. The gestational parent bears all the burden and makes all the decisions." S/he looked down at his/her patient. "Usually. Ideally. Except in extremely bizarre circumstances."

"Maybe you should look after this one yourself," I suggested. "From waking to rehab and all the way through to integration."

Neep's expression was pained. "Full-time custodial care isn't part of my job description. I'd have to ask permission from Maintenance and they're not much in favour of mixing responsibilities. Once he wakes up, I have to give him over to your department."

"Unless you need to keep him in quarantine," I said.

Neep's red-gold face was skeptical now.

"Sure, the intake pen disinfects every arrival and whatever comes in with them," I said, "but this is someone who's been cross-pollinated. Spliced. By the *Dacz.va*, who can't boil water without burning it. Who knows what else they've fooled around with? This poor abductee could be incubating a lot more than a hybrid baby, and if it's at the molecular level, it won't show up for a long time. Maybe not till something happens. Like we all start getting sick or pregnant."

"If you're not a genius, Hannah, you're above average," Neep said, sounding almost happy. "I should have thought of that myself." His/her face fell slightly. "I'm afraid that means you'll both have to spend two days in quarantine yourselves, after which I'll have to implant all-over monitors and paint you with weather-proofing."

I chuckled a little at the slang but Charlie looked worried. "Is that really necessary?" he asked. "The weather-proofing, I mean."

"You'll never notice it. It'll only activate if your insides change suddenly and uncharacteristically," Neep told him with a reassuring pat on the arm. "And if nothing happens within thirty days, it disappears. You'll never notice that, either."

"I know," Charlie said, still not too happy. "Up here, I know." He tapped his forehead with two fingers. "I just can't seem to convince the rest of me. My skin insists it can feel all the molecules sitting there on the surface, waiting for any excuse to seal me up. It gives my stomach claustrophobia." Bodypaint and cosmetics are unknown among Charlie's people. They do, however, have more different kinds of combs and brushes than I ever imagined.

"I'll give you a mild anti-anxiety med with an anti-nausea additive," Neep told him. "Sorry. I know how you feel but it's part of how I can justify keeping him in quarantine."

"I know," Charlie said. "I guess you'd better contact Tiller and Ophelia, too, then."

"And put the other abductee in quarantine, too," I added.

Neep plumped down on a stool near the console and let out a heavy breath. "Oh. Right."

"Sorry," I said, "but conspiracy's always a lot of work."

S/he shook her head. "It's not that. Syd's got the other parent and I don't know how s/he'll feel about this."

"Syd wouldn't back you up?" I asked, surprised. Even out here in the Big Dark, doctors were a tight-knit clan who looked out for each other. I used to think the similarity was a remarkable coincidence but as I said earlier, coincidence is a euphemism for symptom.

"I would never openly assume one way or the other about anyone," Neep replied. "But besides that, Syd has been both a fertilizing and a gestational parent. S/he may find this…upsetting." Neep stood up. "Which is why I'll have to go over to her/his area and talk to him/her in person…

The console chimed and Syd's face appeared on one of the screens briefly, followed by a dense block of symbols I couldn't read. The translator didn't extend to written language. Neep glanced at it and then did a double-take, something that only looks comical to me when someone from my own planet does it.

"Okay," s/he said, "open it up."

The room shook a little as the far wall split in half vertically, softened, and drew back like curtains.

"I was fairly sure you'd want to work in tandem." Syd motioned for Tiller and Ophelia to move the other abductee's hospital bed closer to us. "I just didn't want to assume."

"No quarantine, then?" Charlie said, sounding both nervous and relieved.

"We're in quarantine right now," Syd told him. "All eight of us."

"Oh. That's...uh, unexpected." Now he was dismayed and relieved. Charlie is the king of mixed feelings. I was busy being surprised at how close Syd's area actually was; the way Neep had been talking, I'd thought it was a mile away. Or perhaps it was even farther away than that by the standard route of travel. The Big Box has some topological quirks that never show under normal circumstances. Today, however, circumstances were getting more abnormal all the time.

"Hannah." Syd beckoned to me from where she stood beside the man's bed.

I hesitated, bracing myself for some other topological quirk or at least an orientational anomaly, then felt the strong urge to celebrate with a victory dance when I walked the twenty-odd feet without incident. "He still doesn't look familiar," I said, just for the sake of saying anything at all.

"Are you sure?" Tiller said. "Because the way you look, it's like you almost recognize him."

"Maybe it's just because he's from my Earth," I said.

"Aha!" Tiller turned to Ophelia. "See? What did I tell you? The planetary face."

"The what?" I asked, looking from him to Syd and then to Ophelia, who yawned but seemed more alert.

"Planetary face is Tiller's slightly weaker tie-that-binds," she said. "His theory is that all facial expressions travel around the world – a world, your world, for example – person to person. They circumnavigate any given globe by going from one face to another, so that even if two people have never breathed the same air, they are bound to each other because they've shared the same facial expressions." She yawned again, a little less widely. "The implications for us here in the Big Box are momentous. Anyway, that's why this guy almost looks familiar." Pause. "If he does."

Abruptly, a holo display appeared over the unconscious man. "Oops, wrong file," I said after a couple of seconds. "Did you two already get the records mixed up just because we're all in quarantine togeth..." I broke off. The foetus was at an earlier stage of development, and in a different position, growing in a cavity that had never been meant for childbearing.

I gave an enormous sigh that actually drowned out Ophelia's yawn. "Wait, don't tell me," I said to no one in particular. "The other abductee, she – he – s/he's the f-f-f ..." My speech centre suddenly snagged on too many f-words.

"Fertilizing parent," Syd said helpfully.

I started to feel a bit lightheaded and it must have showed. Tiller slid a chair under me and Charlie appeared on my right with a glass of water.

What I was thinking about was Nazi experimentation, of course. I was too young to remember the revelation of the Holocaust first-hand but it had been fresh in living memory when I had involuntarily left Earth and as near as I could tell from those who had arrived here after me, it was still the definition of human evil.

The thing I wondered about most when I was first adjusting to life here was whether human evil existed as a standard in the Big Dark. The invaders with the superior knowledge and technology and power, who treat the members of the less advanced civilization as animals at best and objects at worst, to be used and discarded – it was an old story on Earth and the aliens involved were only from a different part of the same world.

But out here, all bets were off. If aliens saw you as an ant, you couldn't appeal to the humanity in them so they wouldn't step on you. Demonstrate sentience? Even if you could make yourself understood, maybe it wouldn't matter. What if they had no concept of evil?

I worried myself into a breakdown over that one. That was before I understood the living arrangements in the Big Box.

But the Dacz.va didn't live here. They only stopped by long enough to drop off people they had abducted on whatever whim had moved them. Considering the Dacz.va aren't even humanoid, their penchant for human company is completely baffling. They do keep records – what Charlie referred to as CVs always contain a video log of the time the abductees spent with them. We had never seen anything in any log that qualified as even mildly abusive. Unless, of course, you count the abduction itself and the fact that none of the abductees know they're going to spend the rest of their lives in a way station in interstellar space. That's pretty lousy. But it's not the same level of cruelty as planting a developing foetus in a male's peritoneal cavity before dumping him in a shelter where he'll wake up with no memory of what happened.

"Relax. Can you relax?" Neep's voice sounded as if it were coming from somewhere very far away and yet her/his red-gold face seemed to be close. Was I looking at him/her on a high-res screen? Was I having a breakdown?

"I really hope not," Neep said. "You've been stable for so long, I'd hate to see you take a step back."

Charlie said something I couldn't make out.

"Oh, him," Neep replied and I knew s/he meant Jean-Christophe. No one else can inspire the same inflection on him; the translator renders it perfectly. "Hannah? Wake up."

I turned to look at him/her and instead found myself raising my head and opening my eyes. I was still in the chair Tiller had got for me. On my left, Neep was perched on a low stool; there was a coolness on the back of my hand where s/he had applied some medication.

"It wasn't the Dacz.va," s/he said. "Did you hear me? It wasn't the Dacz.va."

I couldn't say anything.

S/he slid a flatscreen onto my lap and turned it on. "We looked at the records. They did it themselves."

I watched as she ran the log for me, skipping through sections to show me the highlights. The person from Neep's world had already been with them long enough to put together a fairly complex laboratory by the time they scooped the man up, taking him right out of his bed in a motel room in the middle of the night.

The Dacz.va had kept the two of them for a long time. I made Neep skip through as much of their developing relationship as possible; it was like watching a car go over a cliff in slow-motion. If

Neep hadn't pointed out the fertilization sequence, I might have skipped through that, too. It happened in the laboratory and even when I knew, I still couldn't tell what they were doing.

But it was true – the Dacz.va had done nothing, except hover around like opaque jellyfish, watching.

"I suppose I should have realized," I said finally, pushing the flatscreen into Neep's hands. "The Dacz.va probably didn't even understand what was going on."

"Or if they did, they didn't realize the significance," Syd added.

"We still have the problem of what to do with them," Neep said. "Obviously they were in love. Now they won't even remember each other."

"Never mind that," I said. "He became a man who thought it was reasonable to adapt his body for childbearing – who wanted to. From a world where this wouldn't have even occurred to him. Is wiping his memory really going to change him back?"

Everyone was silent.

"What if he wakes up pregnant, with no memory of how it happened – or why he wanted it to? I can't imagine what the effect on him would be," I said.

"Obviously we have to take the foetus out for external gestation," Syd said.

I turned to him/her sharply. "And if he wakes up expecting to be pregnant?"

Syd frowned. "The Dacz.va wiped his memory. He'll have no knowledge of it, as you just pointed out."

I shook my head emphatically. "No, I said what if. For a man from my world to change so drastically that he wants to have an alien's baby – *literally* – I don't know that just wiping his memory can put him back the way he was."

"But we also don't know that it can't," Neep said after a long moment. "We don't know either way and we have to do *something*."

"This is so *irresponsible!*"

We all turned to look at Syd in surprise. S/he was standing with her/his fists on his/her hips, glaring at the person from her world, still unconscious the bed in Neep's area. "What?" I said blankly.

"There's no excuse for him," s/he said angrily. "It's not right to have more than one parent gestating simultaneously in the same family. It puts too much strain on everyone, including the developing children. You can see how hers is so much smaller." She pointed at the man. "It's growing more slowly, there could be problems."

"I think that's an actual biological difference," Tiller said, looking at the holo display thoughtfully. "Some humans take longer."

"You're not a doctor," Syd told him sharply.

"I'm sorry," he said, sounding sincere.

I covered my eyes for a moment; the surreality was threatening to overwhelm me.

I didn't hear Neep tell Charlie to take me out of there. Perhaps s/he hadn't needed to.

A few hours later, I felt silly. After all, I've been out here long enough to have seen things a lot stranger than a man from my own world pregnant by his alien lover. Or, well, at least heard of them, anyway.

The thing is, I knew that wasn't actually what had freaked me out. It had been the idea of the Dacz.va performing experiments on unwilling subjects. And despite the fact that this hadn't been the case at all, I couldn't seem to shake off the effects of the initial horror, not completely. Because that's what I was most afraid of when I first woke up and found myself in a hospital bed thousands of light-years from home with no way back.

No way back...I guess that's my second greatest fear. Well, not that exactly. I already know I'll never see Earth again. But what I've been dreading without realizing it is the day I meet a new arrival from Earth who is more alien than Charlie or Neep, or even those damned feathered bipeds. Perhaps one man from Earth willingly pregnant by his dually-sexed alien lover is too small a sample to be representative; perhaps for now he only counts as atypical.

I was so deep in thought that when the pick-up signal chimed, I practically jumped out of my skin.

"Wouldn't you know we'd get another one this close to the end of our shift?" Charlie said. "You want me to pass this one to someone else?"

"No," I said. "Let's take it. I can't imagine it's any stranger than anything else we've seen today. And if it is, I'm dying to know how."

"As long as you won't have a serious episode of brain crisis from the impact," Charlie said as we headed toward the intake pen.

No buzzing or humming from the translator. "You mean as long as I won't freak out?" I asked, slightly puzzled.

Now he gave me a look. "That's what I said. As long as you won't have a serious episode of brain crisis from the impact."

I let it go and made a mental note to have Neep check my translator. We had the usual journey through the usual traffic, although for once none of the wardens tried to assert their feathered authority by making us stop for tour groups or cargo chains. If we had the same luck on the way back, I told Charlie, we'd end our shift on time.

Then I saw the man lying on the floor and forgot all about that.

"He said he was leaving. I told him not to bullshit me." His hair was short now and the beard was gone. Without it, he looked a lot younger.

"If I were going to bet that someone could find a way to leave the Big Box, it wouldn't have been him." Charlie adjusted his arm so the stretcher could scan the information on his bracelet. "Maybe this is just someone with a startling resemblance to Jean-Christophe. That's possible, don't you think?"

I shook my head. "Jean-Christophe has been bad for me often enough that I would know his body anywhere. This isn't the most unlikely double in the w – universe. This is Jean-Christophe." I covered him up. "He said he was leaving. I thought he was just trying to get my clothes off. And now here he is with his clothes off and not because he wants to be bad for me." I looked over at Charlie. "Just tell me it's not the Dacz.va."

"It's not the Dacz.va," he said promptly.

I gave a heavy sigh of relief. "Thank God. Or whoever. Because that would just drive me crazy, if Jean-Christophe figured out how to talk the Dacz.va into taking him –"

"It wasn't them or any other crew." Charlie looked up from the readout. "It was Maintenance."

My mouth dropped open. "*Who?*"

"He didn't leave. Not the way you're thinking. And not the way he expected, maybe. He didn't go anywhere – they just re-wound him."

My stomach did a very slow forward roll. Re-wound; Maintenance had cleared his memory and put him back at the beginning. When he woke up, he would think he had just arrived here. "I wonder what he did that made them do that to him," I said. "Remind me never to get on Maintenance's bad side."

"It isn't a punishment," Neep told me when we brought him in. "He wanted to leave, to go home. He was suffering."

"So Maintenance just wiped his memory of being here? All those years, just gone?"

"Maybe he'll adjust better this time through," Neep said. "Who knows – maybe when he comes out of rehab, he won't be bad for you any more."

"But I remember the years he spent here. I know he didn't just arrive."

Neep shrugged. "You're a professional, you can keep a secret. Can't you?"

I looked from him/her to Charlie; he was studying the floor. *Have I ever been re-wound?* I wanted to ask but the words wouldn't come. Instead I heard Neep saying, "Your shift's over now, don't worry about him. Leave him to me."

Charlie and I went back to the shelter in silence. The next shift was already there and monitoring patients in various stages of rehab. I picked up my handbag – the way things work in the Big Box, there's no real reason to carry one but I've never broken the habit. By contrast, Charlie has always walked around empty-handed so there was no reason for him to come with me. Except to come with me.

"You are going to find your way to be all right, aren't you?" he said finally as we walked down the corridor to the nearest main thoroughfare. Someone passed overhead in a high-wall transit, going fast.

I looked over at him. "Did your translator buzz on that one?"

"No, why? Did yours?"

"No, I just – I was just curious."

He frowned a little. "You mean you were just curious," he said, as if he were correcting me.

"Right. Just, uh, curious." I gave a short laugh. "Not freaking out."

"Oh," he said, a bit unsettled. "Maybe there is something wrong with the translators. Like you said."

"No, I don't think so," I told him. "It's not the translators – it's what they're translating. There's nothing wrong, it's just different. Changed. The translators are catching up."

Charlie's troubled expression deepened. "I was waiting to get a buzz on that. Because I think that not long ago, I would have. But I didn't."

I nodded. "Sometimes the surprise is not what you don't understand, but what you do." No buzz on that, either.

We reached the end of the corridor and went our separate ways.

Pat Cadigan has been producing original and exciting fiction since the 1980s. Her fifteen books (including two volumes of non-fiction) have chalked up an impressive series of accolades and awards and, to date, Pat can lay claim to two Arthur C. Clarke Awards, two Vector Awards and half a World Fantasy Award. In *disLOCATIONS*, last year's NewCon Press anthology, Pat unveiled the first of her 'Tales from the Big Dark', and we are delighted to now be publishing "Lost in the Translation", the second in this wonderful new series of stories from 'the Queen of Cyberpunk'.

Touchme™:
Keeping in Touch

Heather Bradshaw

Tuesday morning, ordinary in the same way that ants in the kitchen in summer and politicians on the radio on ego trips about social security are ordinary. Taking my seat in the corner of the call centre I'm feeling just slightly worse than usual. I estimate the day will merit a four or so on my private how-close-am-I-to-quitting scale. A two-cups-of-coffee, one-chocolate-bar-and-a-redraft-of-my-CV day. But there just is no way of making TouchMe ™ Lost Devices Location Tracking Operative look like the sort of job that a budding manager should have.

I've left my own TouchMe™ at home. I've been leaving it at home for weeks now. Paul doesn't seem to notice. I hope maybe one day he'll call the 'Lost Devices' number about it and actually speak to me.

My headset bleeps.

"Good morning! TouchMe™ lost devices tracking, how can I help you today?" I asked Pavlov cheerfully.

"I think I've lost my pink one," the teenage female voice whines. It is uncannily familiar. TouchMe™ has sold 1,247,896 Devices on 765,431 separate contracts as of that minute according to the foot-high display projected at one metre intervals round the walls. But the name 'Minnie' is knocking persistently at my frontal lobes.

"Oh, I'm so sorry to hear that. That must be so annoying Mi...., do you have its DeviceCode there for me?"

"Its what? Croz bought it for me, he just gave it to me last week. At least, I think it was Croz."

Last Thursday it had been a blue one from Jase, I was sure of it.

"The number printed on the back that you have to write down?" I say hopefully, tapping 'M I N...' onto the keyboard projected on the desk.

"Oh, I never do that, they always rub off. Can't you find it for me anyway? I think someone stole it at Mimoza's last night."

Where were you wearing it, you little tart? Or were you so sloshed you didn't even notice that bloke who put his hand up your skirt? Maybe he removed the wrong one.

"Oh dear. I'll make sure I let the production team know about the problem. Do you know what its call number was? Or the number of the phone it was tied to?"

"Nah, I just think it was Croz Patel who give it me, though it might have been Toady Jones...Can you check both?"

"I'm afraid we can only search by numbers and not names, for reasons of data protection..."

"Ah, you're always fricking' useless, nasty cow!"

My wallscreen flashes: 'Call lost without solution, -5 bonus points' at me and the record for Minnie Johannah Jones, 14, appears. She's running sixteen TouchMe™s off one pay-as-you-go account and another six off a monthly rental. None of them are registered by the recipients. And sure enough there *is* a log record for last Thursday morning in my name. I initial the transcript of this morning's call.

'Bleep'

"Goo..."

"I have a device number for you." The voice is full of female fury. 'Uh-oh' go my frontal lobes.

"400,095,712."

"Is that lost or found?" I ask syrupily.

"Lost," she snaps. I don't for a second believe her.

"Oh, I'm sorry to..."

"Just confirm who it was last registered to for me. None of this script bull." The voice is icy.

"And your name, please?"

"Never mind my name, I want to know who this thing belongs to."

"I'm afraid that for reasons of privacy I cannot give out any information about a device except to its rightful registered owner." I complete the sentence even though she is talking over me. Once she has finished her string of colourful and creative insults, all delivered in a voice which oozes class, I ask again: "Now, if I could have your name I'll see what I can do?"

"Baker. Mrs Marjorie Baker," she humphs. I type.

Bingo! Paydirt!

"Please confirm the first line of your address? And your mobile number?"

Through gritted teeth, she does.

"The device in question is registered as owned by the *joint* holder of your account, Mr David Baker," I say carefully, thinking that Mr Baker has become careless, very careless.

There is a slight pause while she figures it out. Then she asks the right question:

"Could you please give me a breakdown of all the incoming and outgoing calls on that account for the last week, to all numbers?"

"Certainly ma'am, I shall have to send that out, to what email account should I send it?"

I thought she was going to ask me for the last 24 hours then and there over the phone but she gives me an email address. I select the week's calls and send them on their way with a couple of clicks.

"Anything else for you ma'am?"

"No, thank you. You've been very helpful." The malice in her voice makes me shiver. The linemonitor picks up 'helpful' and flashes "5 bonus points added! Call successfully resolved."

The wallscreen reflects Dennis walking across the office towards me. I flick the 'emergency comfort break' switch on my headset. Another 5 bonus points docked. Dennis has a brain. He's working part time while he finishes a doctorate in philosophy. His dark hair is all disarrayed today and it's falling in attractive waves across his face. I reckon he must have spent some time abroad or outside or something because he has a very weathered sort of face. It has that leathery burnt brownness to it, but good chiseled features and a lovely smile, which you don't see very often. It's a sad smile, but warm too. He's tall. He leans over me and waves into my screen.

"How's Teri today, then?" he says. I can smell him, warm and rich, old leather and something exotic. Cinnamon maybe. The effect is so different from Paul with his hairspray and face cream and implants. Dennis is resting his hand on the back of my chair.

"Teri's okay. How's Dennis?"

"Ahh…well, it's nice of you to ask. Have you had any kazingers today?"

"Any what?"

"Kazingers. You know, jealous lovers betrayed by the very technology they use to display their adoration." He waves one hand theatrically.

"Is that a corruption of humdingers?"

"No, webspinners."

"Romantics."

"Is love just a romance, a fiction, a trick?" His fingers are touching my shoulders.

"It's a source of profit. It's a disease of the brain, a …" But his face in the screen is too serious for joking.

"It causes real changes in the brain," I finish lamely, swallowing hard.

"And it makes us do ridiculous things," he says very quietly, removing his hands just in time to avoid the sharp eyes of the Building Peer Assistant, Ms Mathasingh, who appears to have popped up out of the floor beside us.

"Now then, Mr Phelps, Ms Turner," she singsongs in her remarkable would-be-Indian accent, "your call tally is down for this morning. Is there a problem I can help you with?"

"No… no, not at all Ms M," says Dennis smoothly. "We've just successfully resolved it between us. You see, Teri's keyboard has been fluttering just like mine was last week, but I've shown her how to fix it. It's all steady now, isn't it, Teri?"

"Yes, yes, perfectly steady now," I stutter, flicking my fingers on the desk top to open a couple of menus, just to test it.

Ms Mathasingh's cold grey eyes narrow under her slate-grey tightly-bunned hair.

"I did not see any fault report from Ms Turner," she snaps, "nor an assistance call log." She gives Dennis a particularly ferocious glare.

"The human voice is an amazing phenomenon," soothes Dennis like a lullaby. "It can be heard across whole offices without any assistance from electronic transmission or amplification, you know."

"Log a FAC next time, Teri," she growls, turning on her heel and clacking across the floor towards Jodie McCall's desk. At least, I presume it's Jodie's, because I can hear the Australian twang of her ever-complaining voice from Ms M's headset.

She's switched off my comfort break signal and two jealous (male) lovers, three candidates for dementia treatment and a headmaster all assault me mentally in quick succession with DeviceNumbers requiring tedious Trace-A-Touch™ investigations.

At coffee break, Kari Jones cries on my shoulder because she's had no Touch™ from her lover Oliver for a whole week. Oliver is quadriplegic after an accident (of his own making) involving jet-ski racing and no amount of stem cell therapy has been able to help him. Since, contrary to the politician on the coffee dispenser's 24 hours news feed, security is still the last thing provided by social security, he consented to undergo modification to become a NET-ship pilot. The Near-Earth-Transport company used to really struggle to find pilots willing to work away from earth for years at a time. Then they hit on marketing human-ship integration as a great way for the 'gravity impaired' to have 'star-spangled careers'. They have a 50-year development and sales deal with TouchMe™ so that their pilots can have 'sex and the stars'. But it's no help to Kari, who knows all about their dreadful safety record. She wants me to do a clandestine Trace-A-Touch™ for him but I don't think I have extra-terrestrial access permissions.

The coffee is a weird brownish-grey emulsion with pulpy bits in, like coffee and mayonnaise mixed up with a hint of hydrocarbon. Investigation shows that this is occurring because the service robot has shoved the 'New! Now even cheaper!' recyclable cups into the hole for coffee beans and the machine's fire retard system has gone off. I have no idea how to locate someone to fix this and so just leave it, warning Dennis not to use the machine as I head back to my desk. I do log an FAC for the coffee machine but all I get in return is a note telling me I'm not authorized to report catering machinery faults. So much for the two cups of coffee today.

Somewhere in amongst eighteen misdirected Technical Fault calls (each FAC'd) all from two accounts, and a sequence of five dissatisfied customers (personal daily rating: -50), Ms Mathasingh comes over to tell me that: "The non-environmentally destructive conveyance devices are not locatable at CM490026 in Recreation Room 1." She's called away before she can 'progress' this with me.

I'm still unsuccessfully trying to understand what relevance, if any, this technical gibberish has, when my headset bleeps:

"Good morning! TouchMe™ lost devices tracking, how can I help you today?"

"Yeees! Woohoo! Cha-ching! What a success! Well am I glad to hear you!" For one picosecond I think it might be Paul but the voice continues: "You are a real live human, aren't you?"

"Actually, yes," say I.

"Grrrreeaat! We're playing Random Dial and you get two thousand bonus points for each real human you get on a first dial attempt. You're wonderful! Amazing – say, what's your name?"

I think quickly but the frontal lobes are out of commission so I resort to:

"Teri."

"Well, Teri, you've absolutely made my day, I am 150% satisfied with your service, I think TouchMe™ are a truly wonderful company and I'll recommend your products to all my friends and customers just because of your excellent, helpful, efficient, and glorious service today! You have a grrrreat day!"

Line goes dead. That ridiculous piece of software that runs the linemonitor is clicking up bonus points as fast as its little L.E.D.s will allow. It settles on +5. I reflect that technology really is at a significant disadvantage in interpreting human behaviour and that management measures are no substitute for managers.

My headset makes a strange screeching and my screen delivers an internal email. Antiquated! The written word. Only a genuine old-fashioned geek could do that. The missive informs me I am to report to Technical Service Desk 14 on the 3rd floor of the Soft 'n Feely Building to explain my destructive interference with the Recreation Area 1 coffee machine.

The reply address is one of the semi-intelligent server programmes, P2. I write an angry message, using the correct pronoun protocol, explaining that if P had any understanding of the humans P's supposed to serve, P would realise that depriving them of crucial life-sustaining nutrients such as caffeine is extreme cruelty and also severely affects their ability to function. If P had any sense, I continue, let alone morality, P would see to the health of its poor abused compatriot in the kingdom of electro-mechanical widgetry and get the cups extracted from the dear thing's coffee bean orifice. At the same time, it might also want to discipline the psychopathic service-bot which got the orifices confused in the first place!

I feel much better after that, forward a copy to Dennis, reach for the emergency comfort break button again and go in search of Recreation Room 2 or the mobile chocolate machine.

As I make my way up the stairs to the next floor, a fleet of service-bots appear. They filter down the stairs and surround me. I'm just beginning to wonder if the office systems have reached critical mass and gone conscious when a harried young man crashes through the 2nd floor fire escape doors waving a control wand and muttering about: 'Blasted beta versions with bloody great bugs... STOP – WHEN I tell you to, you lot!'

He slowly lifts his eyes from my worn-out cowboy boots up my multicolour nanoweave stockings to the miniskirt and beyond. He goes all pink under his ginger hair.

"Oh, I am sorry er... er..." He peers at my left tit. I've left my security nametag on my jacket downstairs.

"Teri, Teri Turner," I say reassuringly, trying to shake off one of the 'bots – the one which is attempting to copulate with my left ankle.

His freckled face turns a deep shade of puce. His name is Burt Bridges and he'd *never* forget his security badge. My frontal lobes start signalling "uh-oh".

"*Ms* Turner, Mr Broadscrew wants to see you. We've been paging you. Please come with me immediately."

"*Mr* Bridges, what on Earth for? And would you please get your 'bot to stop screwing my foot?"

"It's not screwing, it's..." and he bends down to squint at it, "conveyance device refilling. That's interesting, the attitude assessment subroutine seems to have gone into negative hexa."

I'm half tempted to ask him if he 'conveyance device refills' his girlfriend too but a sinister black light bulb has just clicked on in my head. I realise the strange noise I can hear is not one of the 'bots, nor in my head, it's the Building pager system trying to locate me.

"What does Mr Broadscrew want to see me about?" I repeat.

Burt has now joined the 'bot on the floor. It has put a pair of pincers, of about 85 mil diameter, round my boot. My boot is 90 mil in diameter.

"That's interesting!" says Burt, "That's a nasty n-loop in the free-stuck-device subroutine."

I'm very tempted to explore f-loops in the free-the-stuck-bot routine my brain's emotion centre is suggesting, where 'f' stands for foot-propelled.

"Burt, please get that thing off my leg before I am tempted to vandalise company property," I hiss.

"Oh yes, that's it," he says absently without looking up.

"That's what?"

"What Mr Broadscrew wants to see you about. Just stand still, I need to recalibrate the attitude sensor."

"I thought you wanted me to go with you to see Mr Broadscrew!" And can I recalibrate your attitude please?

All the bots suddenly start a piercing bleeping, the fire doors burst open and no less than five burly security guards, human, sweep up me, Burt and the offending 'bot.

"Right, Ms Turner, no more of this hiding in the stairwell!" the biggest guard says crossly.

"But I only wanted a cup of coffee!" I say in shrill bewilderment.

"Mr Broadscrew and Mr Bradbrawl will see about that. Come along, stop resisting."

"But... but... the bot!" I know my protests are useless because Burt is nearly crying about his failed calibration. I just hop along. Luckily Bradbrawl's office happens to be next to the fire escape on this floor, or maybe he has interrogation rooms on every floor. The bots appear to be having a party behind us, then they all hit the closing fire doors and Burt shrieks as though in pain until they figure the swing out and make it through to join him.

Bradbrawl glares at me.

"One falsely malfunctioning keyboard, 200 brand new missing conveyance devices, one damaged service 'bot and what looks like," he gives Burt a rather suspicious look, "one assaulted junior technician. Explain yourself Ms Turner!"

"The coffee cups had been shoved down the coffee bean hole; that seems to have set the machine's fire extinguisher off. The coffee it produced this morning was a nasty sludgy mixture, definitely not fit to drink. I sent a FAC...could you remove this bot from my foot please, I think my ankle is beginning to swell?"

They both begin to talk at once. Meanwhile Burt has crept around the five security guards (who are all, I note, surreptitiously trying to shake off copulating bots from their left feet) to my left foot and is trying to start his recalibration again. Broadscrew is saying in a shrill, nasal voice: "Impossible! FMX450s are totally reliable!" And Bradbrawl is intoning in his bass rumble, "But what about the keyboard, young lady, what about the keyboard?"

I am about to tell him that there'd been nothing wrong with the damn' keyboard – we were just trying to hide from Ms Mathasingh – when the guard in front of the door lets out a loud, "Ooof!" and staggers forward into me. Burt yells in frustration, I fall onto Bradbrawl's desk and Ms Mathasingh says: "Dick Broadscrew! I should have known I'd find my missing prettiest female Operative in your office. What do you think you are doing? And Willy Bradbrawl," ("Bill!" he breathes angrily into my ear as I try to stand up) "you're almost as bad! You even have the poor girl tied down! And as for you lot – are you all peeeeeping Toms? Get out! Get out! I shall have you all up for sexual harassment!

"Burtie Bridges!" she exclaims still more shrilly. "Have they been leading you astray? Stand up! What are you doing down there? You don't need to get down so far to see up Ms Turner's skirt!"

"The bloomin' *recalibration!*" the poor lad mutters, in agony at being interrupted a third time.

"Teri," and Ms M reaches for my arm, "I think you should come with me to see the Office Health Officer, come on Teri..."

As I've only just extracted myself from the guard-Teri-desk-Bradbrawl sandwich and am still recovering, it takes me a minute to figure out whether taking the bot and Burt along to wherever we are going is a good idea or not. I conclude it is because somehow I have a strong suspicion that Burt has been on lates recently and might know more about the coffee cups than I do. Besides, the security guards are beginning to look rather exasperated with the bots and I think they might make rather a mess of little Burt. I grab his wrist and hiss "Come on!" as Ms Mathasingh pretty much drags me out of the door and right across Floor 2 (Technical Faults and Personal Injury) into the lift.

The lift, however, is full of rather green-looking people.

"Move, move!" Ms Mathasingh orders, "I urgently need to take this young lady to the OHO!"

No-one moves.

The doors open and close a few times, reacting to my bot's proximity sensors no doubt.

Then someone says: "That's where...we were going...too, but she's...off...sick...something to do...with the...coffee..." and then, thankfully, the lift departs and, to my great relief, the bot lets go of my ankle.

"That's interesting..." Burt says thoughtfully, scooping it up into his arms. Ms Mathasingh cocks her head and listens to her headphones. In the total calm that has fallen on Floor 2 as everyone emergency-comfort-breaks at once to watch us, we all clearly hear Ms Mathasingh say warmly and politely in unaccented English, "Yes, Professor Dame Ess, yes of course, I'll bring them along to your office right away."

"I thought she was dead!" Burt hisses at me as we pound up almost all the stairs in the building.

She might well be. All we can see is a figure in the simulation screen that covers the whole of her office wall. She is wearing three TouchMe™s down her left arm and a soft, billowy, mauve toga thingy. She has ringlets of heavy, honey-coloured hair piled high on her head and a sweet smile, but her eyes, which are huge and totally black, look so old and deep you could fall into them. Bare feet in a grassy glen.

"Hello Mavis," she says to Ms Mathasingh, gently. "How is your grandson doing?"

"He's much better thank you, Cara. They think the nanotechnology will have completely cleared the tumour by Sunday."

"Good. I'm glad to hear it. You've been working really hard today, I can see. I'm grateful for that. You've done a good job, as always. I'd like to talk to you about a few things we should fix in a moment, but could I have some time with Ms Turner and Mr Bridges in private, do you think? Melinda will find you some real cardamom tea."

A door opens somewhere and Ms Mathasingh wastes no time in using it. This penthouse suite has a real window and beyond it I can see clouds scudding along against a salmony pink sky. It looks as if there is another typhoon heading our way.

Professor Ess seems to drift right to the front of her screen. I notice Burt shiver and wonder if he feels cold.

"Teri, do you not believe in the technology you shepherd?" she says slowly. The voice seems to come from all around.

"The technology's fine," I reply quickly. "It's just my boyfriend's nearly an ex."

"Oh, I see," she replies with a sympathetic little nod, eyes twinkling. "Now, Burt, what's that you're holding?"

"It's an FMX 500," he says proudly.

"Aha. And Teri, did you have something to say about the coffee machine on the first floor?"

I am about to shake my head and deny it, because I'm sure she understands the situation better than I do, but she continues, with just a hint of humour on her softly lined face: "Something about its health?"

Oh no! I feel the embarrassment creeping up from my toes all the way to the top of my head. Oh what the hell...

"No actually, I wanted to say something about the service bots that amazingly managed to ram the coffee cups into the wrong hole in the coffee machine. I didn't know who to go to in order to sort out the problem so I sent a FAC."

"And you have also found the answer to the problem, haven't you, as well as the person responsible? There's always a person responsible. People are far less inhibited with their emotions when they're talking to a machine, you know."

Burt is staring at her, clasping the bot as though it's a favourite teddy-bear. I haven't the heart to accuse him.

"Well, go on then," says the apparition on the wall. "You are the one who wants to be a manager."

I look around desperately. This is awful, what if I'm wrong? There's a desk and two chairs.

"Burt, would you sit down a minute please?" I say, gesturing at one. Luckily the screen's gone dark, and after a moment's headshaking, he does.

I sit in the chair on the other side of the desk. It's a nice desk, not too large but a real wood surface, quite old and scratched. He yawns, and covers his mouth with his hand, muttering an apology.

"Are you tired? Were you working late last night?"

"Ummm, I was covering for Giggy, he had an ig," he says, then looks confused. "I mean, Iggy had a gig. Actually, I didn't mind and Mr Broadscrew thought it was a good idea as I could get these new FMX 500s commissioned. They only arrived yesterday afternoon." He wriggles a little uncomfortably.

"They're very clever, aren't they? They look rather small though. Can they only work on the floor?" I say, trying not to giggle at Iggy's gig.

"No, look..." He places the bot on the floor and presses something on his handset, causing the bot to grow three spindly telescopic legs and leer at me over the desk. "They have to be able to get up to the ceiling to service the fans, you know, but mostly they just go to this height, to get at the coffee machines and..." He suddenly goes wide-eyed, and his freckles stand out as he turns white, then they disappear one by one as a tide of pink rises up his neck.

"Oh no! It's all my fault! And all those people in the lift..."

For a second I fear he might actually cry.

"Actually, it's not your fault..." I begin, thinking with relish of laying lack of proper human supervision and lack of responsibility for semi-autonomous artefact charges on Richard Broadscrew.

"No, it is," he wails. "I set them off and I never checked that they'd done things properly because...well, because. And then it was lock-up time and I didn't come in till lunchtime today and forgot and I didn't use the coffee machine! And all those people are sick!"

"Um...Burt...why didn't you check?" I can't resist asking.

He looks very sheepish and wriggles some more, rubbing his fingers together nervously and looking all around the room.

"C'mon Burt, you can tell me – I'm not even cross about you feeling up my leg to get that bot off, am I? And you haven't even asked what I was doing on the back stairs on Floor 2."

He looks down at the floor and turns even redder before taking a deep breath and saying all in a rush: "I didn't feel up your leg! Bradbrawl's lads have got a... a poker ring going for money on Floor

8 in a surveillance-free spot they've created and I caught them and they gave me ForgetIt™. Except they didn't know that I'm genetically immune to that stuff, so I just pretended to curl up and go to sleep as if I wasn't... and then they forgot about me and went home and I only just managed to get out before the autolocks came on."

He sits there shaking and I very nearly got up to hug him, but Melinda comes in with two lovely steaming cups of real coffee. When she spots how shaken Burt is, she takes him next door.

Professor Ess reappears as the door closes.

"You've done a really good job for me today, Teri. You've got to the bottom of something I've been wondering about for a while and you've shown some excellent interpersonal communication skills. You have some qualifications in management too, don't you?"

I am feeling rather sour about how she's just used me to get information out of Burt. It all seems so pat, somehow.

"Yes," I say shortly.

"Well, I'd like you to report to James Lovelock over in Finance tomorrow morning. He has a manager off sick at the moment and I think you might be able to help him out. The New Accounts team seems to have got into rather a muddle recently. Do make sure you have a good dinner tonight, Teri."

I am still dazed when I finally make it home; so dazed that even an answerphone message from Paul saying that he's fallen deeply in love with some guy called Lindsey doesn't make it any worse. I still haven't got around to making that dinner when my doorbell rings. Dennis, with flowers and wine and a beautiful pair of matched TouchMe™s. Later he shows me exactly why Professor Ess had once, long ago, thought it such a pity when lovers are parted. Which is why she found a way of sending touches by telephone...and why it is so much better not to be parted at all.

Heather Bradshaw spent much of her childhood on remote construction sites in Iran, Libya and Pakistan, whilst her teenage years were misspent working as a mechanic for rally teams in the US and UK, before studying engineering. Work promoting British

141

exports then led to a degree in philosophy, and Heather is currently working towards a PhD in bioethics at Bristol, although traces of her can still be found at the University of Oxford. Her first memory of creative writing is completing a one page description of a monsoon storm with a blunt pencil at midnight in Pakistan when she was six. All of which has led to this, her debut as a published fiction writer.

We Shelter

Leigh Kennedy

The alarms rang just before our usual rising time, warning of incoming craft. Dazed with sleep, we leapt out of our beds to the windows and looked down onto the snowy fields. Our hands were cold on the glass and our breath made misty spots if we breathed too closely.

In just a few seconds, the air cracked like thunder. A craft steamed down, roaring with resistance to the ground. It twisted and juddered, then turned in a long arc so that the silvery nose with a red symbol came to rest across the field, at a distance, but close enough that we might have seen a hatch open or some sign of crew. But we could see no further movement.

"A strange craft," one of us said. "We don't recognize that symbol."

Surprise made us stare longer than we should have. When the alarm blasted we jumped with fright. At the second blast we hurried back behind our screen to get our outdoor gear on.

Our stomachs weren't awake yet, our eyes still sandy, as we ran down the open stairway, our many boots ringing on the metal steps, our hands cold on the round rail. We were divided by the doctor, half of us staying inside on alert, half of us herded into the hangar, where we ran for the opened back of a van. As soon as the door rolled down loudly, we sat cross-legged on the floor and braced ourselves, looking out the two small rectangles of window on either side. We lurched out of the hangar and into the slippery dawn-blue field. The ice cleats made a rumbling sound, vibrating the whole van until we felt nerve-sodden. To preserve energy, we moved closer together, our thighs and arms touching. Our breath was heavy and bitter with fasting.

It only took a few minutes to reach the ground transport umbrella. We heard the doctor say to the driver, "Still no response. Either they've had a complete equipment failure or they're all dead."

We put on our hoods and masks and, when the door slid open again, jumped off the end of the van. The umbrella was only half the height of the strange craft. When we tried to look up at it, sleet pelted our faces. The craft was unusually far away from the umbrella so, after unlocking the flexible tunnel, we dragged it to the craft with so much effort that our hands and shoulders hurt and our legs grew tired. The doctor decided which portal to use. Sheltering inside the flexible tunnel, we shot the grip lines until they stuck fast beneath the door, then we pulled the folding stairway up to it. Our faces stung with the ice, our toes and fingers were becoming stiff, as we climbed up the stairway.

The first of us hammered on the door and we waited. Nothing happened.

The doctor turned on his loudspeaker. "¡Hola, hola!" he shouted. "¿Quiénes son ustedes?" Then, "Who are you?" Then he shouted again in the language that not all of us understand. The door finally slid open.

Even inside our suits, we could smell death and rot within the ship. Just beyond the airlock, beings huddled; we almost might have thought them not human, but some many-limbed creatures with fungal-textured skin. In fact, they were probably like us in the van, conserving warmth by clinging together. They called out in feeble, different voices: a howl, moans, mutterings. We saw opened mouths with no sound coming out. Dark hollow eyes full of tears or shock.

The doctor, in his full protective suit, pressed his phone. "Prepare seven isolation units."

Some of us knelt down, rolled out transport bags and began to disentangle the beings. Some of us felt slightly sick and light-headed, hands shaking as we tried to remember everything that had to be done.

One of the beings, his face a waxy grey, his cheekbones sharp under circled eyes, whispered, "No trade goods. Turned away everywhere. Hot lands, cold lands." He waved his fingers in a helpless gesture, his voice parched. "In our last shelter we were poisoned, starved. Suicides." He waved his finger towards the back of the ship.

We lifted his shoulders and his feet and held the back of his head and slid him into the bag.

"Warm," he said.

Then one of us realized that only that one of us understood his language.

Either unconscious or asleep, a young girl curled up next to an opened-mouth woman, whose lips were dark grey and eyes fixed. A second waxen older man seemed still to be alive.

A young man held his hands over his face, as if ashamed or blinded by the light we brought. We touched his shoulder and he pulled his hands down and stared at one of us. Just one. This one.

"Mulli," he said. "Are you Mulli?"

I shook my head, my heart hammered.

We lifted his shoulders, his feet and the back of his head and helped him into the bag for transport. His face relaxed; perhaps he fell into unconsciousness.

After we tended to the live beings just inside the ship, some of us helped take them down to the infirmary while the rest continued to search for survivors. The smell grew worse when we began to open doors and move through the craft; the number of those living had been a tiny fraction of the dead. We found many bodies carefully arranged in a cold, unused section. Fresher corpses lay in their bunks or on the floor, remaining where they had spent their last moments. We shone lights into their pupils hoping for reactions, then took DNA snips and face photos of each one. There were fifty-three bodies.

The doctor said, "Most seem to have died of dehydration or an infectious disease."

We found some empty, folded boxes from another Shelter. One of us said that the strangers might be pirates.

The doctor laughed. "Not very successful ones!"

One of us said they might have been poisoned.

"If they have infected us with plague, I'll have those survivors done as anti-humanitarians. Imagine coming *here* in this condition!" The doctor waved his arm angrily. "We save lives and they just waste theirs! Look at this!"

We left the dead behind where we found them and began to collect their data and equipment, taking it down to the van, up and down the stairs, back and forth through the tunnel. A catering robot drove out to us but we didn't feel hungry, just thirsty, and meals were left unopened.

Because we were possibly contaminated, those of us who went to the craft moved to the infirmary, becoming health care for the five survivors, attaching fever patches, coordinating monitoring equipment with spreadsheets, drawing blood samples from tubes, administering medication and generally wiping, tidying, offering and fetching. Only the young girl was alert and aware of her surroundings; the others seemed to be drifting at the edges of comprehending their situation.

When night fell, the doctor came in with an expression as if he were trying to swallow a rancid nut whole. He looked over the spreadsheets and examined each survivor, then went to sleep in his own isolation bed behind the office. Half of us went to bed for half of the night in another room of the infirmary. Some of us slept but some of us found it too hard to sleep. To close our eyes meant seeing all those dead faces again. We got up and stood in the kitchen, drinking tea together. One of us said that once, when we were turning bodies face-up to record them, an arm came away, loose from the body. We agreed that the smell was still inside our noses and the citrus tea didn't kill it.

We tried again to go to sleep because in a few hours we would have to let the others sleep. Some of us succeeded.

I dreamt of home, feeling the burning sun of one of the places that is Too Hot. I saw my sister, Mulli, so clearly that it hurt my stomach and I woke up gasping, then never returned to sleep in the time left.

We washed and dressed to replace the tired ones who had stayed up. One of the survivors had died, one of the older men. We heard that the doctor had come in earlier and said that they might all die, apart from the girl, who seemed quite healthy, so we should think of her as a future colleague. We learned that he was no longer angry with the refugees. The laboratory tests showed that they had eaten poisoned food. This meant that we were no longer in isolation so could return to usual assignments when the designated shift arrived to work in the infirmary at daybreak.

All the patients were sleeping or quiet, so we sat at a small table and ate some fruit, bread and paste for breakfast. We were still tired from a short, restless night. The food refreshed us enough to perform the duties remaining to us for a few hours.

The adult woman died next. We closed her eyes and took the tubes out and pushed away the monitors. We composed her back in her transport bag, admiring her hair, which had probably been lovely when she was healthy. We let her wear her ring to the crematorium, as the minerals would be reclaimed anyway. Then we closed her bag and never saw her face again.

One of us lifted the curtain to see the progress of the morning. It was still dark outside, but we saw that some of us were in an operation around the strange craft. The flexible tunnel was lit. It looked like we were carrying bodies from the craft to the hangar.

"Mulli," the young man said.

We gathered around his bed. He looked at one of us. This one. I sat on the edge of his bed and took his hand.

"Mulli, I never believed I would see you again," he said.

Most of us wondered what he was saying.

I squeezed his hand and smiled at him. I stayed on his bed, holding his fingers until he died.

One of us began to weep with terrible sobs, remembering. Some of us came closer and put our hands on our shoulders. Then, we all gathered at his bed and we all wept, each of us from our own experiences.

The girl woke and made a noise of alarm. All but one of us went to her bed to soothe her, to tell her that she had a home, that she could be one of us, that there was a lot of work but she would be safe.

I couldn't let go of his hand until we had to help elsewhere.

Leigh Kennedy started out aiming for the top, and her first published short story, "Faces," appeared in *Analog* in 1977. She followed this with two highly regarded novels and a string of well received shorts in various venues, including *Asimov's, Shayol, Interzone* and *Omni*. Born in Denver, Colorado, Leigh moved to England in 1985 and now lives in Hastings with her husband (the author Christopher Priest) and their family. Due to other commitments, Leigh has done little writing in recent years, and we are delighted that she has agreed to be a part of this anthology.

Dinosaur

Deborah J. Miller

The sun beat down on the red sandstone shelf from the bluest of skies; it rarefied the air and the quality of the sounds in such a way that the tapping of the hammer could have been heard at the other end of the canyon, but the hammerer and a small girl were the only people for many miles. A stream travelled sluggishly along the basin floor, almost dry now, but deep enough to provide drinking water for a campsite and other denizens of this parched landscape.

The campsite consisted of just two dusty tents but still had an air of gaiety about it somehow, as someone had hung laundry, flag-like, from the lowest branches of the trees and large bunches of meadowsweet were drying, suspended from the guy ropes. A lone solemn teddy sat on guard duty on the bonnet of the nearby jeep.

From the shelf near the top of the ridge you could look down on the camp and see both ways along the canyon for miles. However, James Harlowe and his daughter Mina were far too absorbed to admire the view.

"I've got it, Mina."

She wasn't listening; instead she was smiling at the square green face of the Brontosaurus which was watching their progress through a gap in the trees at the top of the hill. At the sound of her father's voice, it turned to go.

"Bye..." she whispered.

"Look!" He held the prize forward for her inspection and she studied it eagerly. "Do you see, Mina, how its hips and thighbones spread outward like the lizards of today? Not so very long ago we used to think that nearly all four-legged dinosaurs walked like that." To demonstrate as he talked, he put the hunk of rock on his knees and made a bow shape with his arms, rocking from side to side. "Of course, now we know..."

Her giggle interrupted him. "You look funny, Daddy."

"Do I?" He grinned back at her fondly, his weather-beaten face and ashen bleached beard belying the fact that he was still a young man. His eyes still shone with the laughter and zeal of youth, only softly tainted by the visceral touch of a deep sadness. His gaze lingered on the top of her head as she pondered the specimen, tracing the lines with her finger, his thoughts elsewhere.

As she traced the lines, Mina brought the tiny creature into being. She had done it before and knew her father was unable to see the electric lines of animation which sparked from her charmed fingers.

First cartilage, then muscle, fats and blood, then finally, the best bit, skin. Not until you reached the skin could you tell what the creature was going to look like; its texture and colour were so important that Mina always held her breath as the skin appeared. It gave them their character, she felt. Slowly the lizard sloughed the timeskin of aeons until it blinked at her with dumb, jet eyes. It shuffled off the warm stone, reborn by the touch of the sun and its animator.

"It was yellow, Daddy," she remarked, watching it move, paddling its legs in just the way he had demonstrated, "with little black lines down each side."

"Well, we'll never know, Mina." He sighed. "It's nice to imagine what colours they must have been, but it's extremely difficult to tell."

She scowled at him, *'I know,'* she insisted. She was a truthful child and it hurt her to think she was disbelieved, especially by her father whom she worshipped. Her blue eyes filled with tears. "I do."

"Okay, Mina." he soothed, utterly perplexed. "Shall we break for some lunch now? Peanut butter and jelly sandwiches..."

She brightened immediately. "Okay, Daddy; while we're eating could you tell me a bit about Brontosauruses?"

"Course I will. They haven't found anything like that around here though, just small fry really, fish and amphibians. Funny, it seems that it was a wetland environment, with lots of tall trees, ideal for high grazers like Brontosaurus, Brachiosaurus and the like..."

His voice fades with the distance of time, but seems to linger on in the stones of this place for those few who would wish to hear. It seems the fiery rays of the sun have scorched the memory of that day indelibly in the brain of the young girl, in all its love and clarity.

Dr Mina Harlowe stands on the very spot and sheds the tears she would not shed at his funeral. She has not come to mourn him; in fact she does not really know why she is here. Not usually a sentimental person, she lays a crumpled yellow rose on the picnic stone rather woodenly, feeling self-conscious at the statement she is making.

"I love you, Daddy."

She knows that she told him many times when he was alive – she has never said it to anyone else since his death twenty-three years ago. Mina does not like men – all small fry really.

Sitting down, she folds her angular legs beneath her as though consulting an oracle and takes her peanut butter and jelly sandwiches from the rucksack, feeling better for reminding herself that she *can* feel, as other people do.

Chewing and thinking.

"God, do I need answers..."

"I think there were Brontosauruses here," she pronounced proudly. "I think if we look over the top of the ridge, we could find them."

Her father's eyes followed the direction in which she was pointing with such firm conviction, and he frowned. "It's not possible, Mina. Don't you remember about how the rocks are younger nearer the top? You've known that for a long time."

"Unless it's *folded*, Daddy, you said." Her face was perfectly serious as she corrected him, and not for the first time James Harlowe felt almost as at home with his daughter's wisdom as that of his colleagues. He considered her proposition fairly before dismissing it.

"No, I don't think so, there wasn't much tectonic activity in this area for millennia, it was a very stable environment..."

"But Daddy..."

"Mina..." He was growing tired.

"But, Daddy, listen. What about something like a big mudslide? Look, if all the Brontosauruses were feeding in a big herd on the banks, which were much steeper then..."

She never knew where all the words came from, tumbling forth as though they had awaited her utterance with impatience. And she could see them, on the ridge as she spoke, bobbing their huge necks, urging her on.

That's right Mina, tell him how it was...

"...a pocket of mud..." she was saying, "...they all died. The mummies, the daddies and the babies... all higgledy-piggledy... in a great big heap of dinosaurs..."

James Harlowe was aghast. He knew his daughter was a bright child, different somehow from other children her age, but this was something else; how could she possibly know this?

"Let's go and look then, shall we?" He kept his features deliberately passive, the mixture of envy and pride he felt sublimated by his reason: envy, because at the age of ten she had more instinct for his subject than he could ever have – and pride, because even if they found nothing, in her youthful passion, she had never looked more like her mother.

"C'mon," he said. He took her hand and together, they walked toward the top of the ridge.

She swallows hard, the ball of dough and peanut butter suddenly dry and thick in her throat. Gulping lukewarm tea from her thermos, she thinks wryly, "The rest, as they say, is history. Prehistory even..."

They were there; the biggest heap of bones found for years, the best example of a Group Catastrophic Extinction ever. Every morning for weeks James Harlowe stood at the edge of the pit, watching the dig, watching his daughter. He never asked her after that first day, how she knew. He suspected it was simply a gut feeling, occasionally expressed by older, more experienced scientists which the child did not know how to explain. In less guarded moments, he caught himself thinking she had been 'visited' somehow by her mother who, dying, had promised always to watch over him if she could. Her warmth had lingered on in a more tangible way in Mina. A quiet, serious child with a smile just like hers, but already, her own woman. The dig changed his perception of Mina in a small but subtle way. His child, Hazel's child, had the ability to amaze him, just as her mother had done – he could only find her more precious for that.

The first report, of a possible Tyrannosaurus on Bodmin Moor, had come inexplicably when Mina was at a conference in London. She was talking to another American delegate whose vivacity in the face of her own jet-lag made her feel old and stale.

He blurted keenly, "Dr Harlowe! I've been a fan of yours for many, many years." A tiny speck of saliva landed on her cheek having shot out from between his earnestly protruding front teeth. Resisting her immediate impulse to whip out her handkerchief and wipe her face, she smiled graciously, extricating her hand from his clammy grasp, whilst shrinking inwardly.

So what am I? A fossil myself? I'm only forty years old for chrissakes.

She knew what her colleagues all thought of her – a spinster, married to her research. Why at her age she wasn't considered a sharp career woman was beyond her. Perhaps her diminutive, and constantly shabby appearance had something to do with it. Mina had matured into a quiet, serious woman whose permanently mournful expression seemed to reinforce her serious disposition. Although she was by no means ugly, she knew the word 'plain' could be used to describe her. Her ashen blonde hair often looked dead and lifeless, and her passion was a small quiet voice mostly apparent in her dealings with bones. Occasionally when one of her students engaged her enthusiasm she favoured them with a smile, which was like the sun coming out, and by virtue of its rareness, invariably blew them away.

She knew they called her the Mock Turtle, and she was sanguine enough not to be too hurt by this, since it was obviously affectionate. She told herself repeatedly that she didn't mind their fond but incorrect view of her, that all she wanted was the continued respect of the scientific community. After all, age was an attitude of mind; whether it was theirs or hers, she hadn't quite decided.

Her companion was wending his way toward her through the crowd, two glasses of red wine held aloft. He shouted something to herself and the young zealot. "...a fucking Tyrannosaurus!" was all she caught. She smiled anyway, enjoying Robert's blusterous enthusiasm second-hand. He shoved the wineglass at her clumsily and began to gesticulate as he spoke with the free hand, spilling his own drink everywhere.

"Would you believe it? A real live Tyrannosaurus Rex has been spotted on Hampstead Heath! By four people... wonder what they were drinking, eh?"

"What do you mean, Dr Dunbar?" zealot sniffed, unimpressed.

"It was just on the News. Like one of these UFO sightings or abductions, only a Tyrannosaur instead. I must admit, those guys looked pretty shaken up. All telling the same story though. Apparently it was red."

He cocked a bushy eyebrow at Mina over his glass. He was very fond of Dr Harlowe, respected her work, even if she occasionally wrote controversial papers citing the case for purple iguanodons and luminescent green petrodon – it would *matter* to her that it was red, real or imagined.

The young American was waving to someone over Mina's shoulder. "They must be some kind of dinosaur buffs those four guys," he remarked, "in order to get their story straight. God save us from amateur palaeontologist, eh? 'scuse me."

"I don't think so," Robert muttered, watching him go. "They didn't strike me as the type..."

The story was obviously circulating the conference reception area; people were laughing or making dismissive gestures and the hall was more animated than previously. Mina stared into her drink. The shag pile carpet suddenly seemed bouncy and unstable beneath her feet, and her fingers were tingling in a way that felt oddly familiar.

"Are you alright, Mina?"

She looked up at the looming figure, as if from a great distance. These people, her friends, her peers, really didn't know her at all. Someone tapped Robert on the shoulder.

"They want a token expert, old boy. To go and interview the plebs. Are you game?" He started humming the theme to 'The Twilight Zone', still laughing.

"ME!" Her high, thin voice rang out like a gunshot. Mina squirmed and coughed uncomfortably as several groups of people turned to see who had shouted. "I mean, I'll do it... I'd like to do it... It'll be fun," she ended lamely.

"Good girl, Mina. I'll give you a lift into London if you like," smiled Robert.

"God, it's not one of those tabloids, is it?"

"No, no, quite a respectable one really."

Against her better judgement, Mina liked Terri Turner straight away. Usually, extremely attractive women made her feel uncomfortable and on edge, but the tall redhead exuded such energy and drive it was a refreshing change after leaving the company of some of her more 'comfortable' colleagues. She was also direct, and Mina liked directness.

Terri stalked down the corridor, covering a seemingly vast distance in each stride, while Mina almost jogged to keep up with her. She talked fast, but not rubbish, and she knew all about Mina. Despite the speed at which the story was breaking, the journalist had done her homework well.

"We removed them from the scene as fast as possible. We were lucky enough to get there first; news crews and public are swarming all over the place now, of course. I was going to interview them all separately but then decided to wait until you got here and do them together. There's an even chance they'll contradict each other. Watch the big guy..." she glanced at her notes, "Alistair Winter – he knows there's big money in this story. Even if it *is* true, he's liable to embellish it further. I've told them if there's even a *hint* of this thing getting on the internet, deal's off." She stopped abruptly, causing Mina to skid to an ungainly halt, and flung open the door to an interview room. "Well, here we are then..."

The words hung on a cloud of illegal cigarette smoke and an uncomfortable silence. Two young couples occupied the dingy beige and brown room which was furnished with a number of tatty armchairs and some ailing pot plants. Late evening sun streamed in through a narrow, plate glass window, set high in the wall, illuminating the dirty curls of the smoke. The group had obviously stopped what they were saying in mid-sentence, and were gazing unblinkingly toward Mina.

One of the girls was sitting across her boyfriend's knees, hunched up and tired-looking. She held a mobile phone, her thumb poised over the buttons as though she had been texting someone. "We're not being held here or anything are we?" she demanded.

"Don't be daft, Mary" the other girl chided. "This is the press, not a police station. And we haven't done anything wrong." She sounded exasperated and fed up, as if the other girl had been whining all day.

"Leave her alone," the boyfriend growled, "she's just tired."

"Oh, and we're..."

"Ahem..." This stage cough was accompanied by Mina's companion throwing the door wide to its hinges and gesturing down the corridor. "You are all free to go at any time," she said, somewhat acidly. She stalked across the room and snatched the phone from Mary's hand, switching it off with great emphasis. "Of course, then you wouldn't get paid for your story. You also *will not* get paid if you tell all the details to anyone else first," she scowled.

There was a short pause as the group considered this, but no one moved. Terri nodded, satisfied that they understood one another. "This is Dr Mina Harlowe," she said. "She's a palaeontologist and she's come to talk to you about the dinosaur. I'll go and get some coffee and biscuits."

As the door closed, Mina sat down facing the group. She felt awkward and decided to take a confident sounding tack. "Do you know who I am?"

"Yeah, she just told us." The big guy laughed sarcastically, this was presumably Alistair Winter.

"Shut up, Ali." His girlfriend dug him in the ribs.

Mina ignored his sarcasm. "Let's just say I'm a *world class* dinosaur expert." She smiled, trying to bring a bit of friendliness to the proceedings. "Let's also say, I believe you."

"Just like that?" The irritated girl said quietly.

"Yes."

The air of hostility ebbed from the room somewhat and there was a short pause as battlelines were temporarily suspended. "Perhaps I should introduce everyone then," the girl said. "I'm Caitlin, this is my partner Josh," she waved toward the other couple, "and Ali and Mary."

"Great. Now tell me what the dinosaur looked like."

"Huh? Don't you want to know if we'd been drinking, doing drugs?" Josh sounded almost disappointed.

"Yeah, or we might know loads about dinosaurs for all you know," Ali added.

Mina looked at his stupid, if rather handsome, face and speculated that, for him at least, this seemed highly unlikely. She smiled.

"I've already told you; I'm starting from the assumption that you are telling the truth. I'm not here to waste my time. I left a conference to come here. I expect someone else will ask you all about yourselves."

"Sorry."

It turned out that Caitlin was an art student, and very observant about colour and detail. By the time she left the interview room, Mina was holding a plausible drawing of a dinosaur and pages of scribbled notes.

Terri frowned at the drawing Mina had produced under the noisy and argumentative instruction of the group. "But reports said it was a T-Rex. This isn't a T-Rex, is it?"

"No, it's not. That's why I'm inclined to believe them," Mina replied, still staring down at the picture. "Any idiot knows what a T-Rex looks like. This is a Megalosaurus, almost as big and vicious as a T-Rex, but notably *not* the star of any Hollywood blockbuster. They got all the finer details correct, see, three fingers…" Unconsciously, she hooked her own fingers into a claw to demonstrate as she spoke. Terri grinned, enjoying Mina's obvious delight and passion, but she did not interrupt her. "The stance is less upright than a Tyrannosaurus too, heavier upper torso. Caitlin also said it was a bright, bloody red colour, something which the latest," she paused, "actually *my* latest research is suggesting. There's no way they could actually have known that, my paper hasn't been published yet."

"So, where do we go from here?"

"You tell me."

She sits on the picnic rock, back against the baking cliff face. Remembering. Feeling sorry that Terri's story was so soon irrelevant; wishing that was the least of it. Her eyes are closed, facing into the desert sun. She is burning. Her fair skin baking in the heat, ash blonde wisps of straw-like hair catch the tiny breezes, or stick to her neck and face. She doesn't care. She is speaking to her father.

"God, Daddy, can you see what's happening? Do you know what I've done?"

Her hotel room was dark and quiet. Normally the sound of the rain trickling down the windows would have touched her in a small, subtle way, born of her keen sense of detail and love of all things elemental. Tonight, the rain whispered a different story. Tonight, quite simply, it reminded her that she was alone.

Mina had stared at the drawing, thinking disjointed thoughts, which eventually blurred to white noise, the occasional word jumping out of the monologue to assault her. Now, her reverie had nothing to do with the picture any more; all vaguely coherent thought had finished half an hour ago.

Stirring from her cross-legged position on the bed, she noticed the growing darkness for the first time as she chafed the feeling back into her right foot which had gone to sleep. Soft outlines of the high-backed couch and chairs loomed like cold sentinels with their backs toward the overlarge bed. The resonance of other transient souls who had spent the night here seemed vaguely tangible to Mina in her state of mind.

Occasionally given to pure melancholy, Mina perversely enjoyed feeling miserable. She knew her colleagues were all downstairs, laughing and drinking, and that she would be most welcome to join them. However she had always felt different, as if by her aloofness she had exercised some noble moral or intellectual strength. Only recently had she begun to question this. Tonight, she felt alone more keenly than she ever had, and that feeling surprised her. She glanced obliquely at the discarded drawing; there was something else, an irritated feeling, of almost . . . responsibility for the manifestation of the dinosaur.

Ridiculous.

Absently tossing back the remains of her drink, she prepared to get into the bed on which she'd been sitting for the last hour. On the bedside table there was a fossil, *Gryphea*, Devil's Toenail. Her hand closed around the grey stone as she settled back against plush mountains of pillows. She liked the fossil's cold, dense feel, found it soothing. It fitted into the palm of her hand snugly, the striations on the curl of the shell almost worn smooth by her years of absent caresses. Tonight though, it was warming up remarkably quickly. Lifting her hand from against her chest, she stared, opening her fingers slowly as if seeing the stone for the first time.

Gryphea was alive. Lazy blue lines of luminescence still circled the shell, no longer grey fossil but red, brown and white. No longer dense stone, but light, impossibly light in her palm. Gently, she prized open the top hinge; inside the little bivalve squirmed, muscular and wet.

Mina didn't feel too surprised. Vague and sunny memories of her childhood gift assailed her, making her smile. She remembered all her creatures; how they had basked in their unexpected existence for a short time and then simply disappeared. She had never questioned her strange talent, nor analyzed it in any way. There were other, bigger questions, she had come to believe as she grew older, and so, when at the age of fifteen she had tried and failed to reanimate an *Archaeopteryx*, she had simply shrugged and walked away. The joy of creation had left her, and only the burning questions of her chosen science remained.

She popped *Gryphea* into a glass on the bedside cabinet, wondering how long he would survive in the fluoride-laced water. She watched him for a while as she fell asleep. Tomorrow, she would phone Caitlin McGhee and go to the place where the dinosaur had been. She had no idea why; she would just like to be there.

"Mina? Is that you?" The voice on the other end of the phone gushed on in a somewhat rhetorical vein. "Are you awake? Have you heard the news?"

It was her research assistant, Tim Weisner; he never paused for breath much anyway. Mina was home again, in Princeton, and still sleeping off the jet-lag from her trip to England.

"A Pteranodon for chrissakes!"

"You what?!"

"Over New York! They're calling it a Pterodactyl, of course, but... Listen. we've got to get over there! It's killed three people!"

"But they don't... they wouldn't..."

"I didn't say it'd eaten them. Put your telly on while you get dressed. I'll come over and get you. Hey, isn't this amazing? It's history, Mina, history!"

"...and this is Aileen King reporting for CBS on what must be the news story of the century. A prehistoric nightmare has begun on the streets of our city. This is no hoax. A winged dinosaur, yes, a winged dinosaur, possibly an actual Pterodactyl, has killed three people, one a young boy of three, here on the roof garden at 22nd/3rd St... You can see all around me the wreckage caused by its wings in this once peaceful haven... and here, next to the fishpond, the tiny, bloodstained sunhat of little Ricky Gonzales..."

The reporter went on in graphic terms to describe how Ricky's mother and father had apparently been swept off the edge of the roof. The camera panned over the edge of the building to the scene below, where tarpaulins now hid the splattered remains. Blood, like a red inkblot, escaped the neat lines of the covering and the cameras lingered seconds longer than mere reporting called for. Richard Gonzales' body was not there; it had been dropped two blocks away, causing a multiple pile up and another casualty of the incident. Although there was little need to embellish the already incredible facts, the reporter was making as much dramatic mileage out of the 'story of the century' as time allowed.

"Remember, you saw it here first on CBS, eyewitness accounts to follow..."
And finally, the somewhat tasteless...
"...New Yorkers, look to the sky."
Mina went with Tim to the scene, with no doubt in her mind. She knew it was all completely true. Already, the tone of the reporting was irritating her; they didn't seem to realise the significance of what happened here. They were much more interested in sensationalism than fact . . .

Those poor people hadn't deserved to die, of course, but she felt curiously detached and ambivalent about their fate. And she could not deny the surge of vindication she felt when an old down-and-out who had been an eyewitness commented, "It was like a giant seabird."

Mina picked the man out from amongst his cronies, they were all willing to sell the story for the price of a bottle, but this one seemed lucid. He was shaken by what he'd seen, but awestruck by it. His amazement remained undiminished even hours later; he had a sense of wonder that it seemed everyone else in this damned city was lacking. She liked him.

"Do you mean its coloration," she asked, "light underneath and dark on top?"

"'s right Miss. Like an Albatross."

"Can I buy you a burger? We can discuss the dinosaur a bit more."

He grinned an ulcerous grin "Sure can."

That had been a year ago, one year and eighteen deaths. Mina still sits on picnic rock, her mind wandering. Her lips are still moving. She is repeating the names of the dead. She knows them all. She killed them all.

It took five separate incidents before the connection was irrefutable: London, New York, Paris, Edinburgh and New York again. She almost refused to take responsibility for the second New York death when some fool (some said hero) decided to play toreador with a Triceratops and was gored to death after running up a blind alley... but still, the fact remained, they were coming for her.

She was the common factor; the percentage chance against one single person in the world being within a fifty-mile (and decreasing) radius of each visitation was incredibly high. They were coming for her.

There had been twenty-one happenings now. Thankfully, people were not killed every time. A huge woolly mammoth had stood for all the world like a dumb cow, chewing the vegetation for close to an hour in a municipal park in Florida, where Mina was on holiday. It was the most celebrated case in a way; scientists rushed to the scene and took leisurely photographs. The Daytona Mammoth prompted a plethora of papers and became the most documented 'dinosaur' in history.

After being asked to be an independent expert by the media for the first couple of cases, Mina kept her head down and, after making the connection between the events, she took a year's sabbatical.

Imagine then, the anger and impotence she felt about not actually seeing a single one of the creatures. They were getting closer each time but… The last one, a Diplodocus, had been *so* close…

She was back in New York, and buying a pretzel on the corner of 79th Street, when she heard noise and the screams coming from almost a block away.

"Jeez, not again," the vendor moaned.

Streams of panicked people came rushing up the sidewalk, some of them running out into the traffic. Someone jolted her arm as they ran past.

"It's freakin' huge!" he yelled, to no one in particular.

Mina ran into the crowd, fighting against the current of fleeing bodies. Suddenly her frustration overwhelmed her, the totally illogical desire to confront the beast took hold.

"I'm here!" she screamed. "Godammit, I'm here!"

She was almost at the end of the block and could even see a flash of deep emerald hide, when someone hysterical, desperate to get out, became caught on the shoulder-strap of her bag and, as they struggled to free themselves, shoved her back towards the building. Mina felt her feet slide from under her as she lost her balance, and knew in those few seconds that she was about to crack her head against the wall.

Everything seemed to slow.

She could see her own arm flailing in front of her, her hand grabbing at the air as she fell. At that final instant, before she gained a major concussion, she looked up to see the disappearance of a long, mottled green tail.

In the desert, Mina awakens from her trance not understanding why this physical knot of anger refuses to leave her, why the anger she has felt since her father died has something to do with all this. She has tried to make him proud all these years, but he was never there. She remembers crying when she received her Doctorate, and later, in her room, ripping the parchment to shreds.

Someone is calling her name from the top of the hill. She rises, dizzy with the heat and dehydration. Up there is the old Brontosaur dig. Swaying, she peers up the narrow path – did she see a movement at the top of the ridge? She climbs.

Almost at the top, and she is crying silently for no reason. She didn't want to come here, so why is she here? But she doesn't stop her climb.

And now she is on the crest, looking into the pit.

There they are, 'the Mummies, the Daddies and the babies', alive. Green, black and dark brown, she notes. Whistling and swaying their long necks in an undulating, gentle movement.

They turn toward her, looking up out of the pit to where she stands like some Saurian Oracle.

"Why?" she says aloud. "You don't belong here..."

She sits down and watches them for a while. They are doing nothing much, but are watching her in return, and Mina is struck by their beauty. They move slowly, but not the stupid crashing or plodding attributed to, they're just in no hurry. A male and female pair intertwine their necks as giraffe do and Mina is both privileged and entranced. Taking out her field notebook, she draws.

The sun is setting, red flame lances off the far side of the pit, touching the herd, turning them orange and softening their outlines to warm monolithic mounds. The calves begin to curl up to sleep at their mothers' sides and most of the adults lie down, bending their legs under them, their necks lowered carefully in an effort to find a smooth spot. Some of the cows form a 'nursery' and, Mina, delighted, draws frantically.

Their whistling is quieter now as sleep descends on the herd. Sensing her audience is at an end Mina puts her book down. Tears course through the desert grime of her cheeks, but she is smiling, thanks and forgiveness, to them all for coming.

"Mina."

He is calling her from in the pit. Over on the other side she sees the tiny figure almost silhouetted against the weak dying sun, but there is no doubt in her mind. He stands, legs widespread, arms flapping over his head in that huge expansive gesture of his, she can almost hear his smile.

Feeling joy but no surprise at his being here, she stands up and waves back. Funny, that he should be standing exactly there, where she had stood that day.

"Mina!"	" Daddy!"
"Come and see, it's wonderful."	"Come and see, it's wonderful."
He smiles and waves her on.	She had smiled and waved him on.
Distracted.	Distracted.
Mina walks forward,	James Harlowe walked forward

into air   into air
into nothing   into nothing
into the pit.   into the pit.

At the very last moment her step acquires a sense of renewed purpose.
She is falling . . . at peace. Knowing that her fall will stop.
And it does. She lands softly, featherlike, clasping her arms around the
warm gargantuan neck, which has risen to meet her. The creature snickers with
delight at his precious catch and languidly deposits her on the ground. He brings
his face to hers, no 'terrible lizard' or 'thunder lizard' but no romantic storybook
creation either. He cannot smile at her; his features and thought processes not
capable of such expression, but there is something beneficent in the massive face...
Some unspoken understanding passes between them.
"I understand" Mina says. She touches his face, just once, and walks off
into the herd to meet her father.

Mina's sketchpad was found during a field trip, coincidentally led by Tim Weisner, two weeks later. Her body was never found.

Her pictures of the Brontosaurus herd were beautiful, shining. Drawn with simple lines in charcoal, they held all the love and passion and science of the woman who had rendered them.

The images did work of which Mina could only have dreamed; all who looked at them (and they were widely published) were unaccountably moved. Together with the dinosaur appearances, they touched a generation and subtly changed public perceptions; made people shiver once more at the marvel of such creatures.

In a world gone dry of magic, a dustbowl of computer generated ennui, people once again spoke the word *dinosaur* with wonder.

Deborah J. Miller was born in Edinburgh and has now returned to Scotland, having lived in England for several years. In 1993 an earlier version of "Dinosaur" was shortlisted for the Ian St James award. Subsequently, Deborah has concentrated largely on novels. Writing as Miller Lau, she created 'the Last Clansman' trilogy, which began with *Talisker* (2001), and more recently has published *Swarmthief's Dance* – the first of a new series – under her own name.

Further Orders

Elizabeth Priest

I've been sitting in this little meadow in the middle of the great forest for what must be a few weeks now. Okay, I lie. I know how long it's been, but I can't think about the real number without wanting to scream. I am completely bored, beyond anything I've ever known before... They told me to wait here. I'm not sure what for – they only said to wait for further orders. And so here I am, waiting.

It's just me, forty-seven entirely visible trees and three hundred and eighty eight trees that I can make out behind other trees, before the they all become lost in each other, too indistinct to continue counting. Then there's a family of ducks in the pond at the far corner, just where the ground slopes down suddenly. My bag, my campfire, lots and lots of grass (I'm not quite ready to start counting it, not just yet), wild flowers in blue and light purples, small mammals – predominantly mice and voles, and several varieties of crickets, butterflies and ants, with the occasional woodlouse or an unwelcome spider. There are frogs in the pond as well. They croak loudly all through the night. The frogs and crickets aren't the worst of it though. There's a noise like whistling wind, constantly, despite the fact that every day out here so far has been totally still. Still, hot and stifling. I can't work out where the strange noise is coming from, but I've been hearing it ever since I entered this meadow. As I walk around the meadow, it changes direction, but when I step into the trees (not going far in case the person bearing my further orders arrives), it vanishes entirely. It's a mystery.

I have been spending my time, apart from counting and making lists of the things here in the meadow, exercising, running around the field, practising with my sword, climbing trees... and playing around like a child, talking to myself. I've been writing a story in my diary. It's about space aliens and things, because there's no way I'm going to waste any more of my life writing about this stupid cult and the missions they send me on. There's been enough sycophantic fiction about them to fill our library, and I don't intend to add to it.

When I'm not daydreaming about far-flung planets and speculating ways to get between them, I'm considering a million different ways this situation could go. Maybe this is a test. Maybe they sent me here to die. I'm probably going to run out of food in the next few weeks unless I start conserving it. Winter will come eventually, so I'll freeze. My honour stops me from leaving this field. I swore I would complete this mission. They said I would receive further orders after I arrived here, not specifying when. I have re-read the map and the orders they gave me a hundred times. I'm confident that I'm in the right place. I know I got here almost a whole day sooner than they expected.

I've been speculating about the further orders as well. Why wouldn't they tell me the extent of my mission from the very beginning? I can be trusted (apparently, or why would they have chosen me for this in the first place? There were hundreds of other recruits at my level), and in these empty woods, it's very unlikely that I would run into someone to tell in any case. And if the further orders are coming from my own base, would it not have been wiser to send an elder, or a mystic with me, who could then tell me what to do once we got here? Perhaps it is something so dangerous it wouldn't have been wise for us to travel together? Or maybe they will approach from another direction? Another base? Have I been selected to finally go on to a more advanced base, where I might learn a different craft, or have the chance to go on many missions of my own? A promotion from my endless servitude as a novice? I wait, and wonder.

I meditate as often as I can, although I soon get distracted by relentless birdsong or the croaking of those damn frogs. And don't get me started on the crickets or that wailing noise. I can't do anything about the last two, but I have a bow and arrow that I am required to carry with me at all times, and I often consider changing the bird and frogs' status from natural creatures of the world, with whom we share this wonderful Earth, to enemies of the sacred order of our gods, and shooting them all. This would be unethical, but after the twentieth night here, I would have challenged the gods themselves to tell me that I acted rashly. Anyway, I could just claim madness induced by the faint whistling.

I plait the long grasses together, making a long rope. Such is my concentration on the task, the desire not to think about staying within a few meters of this meadow at all times, that the rope grows long enough to go at least half way across the field. I cut it in three, and begin braiding it against itself. I hum old songs, ones that are nothing to do with the gods, and the great work they do, and I realise that I've forgotten most of the words. It's been a long time since I've heard the older songs.

Maybe, I realise, after a week wandering around this meadow, mapping every inch of it in my head, the further orders will focus on the meadow? Maybe the door to the secret base is here? Maybe I have to do something about the mice problem? Maybe I have to reach a Zen state of numbness – I mean, *oneness* – by counting every blade of grass here? I leave that one for last, and search every inch of the grass over the next two weeks, tapping the ground and surrounding trees. I'm not sure what I'm trying to find – either a secret entrance to something, or a source to the weird noise. I drop a stone into the pond, to test how deep it is. I count the flowers again, as more have bloomed, and watch the bees in case they spell out messages in the air or with their journeys between the flowers. No pattern reveals itself, although I realise more blue flowers grow in the north of the meadow, and more purple flowers grow in the east. Nothing grows in the west, where the grass is thinner, and I can see moss. I peel back the moss, in case there's a trap door down there, but there's nothing but mud and insects. I hurriedly replace the moss, and retreat to the area that has become my campsite. For some reason, it feels safer here.

The twenty-third day is the eighth day on which it has rained. I huddle under my cloak, and wonder if I should think about building a house. I'll probably have more than enough time. Heck, I could turn this whole place into a big mansion, constructed entirely of grass, twigs, and mud. But this particular twig I've been sitting on for four hours is going on the fire. As soon as I can get the soggy thing lit again. I can't be bothered moving, and anyway I'm still practising my mental powers.

Theoretically, with enough concentration, I could have moved that twig from under my rear or dissolved it or something, but I think I am worrying too much about the pain and discomfort ("Suffering is all part of the learning curve of life," as my teachers would quote) to cause anything to happen apart from becoming even more acutely aware of the fact that it might have thorns as well. I've moved things with my mind before, in training. It was one of the last things I learnt before I was sent on this mission. Maybe I've been sent here to perfect my skills?

At this point, my cloak finally becomes soaked through, and a fat drop of icy water plops onto the back of my neck, making me scream and jump a foot. And then I land painfully on that cruel twig. Once I've sorted myself out, trying to squeeze more shelter out of the sodden cloak, I start to feel really foolish for screaming, although no one could have heard me. But then, I still have my suspicions that this is all just a test, and that I am being watched.

The twenty-fifth day, at nightfall, as soon as it could be considered even remotely dusk, the frogs begin their croaking again. I slide stealthily up the meadow, moving with the breeze that gently waves the grass, at one with the shadows. I pause a second, assessing my target, hidden in the long grass. Then I jump out, my sword raised, and scream, "For the gods' sake, will you fucking shut the fuck up!?" The frogs all jump back into the pool, startled, and the mother duck gives me a 'Now really, was that called for?' look. "Yes," I snarl, sheathing my sword, and stomping back across the meadow to my campsite (which is still damp from the rain two nights past).

The frogs don't sing all that night, making the other sounds almost bearable, and I sleep almost peacefully, once I've stopped feeling stupid for yelling, and guilty for swearing. And no one heard me. If an angry woman screams at some frogs in the forest, does anyone hear? Probably not, it's so bloody out of the way and empty. I don't think I count any more.

The twenty-seventh day is a Friday. I think so, anyway. I wash my hair in the pond, and then, seeing that the ducks are on the other side of the field eating bugs, I strip off and slide into the pool. I giggle to myself at the thought of further orders, whatever they may be, arriving now. I would probably just stand there; my arms folded across my chest (this pool only looks deep if you're sitting down) and say, "Took your bloody time." Or maybe, "Now what?" although that might be interpreted wrong... I'm still trying to think of a really good witty response long after I've climbed out, dried off, and I'm fully dressed again.

The twenty-eighth day, I wake early, watch the dawn, do a silly dance, and search for mushrooms. There's a disappointing lack of them, although a tree in the northern corner has a weird, fat, wobbly yellow fungus growing on it. I spend a few hours meditating on the way my weapons-training-obsessed, perfectionist, self controlled, calm, slightly icy personality has vanished to be replaced with this crazy woman with the frizzy hair, dirty clothes, and tendency to laugh at anything, to dance in the dawn, to jump naked into pools of freezing cold, frog infested water, and to babble endlessly to the mouse who eats the crusts from my sandwiches. And that's another thing: before I came out here, I always ate the crusts to my sandwiches... It must be the silence. The faint noise of a gale whistling through the trees has faded in my mind, and I can only hear it when I realise I've stopped thinking about it, which is a great relief, as long as I can meditate away all thoughts about it. This gets increasingly harder, and I find myself singing out loud to distract myself instead.

I spend a further few hours searching for the source of the noise. I climb a tree, and look around. The meadow looks a lot smaller from up here. When I first arrived, it felt huge. Now, even on the ground, it seems smaller, more manageable. Up here, I realise just how tiny, in the grand scheme of things (which, from up here seems to be a zillion trees, and not much else), the place which has been my prison is.

For once, the whistling noise seems to be closer, instead of moving bizarrely around. I climb higher, following the noise, and there I find a luminous red bug, as long as my thumb, with huge curving legs, whistling loud enough to make my ears ring. I draw my sword silently, and then bring it down hard enough to cut the branch clean off. I don't know if I got the damn thing, or if I just scared it away, but I spend the rest of the afternoon searching for more of them, having moderate success.

And then the doubts start setting in, as I pace aimlessly about the meadow on my twenty-ninth day, trying to find something to occupy myself with. There's so little out here, I can't piece together any sort of daily ritual. I'm beginning to think building myself a house might be in order. As I look around for a good starting point, my mind doubts freely.

Why am I still here?

Because they told me to wait. I have loyalty to them. This is a test.

What if the messenger with further orders was killed? By enemy spies! No! The squirrels ate him! I've seen squirrels out here, and they don't look half as cute as they're made out to be...

So you'll die out here for the sake of your religion, when they can't even organise decent messengers?

Why not? People have died for stupider things. Besides, I've been with them my whole life, I won't abandon the Way now, when I've come so far, even if I have hit such a strange dead end.

Okay, when I run out of food, maybe I'll leave.

Maybe?

Yeah but... hey, I'm talking to myself now, right? Well, this is new.

Don't worry, it's internal.

Yeah, but now I'm going to remember this, and *know* I broke down and talked to myself... I'm shutting up. Let's concentrate on staring at the clouds for a while, shall we?

I lie for hours, looking up at the sky, watching the shapes of clouds passing slowly overhead, wondering what will become of me... A squirrel hops over and sits on my knee. I look into its little beady eyes, frozen in horror, and then fling one of my throwing stars at it. The bloody thing moves too quickly, faster than someone highly trained in the most deadly combat arts known to mankind! It vanishes into the trees, as does the throwing star. "Crap," I moan, speaking out loud with no twinge of embarrassment, I'm used to talking to keep myself sane. "I'll be killed if I've lost it... those things cost a fortune to replace, and it'll come out of my allowance!"

So I spend hours searching for a flattened bit of pointy metal that a cult I will probably never see again might charge me for... If they do come to find me, I'm blaming it all on the squirrels, and asking to be allowed to go lead a normal life, away from the bases and temples I grew up in, so I may recover from my madness. Or I'll stop asking them for when I'll be allowed to go on a real mission. Which reminds me, for the first time in days, that I'm still in training... I sigh, and draw my sword, ready for many more hours spent prancing around the meadow, blocking and stabbing imaginary assailants. They look like giant, ninja squirrels in my minds eye.

And then, not long into my training session, I see him, waiting nervously on the edge of the trees. The first human I've seen in so many weeks, watching me with a terrified expression. Forget security and being aware of everything at all times; I drop my sword to do a few cartwheels, screaming "Yippee!" and any other happy nonsense that occurs to me. I forget to thank the gods.

Then, finally, I hurry over to him. He's wearing the right uniform, the simple black clothing of mere novices like myself, sent out on these stupid missions, and he has the same standard issue sword hung over his shoulder. He's carrying a pack just like mine.

I stand close to him, my eyes running over his nervous stance, wide eyes, and young face, while I'm getting my breath back. I'm getting seriously out of shape, even with the occasional training. I'm just about ready to talk myself, when he finally gathers up the courage to talk, speaking before I have a chance to get in a word. Looking up at me with his soulful, terrified brown eyes, he says, "Um, a-are you the f-further orders?"

Elizabeth Priest is the daughter of two distinguished authors – Christopher Priest and Leigh Kennedy. Not quite out of her teens, Elizabeth is the youngest author yet to be published by NewCon Press, and this is also the first time we have published mother and daughter in the same volume. "Further Orders" marks Elizabeth's short story debut, though there will doubtless be many more stories to follow.

The Tollhouse

Claire Weaver

On the day everything changed forever, I was in the Outer Ring, eating popcorn.

Of course, it wasn't my job to eat popcorn, but as my colleagues were all on breaks for the next hour there was no one around to tell me off.

Juggling the big bag of Butterkist in one hand and a clipboard in the other, I went from one pod to the next, checking off the contents on the pre-printed form and leaving a big trail of spilt kernels and crumbs. That trail of crumbs, it could tell the boss just how much work I'd done – how many lanes of inventory were crunchy underfoot, how many were clean. If only we had rats to hide the evidence of my slacker sensibility.

The Outer Ring was a large, C-shape warehouse that hugged the edge of the Tollhouse's complex on Asteroid 359. There were 99 lanes in the Outer Ring – long, curved walkways between scaffold racks that almost touched the ceiling. It had strip lighting and no windows, and smelled faintly of wet paint from where they were re-decorating the corridor outside.

Alone, just you and the pods held in the scaffolding, the Outer Ring was cold and echoey and decidedly scary. Not that I'd ever admit to that. I suppose even though I'd been there three years, I still wasn't used to the concept of infinite vacuum on the other side of the wall.

With my popcorn and my clipboard, I was working Lane 75. There were three thousand, seven hundred and eighty-eight pods in the racks of L75, each holding at least one fabric, and it was my job to inventory them all. And the next lane. By mid-afternoon.

Pod one thousand, nine hundred and four: *Red handbag. Broken strap. Contains coin purse, keys, tampon, one pearl earring.*

Check.

Pod two thousand and nine: *One bolt-action Sako TRG41 sniping rifle adapted for a left-handed firer, and one .308 Lapua Magnum cartridge. Faint smell of cordite. Word carved in the side of cartridge, just readable: Sammy.*

Check.

Pod two thousand, four hundred and thirty-seven: *One swollen human brain. Pulsating. Sticky.*

Check.

This was my life.

This was what I was doing when I found her.

I didn't even deal with Incoming: that was the big irony – me, the slacker, hated by the boss and all my peers. Me, the one who found the girl in pod three thousand, four hundred and twelve.

For a crazy, fleeting moment it did cross my mind that being the one to find her might make them *like* me, or at least not hate me so much.

Yeah, right.

Pod three thousand, two hundred and forty: *Unborn foetus. Caucasian. Male.*

Check.

All these things, what we called fabrics, were sacrifices. Gifts from the selfish to ensure they keep control. Bribes to stay alive.

That old saying about life taking its toll is a complete misnomer. We only take what's given up – the things you want to leave behind, consciously or not. The bag handed over to the mugger to appease his knife-hand. The favourite hunting rifle ditched in a river because revenge was more important. The brain sacrificed to find a better party, more booze, harder drugs.

Check.

The child for the career.

Check.

It's all here, in the Tollhouse. All the things you gave up to better yourself, to raise your status, or simply to stay alive. All metaphysically whizzed to this crowded little asteroid and inventoried by a popcorn-eating slacker with a clipboard and a leaky ballpoint pen.

And then the girl showed up, and everything changed. The girl with glassy eyes and singed hair giving off a burnt smell, squeezed into pod three thousand, four hundred and twelve. So scared she looked feral – a little cave-girl in a miniature cave.

My clipboard said:

Pod three thousand, four hundred and twelve: *Chocolate. Various forms – bars, cakes, cookies. Net weight six hundred pounds.*

But instead there was the girl, about fourteen years old, mouth smeared with chocolate cake.

The little box I was supposed to check, left unchecked.

"No, it's a *girl.* Human. Alive." I spoke slowly and clearly, my lips brushing the tarnished wire mesh of the Communication Box. The Box crackled with static in reply: *zjsskzzkkjz!* Statement or question, I could barely tell.

The Box was a black cube glued to the wall, with random-looking antennae sticking out of the top. It was our glorified tin-can-and-string telephony system. At the time of installation, the boss had once proudly informed me, it was state-of-the-art. Before they even *had* string on Earth.

"She must have come through the meta-link."

More static from the boss up in the Dome, sitting in his executive leather chair and looking out at the vast blackness of space. His panoramic view was perpetual night; his lighting the soft glow of starlight. I'd been in his office a grand total of three times – once on my first day, staring slack-jawed at the constellations and missing half of what I was told. Again a few weeks later, after the accident, staring at my shoes and explaining how I didn't *know* the red button opened the airlock – I thought it was the light switch (its convoluted security had made me wonder, but it didn't really sink in until it was too late…). And the last time I'd been there, I was delivering some report to what turned out to be an empty office. The boss wasn't there. I stood for whole minutes with my face close to the glass – but not too close to leave any marks – desperate to soak up the view but too paranoid I'd get caught to really enjoy it. That night I'd dreamt I could fly through the black, cartwheeling around distant suns and laughing in the vacuum.

"No, she's not on the inventory…"

Zzzkkjssizzz!

"Should I deal with it?"

Zzkkzzkjzkizzz!

"Do you want to just send someone down?"

Zzzk!

I understood clearly enough: don't touch her, don't do anything, you'll only make a mess of the situation.

Me, the imbecile.

Me, the slacker.

Everyone always told me they didn't know how I got the job. I guess I just fluked the interview – it can happen.

So can being fired.

From out in the black, the Tollhouse looked like space junk. A vaguely circular shard of rock sixty clicks wide with a clump of dull, scrappy-looking metal stuck to one side and poking a little out of the other side too. Only when you drew closer could you see the architecture – the Dome, the Arches, the gangways and walkways and connecting tubes.

In theory, the Tollhouse should never get bigger: we'd accept the fabrics, process and store them, until they were shipped out to Left Wanting or The Dreamhold to continue their cycle of need and greed. The problem was, more and more sacrifices were being made. Offers and proposals. Bribes and blackmails. It was all still in balance, but happening on a bigger scale. So the Tollhouse had been extended over the years – more departments opened, more staff brought in. First the Storage Warehouse became W'house 1 and W'house 2, then came the Clusters, and now there were the Inner and Outer Rings as well. Incoming had trebled in size in the past half millennium and Outgoing was getting so squished by everything else that it had to move to the underside of the asteroid. The Dome was still the highest point on the Tollhouse, and while the boss enjoyed his view it would stay that way.

I'd have given anything to work in Outgoing. Quiet and hidden on the asteroid's underbelly. The processors working on the underside were always so laid-back – clustered around the cigarette bin before shifts started, they'd tell me, "Chill out – life's only hard if you make it so."

At mealtimes in the refectory, with the tinny sound of cutlery on china drowning everything else out, they'd say, "Work hard, play hard."

In the dorms at night, with the smell of the recycled air making my nose itch, they'd whisper, "Music calms the soul." They had a radio in Outgoing. Can you believe that? The boss would never let me listen to music.

Zzkksjzikkkizszz!

The Tollhouse was so vast and tall, and the corridors and tunnels connecting it all together were so complicated, it could be maybe an hour before anyone came to take charge of the situation.

Me, alone with the girl in the far reaches of the Outer Ring.

Me, with my bag of popcorn.

Or someone could be here in the next five minutes.

You could say I panicked – although, given the circumstances, I maintain that I dealt with the situation as anyone would have. I hid the bag of popcorn behind the station desk – I was starting to feel sick anyway. I grabbed the white plastic bin and dashed up and down the lanes, bent double to scoop up all the crumbs, all the evidence. I checked off all of Lane 78's inventory to make it look as if I'd worked harder than I actually had. I polished my shoes in case it was the boss who showed up, and combed a distorted reflection of my hair in the shiny curved surface of the Box's talk button.

All this dashing and worrying, and I started to sweat. The popcorn churned in my belly and I knew, just knew I was going to be sick. I took short sips from a can of cola but the fizz made my head spin so I sat down, put my head between my knees and took some calming deep breaths. Just like Outgoing might do. Calm and easy.

Oh, god…

I threw up, missing the bin completely and splattering vomit all over the floor. Did I have time to mop it up or should I just cover it with paper towels and hope no one noticed?

Something clattered to the floor over in Lane 78.

OhGodOhGodOhGodOhGod – my mantra as I scurried from the station desk back to the girl. If anything happened to her before someone arrived, I'd be held responsible.

Me, leaving her unattended, as if she'd stay put.

Me, out on my ear. Check.

The station desk was near the middle of the Outer Ring, at the end of Lane 45. It was actually slightly closer to the Core than the

Edge because the lanes became shorter and the pod racks narrower the further in you went. If the girl doubled-back on me, at least she'd have nowhere to hide.

I scanned the tops of the pod racks in case she'd somehow climbed up there, where the rack scaffolding joined to the roof, merging with the lighting rigs and air conditioning pipes. I turned down Lane 71, a short-cut to L78 if you know where to squeeze through, and there she was. Half way down, sitting cross-legged in the middle of the lane. She'd pulled open all the pods on the right hand side, emptied them out onto the floor.

Journals and diaries stuffed full with love letters littered the ground, the pages torn and ripped. A shattered goldfish bowl reflected a dying fish in a thousand glass shards. Paper money twirled and rustled in the air-conditioned breeze.

The little things people give up. The sacrifices to hold onto power. The bribes to change their lives, one facet at a time.

The things we in the Tollhouse simply call fabrics. Meaningless. Stripped of identity. Lost.

People aren't meant to travel the meta-link. With people sacrifices, it's only an aspect of them that's taken to make a fabric – not the whole. A person never actually travels through the meta-link – it's wild and mad and would drive a person insane.

For example, see: the girl. Watching the fish die with confused interest, as if not only had she never seen a fish before but she had no understanding of death.

At the other end of the lane, the boss appeared. His face was red and shiny, I hoped from rushing down here, but more likely from anger on seeing the entire lane in such disarray. The sudden rush of adrenalin made me want to vomit all over again. I managed to choke it back.

Behind him, six processors puffed and panted. Even if the boss hadn't run down here, they certainly had.

The fish flapped its tail once more and died.

The girl looked up at me with glassy eyes from beneath a rag mop of black hair. Seven pairs of eyes watched her watching me.

She looked at me with those wide eyes, opened her chocolate-coloured lips and said the words that changed everything, forever.

The moments that followed were total chaos.

The boss started shouting, telling me to clean up the mess, yelling that I was fired, that I'd never work in the metaphysical industry again. The processors lunged at the girl with a paint-splattered dust sheet they'd brought from the corridor outside, using it as a sort of net. The girl scampered away, crawling under the pod rack, and me, I just stood there, staring.

Me, the imbecile.

Me, the slacker.

Until

"*Stop!*"

And everybody did. Even the boss, his mouth hanging half-open and his cheeks flushed crimson from all his shouting.

Only now they expected me to say something else. To continue. As if I had a point.

Somewhere under the pod racks, or maybe on top of them by now, I knew the girl was listening too. The girl who had said my name.

The girl who wasn't an accident.

The girl who hadn't been through the meta-link, at least, not from Earth.

"She said my name."

Right about then, someone should have said, "What?"

Someone should have said, "Eh?"

But no-one did. They all knew that this would happen one day. They just never expected it to happen to me.

Me, the slacker.

Me, the new boss.

The boss's red cheeks were fading now, the blood draining fast.

The girl from HQ, somewhere in the pod racks.

Outside, the stars shone.

From up in the Dome, the Tollhouse looks so much neater. Compact and concise. Ordered. Structured.

There have been a few alterations since I took over: radios at every station desk, and more varieties of popcorn in the vending machines. Breaks are five minutes longer and it's easier to apply for departmental transfers. I have an open door policy. But really, nothing much has changed. The fabrics still come in, stay for a while, and go out again. They're processed, stored and inventoried. The warehouses are getting too full and we're going to need to build another one, probably strutting out from the Outer Ring on scaffolding. The Outer Outer Ring.

It doesn't make sense, but we figure that's just what the Board wanted – change without change. Freshening up, perhaps. Or maybe there are new laws about employees' rights that they knew the old boss would never go for.

It's traditional for HQ to send a sign – something bearing the name of the new boss. A banner, perhaps, or a buzzing neon light. It's every processor's secret dream, to open a pod and find your name there in glinting, sparkling letters.

It'd never been a fourteen year old girl before, though.

We never found out the HQ girl's name. She went back after the old boss left and I took over. And we never managed to get her to tell us about HQ, or the Board, or anything.

I have the view now. A thousand tiny stars to replace the thousand pods I used to watch.

Me, *the boss*.

Check.

Claire Weaver, who currently lives in London, is probably best known for her three years spent as co-editor of the BSFA's *Matrix* magazine, although she is also a current member of the judging panel who preside over the Arthur C. Clarke Award. A former member of the Northampton SF Writers Group, Claire is a freelance journalist, with articles, interviews and reviews having featured in magazines such as *Death Ray* and *SciFiNow*.

Body of Evidence

Justina Robson

Rachel opened the package at the breakfast table. The device was smaller than she'd thought. It looked just like a wireless ear speaker, the kind you could get free with most personal music players. A small chip in a staticfree wrapper completed the set. She put that into her phone and listened to the instructions.

"Thank you for agreeing to participate in the first public testing of Mind's Eye, the body language and energy reader..." blah blah blah it went on about legal requirements and things she had to thumbprint for – she did – and secrecy and the rest of it.

She made a second cup of coffee as she waited for it all to be over, putting her thumb on the screen at the right moments and authorising the little thing to not only read the 'truth' from the people she met that day, but also to pick up her reactions and transmit them back to the data centre where the trial was being assessed. Finally, and most satisfyingly after all that trivia, she was sent a hundred euros direct to her account in agreed payment for her participation with the promise of another thousand once she had completed her twelve hour trial run.

She put the device over her ear and ran the test and setup as she loaded the dishwasher and got ready for work. The device spoke with a woman's calm and assertive voice in a neutral tone, quietly but loud enough for her to hear clearly over mostly any ordinary noises. The battery worked. She agreed that until the trial period had passed she would not remove or switch off the device.

"In just a few moments, Mind's Eye will commence. Your normal experience and perception of your life will remain undisturbed so that you are able to continue with your day uninterrupted. Only you will know that you are now able to perceive the truth of every situation you encounter. Where matters are not as they seem Mind's Eye will speak to you and inform you of what's really going on! When you are ready to begin, enter the personal code on the outside of the box."

Of course, for the first hour there was really nothing much going on. Rachel was alone in her flat, doing boring things like tidying her bedroom, fixing her makeup and getting her lunch together, so nothing happened. It was only in the last five minutes that she thought she'd put the radio on and just check the weather before setting off. She hated carrying her umbrella, so if it wasn't going to rain, she wouldn't. Her handbag was small and compact. She hated being loaded down. Thank goodness the Mind's Eye was so tiny.

"You hate your job," said the pleasant woman in her ear.

Rachel straightened up too sharply from putting on her shoes, overbalanced and had to grab the wall for support. She wasn't entirely sure she'd heard it right. Why would it say something about her job when she was only trying to figure out if it might rain?

On the radio the weather girl was saying cheerily, "...a good chance of showers in the Sheffield area, with light winds and very overcast. And now, back to Mark with the traffic report."

"She would like to smack Mark," said the voice in Rachel's ear. "She does not like him."

Rachel turned off the radio. She pulled the device from her ear but then it beeped until, slowly, cautiously, she put it back. A glance at the clock confirmed it was time to go.

The morning continued in the same vein. On the bus, in the coffee shop, on the street, Rachel overheard snippets of conversation, and where the Mind's Eye also observed and detected an anomaly it whispered its translation into her ear with the warm confidence of a surrogate deity.

"...so, don't you want to go out with me then, or what?" Please validate me.

"It's not that. It's complicated." No.

"Don't you like me?" Please validate me. You bastard.

"Yeah. Lots." You bore me.

"...and you shouldn't speak to your mother like that!" I'm the boss here. Me. Me.

"I'm not!"	I hate you.
"What size would you like that?"	Venti.
"Grande... no, a tall I think."	
"With whip?"	Yes, and lots of it. Give me it all.
"Er... no. Just as it is."	
"Rachel! Have you got that document ready? I need it this morning."	I've forgotten about my meeting. I don't know if there is a document but if there is you must have it.
"Ehhhh... oh, sure. I'll bring it to your office."	What document?

It was at this stage that Rachel began to settle down and her heart stopped racing. What the device said was really not much different to what she had always thought people meant, in spite of what they said or did. In fact it was reassuring to have her suspicions confirmed. However, the more time went on, the more she became aware that everyone around her was a liar, and so was she. This hadn't mattered when it had all been ordinary conversation, the stuff that politely and efficiently glued the social world together, and the lies were only half-truths or fudges, so they weren't entirely dishonest. She expected as much, so it didn't disturb her to have the subtexts pointed up in clear, perfect prose, though that did spoil the effect and leave her impatient and annoyed. By lunchtime the office was an ugly place of unremitting minor whinges and she was longing for the bloody plain-spoken bitch in her ear to shut up and stop reminding her of it. Only the thought of her overdraft prevented her yanking the Mind's Eye off her head and shoving it into the bottom drawer of her desk.

As soon as she was able to she grabbed her coat and bag and headed for the park to eat her sandwich, hoping she would find a bench far enough away from people to be in relative peace. The very thought of going to her usual coffee shop even for takeout filled her with panic. Outside it was drizzling, a fine, grey English sort of drizzle that kept people indoors with the lights on and the central heating up, so to her relief there were plenty of wet spaces to sit on and hardly any passers by.

She was just biting into the first half of ham salad on rye, trying to ignore the cold, seeping feeling of the bench through her thin coat, when the Mind's Eye said,

"You hate this place."

"Shut up! You're not meant to talk to me!" Rachel snarled, spilling lettuce and mayo on herself and then getting up to brush it off, making things worse.

An old man walking a Yorkshire terrier gave her an odd look and went onto the grass to avoid walking too close to her. She glared at him and sat back down. "As if I didn't already know. Think you're so smart. I knew all that stuff. Nobody needs you to tell them."

The device was silent. Rachel tore into the sandwich, chewing and swallowing with savagery. Why the hell was it talking to her? It was supposed to listen to others, not to her. Anyway, how did it know what she was thinking? Didn't it work off speech only or something? Surely this was a violation of her rights, not to mention false advertising. She shoved the last two bites into her mouth and dug into her bag for the paperwork and her phone, thinking she'd call the Mind's Eye people and give them a piece of *her* mind. Her hands were stupidly shaking and she fumbled the phone and dropped it. Her stomach protested as she leant forwards to pick it up off the soaking gravel.

After an age of turning wrinkling pages she found the number, dialled.

A familiar voice answered, startling her with its calm, precise neutrality. "Hello. You are through to the Mind's Eye answering service. As detailed in our contractual agreements, no calls can be answered until the trial period of your test has concluded. If you would please call again at... nineteen thirty-one hours... we will be happy to speak with you then. Please hang up."

The same bloody woman! Was this some kind of torture? Or, fiendishly, some kind of psychological test that wasn't what they said it was but something completely different to lull you into a false sense of knowing so that you weren't able to do things that made the test invalid, or something? Rachel gripped the phone tightly. She wanted to call someone, but the thought of hearing that voice dissect their every word stayed her hands. She rolled up the paper notes, badly printed and cheap as they were, and rammed them into her bag. She would read them, every damn word, once she got back to the warm. Beside her, the other half of the sandwich was getting wet. She put the lid on the box. She already had indigestion. She should eat more slowly. Chew. Chew thirty times, wasn't that it?

She was aware that she was thinking fast, so fast that perhaps she could pre-empt the device from its self-satisfied commentary by thinking of everything it could say before it could get a word in. It wasn't until some time later, when she realised someone was standing near her, not moving, that she realised she was sitting rigid, staring into space, and had been for a good while. She glanced at the person who was also very still. They did nothing, as if stalled out halfway around the kitty corner that saved a loop of path, bringing them almost to her bench. It was another young woman in business clothing, her neat hair dripping with water into her collar, almost but not quite hiding the dark sluglike shape of a Mind's Eye curled around her ear.

Into the sudden silence the device said, "You are afraid."

"Genius," Rachel muttered under her breath sarcastically, although she felt a jolt of surprise. Fear was the feeling she was having, but left to herself she'd have classified it as something else, or probably not put it into words at all, just stuffed it down and ignored it and been vaguely anxious after. "Hey," she said aloud, before she could stop herself. "Hey! Hello."

The new woman turned, her eyes focusing slowly as if she had been a long way from her body and was disoriented on returning to it. She looked at Rachel, who was pointing at her ear.

"Snap," said Rachel, so glad to see anyone else who might be able to share or relieve even one second of the horrible experience.

Her new friend lit up and came over quickly in that odd springing jog that women have when they are crossing soggy ground in high-heeled boots. "You have one too! Oh, I'm sorry. I was so caught up I didn't even see you..." She stopped at the bench as if Rachel owned it and when Rachel patted it, sat down.

"Should we be talking?" said the new woman quickly, making no effort to stop. "I'm Sally. They are awful, aren't they? I thought they'd be fun, you know, but it's driving me mad." She had a big bag with her as opposed to Rachel's small one. The ragged ends of gossip magazines and dailies stuck out of it and prevented it from closing properly. She clutched this bag to her side as she spoke. "Can't even read without it harping on. Blab blab blab. Non-stop."

Rachel nodded, beginning to feel despair creeping on her. "I wish I could take it off."

"Oh me too!" Sally nodded in an exaggerated way, one that Rachel could see was a habit.

Nod, nod, nod, she thought. Nice girls always agree, always glad to see, always smiling friendly, nice nice nice. Her face could feel that smile as if she were wearing it. She wore it a lot, all day long.

"She can't stand you," said the Mind's Eye in Rachel's ear. "She wishes she'd never set eyes on you. You remind her of herself."

Rachel froze for an instant, and saw the same tiny jerk of the shoulders higher, the hunted expression on the other woman's face that meant the slug thing was talking to her. "What did it say?" she demanded.

Sally looked at her with wide, disturbed eyes. She started to smile, stopped herself, tried again, failed and stuttered, "Said you think I'm an idiot." Then she smiled apologetically. "I was starting to wonder if..."

"No, that's right," Rachel said, frowning. "I did think that. I'm sorry." She glanced down at the magazines and then back up at the other woman's face. "I think things like that all the time but I never pay attention. I mean, it's not very pleasant. And my mother said if you can't say something nice then don't say anything at all."

Sally bit her lips together into a white line but she was nodding. Her hands tightened on the bag. "I know," she said and then, "What did it say about me?"

Rachel tried not to grimace, "That you hated me on sight because I remind you of you."

Sally sniffed, nodded and looked down at the path where the first glimmerings of puddles were beginning to form. A few silent walkers passed by. Sally groped around in her huge bag and eventually found some tissues. She blew her nose. "I hate myself," she whispered. "It says that too. Does it say that to you? No?"

"No. It tells me I hate this place and my job," Rachel said, sorry to find she was comforted by the other's acute pain, and at the same time feeling sorry for her.

Sally nodded and scrubbed at her nose with the tissue, firmly and too violently. Rachel could just see Sally's mother doing that to toddler Sally's small nose; a piece of care that was a warning not to make a fuss and not to ask for any more.

"At first I thought it was just...I don't know... just today," Rachel said. She wanted to give Sally something. "But then I started to realise I do hate it here. I'm not sure that anywhere else is better though. People everywhere are pretending things, just like they do here," she touched her ear where the now silent device sat and then let her hand fall into her lap.

"And worse in places. Or they do worse, and don't lie. I don't know if that's better. I suppose it's honest. Do you know what happened this morning? I went in to work – I work with a law firm – and we were discussing this case and my colleague was talking about the details of it and all the time she was saying in my ear how much he despised the clients and thought they were stupid and they deserved to lose. And when I said something he was saying his point of view about it and she said he didn't value my opinions and even if I was right he'd rather get his own way because he didn't want me to be right. I kind of thought that before but..."

"But it never hurt like it does now?"

"Yes! Because she never stops. You can't not hear her saying those things. I got so mad, I started going through the papers that came with it, looking for ways I could sue the bastards who made it, you know? I thought there must be some wording that would give me grounds to make a formal complaint but halfway through I read..." She did another excavation of the bag, finally throwing the magazines onto the bench beside them so she could get some light into the huge expanse, and pulled out the familiar brochure, opened and folded and marked with a green highlighter pen. "This, look."

Rachel bent closer and read the tiny print.

"Mind's Eye works by reading the energy signals given off around it, from the wearer and from others nearby. It also scans and processes information from a range of well-recognised body language signals when others come within visual range of the camera.

This information is relayed by radio frequency to a local base station where the AI controller interprets the data and returns the analysis to the headset. It is possible for Mind's Eye to make mistaken interpretations based on insufficient data. Therefore the manufacturers do not recommend that any decisions are taken based on information provided by Mind's Eye and its related products, nor that its statements are taken as fact rather than possible interpretation. When in doubt, always rely on your own judgement."

"Possible interpretation," Sally said. "D'you see?"

But Rachel was looking at the last sentence. "The weird thing is," she said, sitting up and staring across the grey park, "I actually feel like it agrees with me. Only I never wanted to know what it was that I already knew."

Sally paused, her sudden moment of confidence engendered by familiar work gone. "But it says my mother doesn't like me."

Rachel shivered and put her hand over Sally's hand on top of the bag. "Why are you still wearing it?" She didn't believe Sally needed cash. Her clothes were good; even the damned bag was one of those that Rachel would only ever see in the windows of couture shops, ugly or not.

"My credit card..." Sally began, distracted, staring off into space though this time Rachel was sure the machine wasn't saying anything. She half lifted one hand towards the earpiece but hesitated and let it fall back. "I... d'you know my lunch hour is just about up and I have to go." She winced and was suddenly standing, turning, trying to stuff everything back into the bag and be off but she was hurrying so much she kept fumbling things. She turned and the last magazine slithered free and onto the bench. She was already two steps away by the time Rachel said loudly,

"No. Wait! Say what it just said!"

Sally turned half back. She was unwilling but against Rachel's sudden determination and her own misery that both drove her to stay and to go she hadn't the strength to win.

"Say it!"

"I... I want to go. I want to leave. I wish I hadn't met you. I wish I didn't have this thing on." By now she was turning this way, that way, looking for a direction but none drew her. She was fixed to the spot and increasingly desperate.

"How was that?" Rachel was almost gleeful. She felt possessed by sudden energy.

Sally cast about, "Awful," she said, nearly crying with her need to escape. She rolled her eyes and head at the same time as if the Mind's Eye had suddenly bit her. "No! You're wrong!"

Rachel thought she had gone too far. Awareness of what she was doing made her sit back down. "Yes, probably... I'm sorry. I'm sorry."

But a strange half-smile appeared on Sally's face. "It was quiet," she said after a moment. "It didn't contradict me. I feel awful."

Rachel wanted to turn things. She also had other questions she must ask before she lost the chance. "Did you try to take it off?"

Slowly Sally began to inch back towards the bench, then she loosened up and came and sat down, the bag on her lap, her bottom on the magazine. "I did, when my mother called. But it said I'd lose all my money and I thought I could at least last until the evening, it isn't so long. And then it'll be gone." As she finished there was a catch in her voice.

"It won't ever be gone," Rachel said.

Sally gave the wan smile of someone who can't laugh. "You said that at the same time it did." Her red eyes said quite clearly too that she knew Rachel didn't mean the device wouldn't be gone. She meant that their new way of seeing and hearing would not be gone. They would not be able to stop the knowledge that they had already picked up with their ordinary human bodies from one another. At least, not for a while.

A few seconds or minutes passed.

"Now I know why drinkers drink," Rachel said. Sally just nodded.

"I did hear one nice thing," Sally said. "I think the trouble is I've been around some unhappy people. Or maybe, like you say, it's the day."

"It's not the day," said Sally, Rachel and the device all at the same time. Rachel found herself looking at the other woman's face and laughing, sharing a laugh at themselves and the instant. It didn't last long but she felt suddenly much better.

"I should probably look for another job," Rachel said, oddly lightened by the thought.

"I definitely should," Sally said.

They were interrupted by the jolly sound of a pop song coming from the enormous bag. Sally picked out her phone and looked at it, then decisively thumbed it off. "My mother," she said and sighed. She got up, picked up her magazine and looked around for a trashcan. "I should be going. Really this time. Lunch is really over."

"Me too." Rachel got up, stretched her stiff back and picked up her lunchbox.

"It was nice to meet you."

"You too."

They both waited, eyebrows raised, but there was nothing to hear. Then with a smile and a wave they parted and went their different ways along the path.

In the evening at the right time the Mind's Eye finally said. "That concludes today's test. Please remove the headset and return it in the box provided. Your payment will be authorised upon receipt."

Rachel packed the device away and sat for a moment, rubbing the space it had occupied behind her ear. She almost missed it.

"But I won't forget," she said into the silence and for the first time in her life she didn't mind the silence, didn't want an answer, or a reply, or an affirmation or anything.

Justina Robson was born in Leeds and studied philosophy and linguistics at the University of York. Having concentrated on writing novels, Justina has produced frustratingly few short stories in recent years, even though she made her fiction debut with one such (*Trésor*) in a 1994 issue of *the Third Alternative*.. Between them, her six novels to date have been shortlisted for an impressive array of awards, including the Clarke, the BSFA and the Campbell. Her seventh novel, *Going Under* – third in the 'Quantum Gravity' series – is due out later this year.

The Ecologist
and the Avon Lady

Tricia Sullivan

Together with her jack knife, sword, mace, pistol, shuriken, hand grenades and blowgun, The Avon Lady had packed an assortment of beauty products for her assignment on the mountain.

"I always like to offer gifts," The Avon Lady had told her supervisor. "I find that they lubricate the process."

The Avon Lady's supervisor thought that bribing local officials with Maybelline was a little cheesy, but as it turned out The Avon Lady had been in the sheriff's office for only five minutes when the sheriff brought up the subject of instant-hardening nail lacquer. The Avon Lady brought out the CVS bag and the sheriff sat on the corner of the desk and rooted around inside.

The Avon Lady took in the bulletin board plastered with pictures of wounded anatomy, posed corpses, death in all its butchershop frankness. Eventually the sheriff selected a pearly chartreuse and started working on her left hand first, from the pinky toward the thumb. She jerked her head towards the window, where the mountain was framed together with a section of blue sky.

"No need to go up there," she told The Avon Lady. "I'll sign your time sheet and you can get out of here."

The sheriff waved her hand to dry her nails and plucked a 'Pele's Service Station' pen out of a coffee cup. She held it poised mid-air, expectantly, and The Avon Lady realized she was supposed to hand over her time sheet.

The Avon Lady said, "Is this a joke?"

"No joke. You don't want to die. We keep quiet between us."

"But I'm under contract to exterminate it. I can't just walk away."

The sheriff snorted. "Why do you think it's still here? The rest either walked away or got drilled."

"Just show me your files, please. I won't impose on you after that."

The sheriff shrugged. "Whatever rolls your thunder."

The Avon Lady already knew that there had been an attack just last week at a service station a few miles away. But she hadn't been privy to the images that the sheriff now showed her. The anatomically identical wounds on the bodies were classic. There was CC footage of a biped in a ski jacket fleeing the scene. At the edge of the frame the perp turned into a wheelbarrow.

"Wheels seem to be a theme," The Avon Lady commented.

"Dead people seem to be a theme," replied the sheriff.

It was like that.

The mountain was always green. Too green, the women of the village said, and lifted their veils to shield their eyes from the sight of it, as from a fire.

The Avon Lady found a sharpening stone in the middle of the village, chained to the well. She drew her sword and got to work. The women came out to watch her, furtively at first, and then more openly as the young women and the children joined them. They drank a tea so fragrant that The Avon Lady could smell it even in the open air, and they were careful to keep their backs to the mountain. The Avon Lady felt funny carrying the sword, but it was necessary.

"You'll need a selection of weapons," The Avon Lady's supervisor had said. Then he had shown The Avon Lady some file footage of the monster. The thing must have had seven or eight heads, maybe even nine on a bad day. Really hard to count when they're all moving at once – try counting kids at a birthday party and you'll get the idea. And that was the least of it.

The Avon Lady's supervisor told her, "This one is slippery. It can shapeshift. Sometimes it manifests as a piece of equipment, sometimes a person, and sometimes a more conventionally scary abomination. You have to be prepared for anything."

On balance, The Avon Lady thought, she'd rather deal with the wheelbarrow than the hydra. But she was a professional. She would do what was necessary.

After she'd checked into her motel, The Avon Lady hiked up from the village in search of the old ecological field station. The sheriff had recommended she go up there first.

"Bring some of them bronzing powders," she added. "The ecologist will like those."

The Avon Lady would have phoned ahead, but there were no phones up here. It was a case of just dropping by – if you could find the place guided only by surveyors' stakes the IBA had left behind.

"The markers function like buoys," The Avon Lady's supervisor had told her. "Always keep them within your sight. Once you've passed the red markers, you're in the exclusion zone."

There was a red marker just uphill of the tower. The tower was in poor condition; its foundations were subsiding. It had only a partial roof and the side facing uphill was exposed to the elements. Rubble lay under vines nearby. Crows sat on the broken wall and challenged her.

The Avon Lady stopped to catch her breath and that was when she saw the monster. It was sitting on a stump dressed in white petticoats and holding itself erect as a prairie dog. An honest-woman face was framed by a lavender bonnet. It leaned earnestly towards the ecologist, who sat on a nearby boulder. They were deep in conversation.

The Avon Lady hesitated. She did not have an appointment.

She cleared her throat and the monster barked, turned into a fish that flopped briefly in the pine needles, and then changed again into a self-directed robot vacuum cleaner straight out of some late-night infomercial. It shot off into the woods, bumping over tree roots. By the time The Avon Lady reacted, the thing had disappeared in the undergrowth.

The Avon Lady pulled up short. She was aware of the ecologist's hostile gaze. The ecologist was old and fat. The skin of her neck had slipped its moorings and conjoined with her jaw in scuttling lines that looked like tide-stranded crabs. Too much white around her irises made her look like a wiki-tiki or some other Polynesian firelight invention. She wore patched moleskin trousers and a plaid lumberjack shirt, despite the heat. Over all of this hung a flower-print kimono.

193

"Are you from the Gazette?" she snapped.

The Avon Lady stepped forward, holding out her hand. She tried to sound professional, but her skin was crawling now that she'd finally seen the thing.

"I'm the hunter," The Avon Lady said. "From the UBI."

The ecologist looked as if she'd found a rat turd in her bran flakes. She did not stand up, and she did not shake hands. After a while The Avon Lady's own hand wilted back to her side.

"Surprised to see you talking to it," The Avon Lady added. "Do you mind me asking what you were doing?"

Now the ecologist stood up. She had a thick local accent, but she sounded educated.

"If you think I'm going to help you, you're out of your mind. I'll tell you the same as I've told all the other hunters. I won't help you kill it."

"But...but...my supervisor referred me –" The Avon Lady was no talker. She'd been hired for her fighting ability.

"Your supervisor is a fool. I keep telling the people from the OBN, my job is to *save* life."

"Actually," and The Avon Lady laughed, "that's *my* job."

The ecologist didn't like that. She had a beady eye, and she buttoned The Avon Lady down with it.

"I think you'd better go now."

The Avon Lady sniffed. "Okay, but I've got a job to do, so stay out of my way." She started down the hill, turned, and added, "Wouldn't want you to get hurt by mistake."

The ecologist just shook her head and watched The Avon Lady go.

The Avon Lady was annoyed, and as she skidded down the steep incline she started to call her supervisor to complain, but then remembered there was no signal up here. When she glanced up from her cell phone, she'd lost her bearings on the markers. None in sight. The Avon Lady halted.

The crows had stilled. Chipmunks made small noises in the dead leaves. A striped woodpecker hopped up the side of a nearby fir, cocking its head speculatively before setting to work. There was a faint smell of smoke.

The Avon Lady began to be creeped out.

Where was the goddamn marker?

She started to go back uphill. She'd lost sight of the tower already. Maybe there was more of a ridge here than she'd realized. Maybe she was walking down the wrong side. GPS didn't work out here. Compasses didn't work out here. That was why the markers were so important.

She was panting a little. Sweating more than necessary. Where…? Ah. Tip of the tower. *There.*

But not where it should be.

The Avon Lady's supervisor *had* warned her about this phenomenon. *Slippage*, it was called. Disconcerting. Made you feel helpless, subjective. Not a way you wanted to feel when you were supposed to be the hunter.

Real grumpy now, The Avon Lady climbed back to the tower. She could hear a clanging sound; made her think of blacksmiths.

Just outside the gate the ecologist was splitting wood with a hammer and steel wedges. Her kimono flared out in a little wind every time the hammer descended. She ignored The Avon Lady.

"Hey, I know we didn't get off to a great start," The Avon Lady said loudly. "But I'm lost. I'm having trouble finding my way back to the marker series. Can you help me out?"

The ecologist set her wedge and hoisted the hammer. Clang…Clang…*Crack*. The wood split. She said:

"Do you think I'm happy about the killing? I'm not. But two wrongs don't make a right."

By now The Avon Lady had had time to think up a retort.

"Okay, I know you're all into the ecology and stuff," she said. "You're like one of those people campaigning to save the great white shark or whatever. But that only works as long as the shark isn't coming up on the beach to eat people."

The ecologist dropped the hammer and straightened. She placed a hand in the curve of her back and took a couple of laboured breaths. Made a show of licking her finger and holding it to the wind, squinting at the sky.

"I think you'll find the marker to the left of that stand of birch," she said at last. "I'm guessing…" and she extracted a tiny, well-thumbed leather book from her breast pocket, flipping through it…"maybe 100 meters downstream from the fish pool."

The Avon Lady looked.

"Uh…on the way up here the last marker was on the other side of the tower."

"That was then," said the ecologist. "This is now."

She put the book away and folded her arms below her breasts. Waiting for The Avon Lady to go. The Avon Lady suddenly remembered her policy.

"Can I offer you some exfoliating cream? Natural sponges?"

She proffered the CVS bag. The ecologist seemed surprised. At length she chose a mascara wand.

"Don't think this means I'll be helping you," the ecologist warned, darkly.

When the Avon Lady got back to the village, her rental car was gone. Online, Avis had no record that she'd ever rented it. Neither did Amex. Moreover, Pele's Service Station was gone, together with all the other cars in the village.

The monster had to be nearby. Reality slippage always accompanied the thing. Luckily, the phone worked. The Avon Lady bitched heavily about the ecologist.

Her supervisor told her to, *"Get over it. She's all we've got."*

"But she's so weird."

"Grow up. Work with her."

In her motel room, The Avon Lady drank a beer and cleaned her gun.

The next day she went up the mountain, following the markers to the borders of the exclusion zone. She didn't dare stray beyond the red, and really she shouldn't have to. The monster frequently crossed over. That was how it killed.

Still, she didn't find the thing. Instead, she ran into the ecologist.

The ecologist's hair was red.

"Is that henna?" said The Avon Lady. The ecologist laughed. She was carrying a big book—a *tome*, really—and when The Avon Lady asked what it was for, the ecologist said it was for pressing leaves.

She said it in a way that made The Avon Lady think of a Mafioso explaining to his little girl what that cinderblock in the trunk of his

Buick was all about. *I use that to rest my foot on when I'm getting my shoes shined, honey.*

The Avon Lady said, "Guess you need some hobbies up here, all by yourself. Don't you get lonely?"

The ecologist's knuckles whitened on the book.

"I read," she said, glancing at it. "And I work."

"Yeah, hard work, that ecology stuff," The Avon Lady muttered. She wondered if the ecologist was an alcoholic or something. She looked so unkempt.

"Since you insist on talking about ecology," said the ecologist coolly, "you might want to consider that the environment and the organism are products of one another. This is nowhere more true than here. Stay here long enough and you'll see."

"Sorry," said The Avon Lady. "I can't stick around. I'm hunting."

"You won't find your monster today," said the ecologist. 'I scared it away.'

'What the fuck are you, Greenpeace?'

The ecologist seemed to think this was funny.

Days passed, but The Avon Lady could not find the monster. When she went looking for the sheriff, she found that the village had slipped again. There was a school where the police station had been. Kids were playing hacky-sack in the dusty yard. A boy, about eleven maybe, came over to the fence and smiled at her. Beautifully. The Avon Lady smiled back, until the kid said,

"You will get killed just like the others."

"How many others have there been?" The Avon Lady tried to sound casual. More kids drifted over.

"Many-many. She bury them under tower."

The Avon Lady snorted. "Come on. Get real."

"It's true. She a witch, right Ivan?"

Behind the first boy, Ivan nodded, black eyes and black curls.

"She powerful woman. She cure my aunt's blindness."

"She bury the bodies. My cousin's friend buried there. He get killed too, and she bury him."

The Avon Lady walked away. She called her supervisor in a panic.

"*What* are *you, stupid?*" he growled down the line at her. "*The whole point about the monster is that it damages reality. Nothing you see up there is reliable. And talking to local kids...*"

"But the ecologist..."

"*Mo Mazlum is our agent in the ecology station, and I'm telling you, he isn't a witch.*'

"A man? But you said 'work with *her.*' I'm sure that's what you said. *Her.*"

"*Slippage, Avon Lady, slippage. Don't talk to locals, and don't believe your eyes. Do what you're paid to do and you can get out. The longer you stay, the weirder it's going to get. You know that, right?*"

"Oh yeah. Slippage... um..."

"*Listen to me. You're an agent with the RBI. You down with that?*"

Her supervisor's voice jarred her back into her bones and skin. Reality. Briefings at Formica tables. The firing range at dawn.

"Yeah," she answered. "Yeah, I'm down."

He used a kindergarten tone with her. "*You want me to recall you and send somebody else?*"

Yes. "No."

"*Remember what I told you about slippage?*"

"Yeah. No. Yeah, I mean..." Slippage was why she was here. To try to prevent it. Along with gruesome deaths. Important to remember to remember. To remember that.

But remembering certain things was like trying to move your tongue on lydocaine. Theoretical. Detached.

"*Don't waste time. Whenever the monster's around, the slippage is always worse. If it spreads, the death count will rise. We can't afford that. Hurry the...*"

The signal cut off.

"...fuck up," finished the Avon Lady, scowling. She was walking through the village, and the urge to throw the phone down the well was so strong that she had to stop and clench her teeth for a moment. The central sharpening stone, chained to the well: it was medieval. What was with this place?

Deep breaths.

The Avon Lady caught the old women watching her from beneath awnings and behind teacups. They had been cooking over open fires. No electricity.

Don't talk to the locals.

The Avon Lady cleared her throat. "How long has the grey-haired woman lived up at the tower?"

Glances among themselves. Then one old woman lifted her chin and in a thick local accent replied: "The man in tower get sick. Very sick. Nikki go up there, take care of him. She never leave."

"Are you talking about Mo Mazlum? It attacked him, too? Did he die?"

The old woman frowned. She seemed puzzled by the question. One of the others spoke up.

"Things go missing on the mountain. Other things come. But you vulgar when talking about. Go home."

"So Nikki is not the ecologist. Or...is she?"

The women covered their eyes with their veils.

The next morning, the ecologist was not in the tower. The Avon Lady called; the crows took flight. The Avon Lady knocked on the window.

Inside: books. Floor to ceiling, shelves stuffed with books. A ladder that glided along the shelves as in an old library.

Books, and the occasional crow feather.

A twig cracked and The Avon Lady jumped. She whirled, lifting the rifle defensively. A squirrel leaped for the nearest tree and scrambled up, scolding. The Avon Lady relaxed fractionally.

Then the ground dissolved beneath her and she was falling. Trees receding, tower shrinking yet also rising higher above her as though lifted into sky. Pine needles sliding beneath as she rolled downhill. She scrambled for purchase, got on to her belly and still felt herself sliding down a near-vertical face.

The hill here should be tilted the other way. The angle of the trees coming out of the ground said so. But she was going down.

No time to deal with that because a mass of rags was coming toward her, multicoloured, whirling – a mass the size of a small car but made of pure turbulence. She unloaded three rounds into it and then it was a songbird, flitting from place to place. Elusive.

The sliding sensation ebbed. The Avon Lady got to her feet, swaying because everything was still moving around her. She could see the red exclusion zone marker out of her right eye.

This is it.

She hadn't packed a suitable weapon. Who expected to be attacked by a sparrow? But she had a knife in her boot. She had been the best in her class at knife-throwing. She could pin it against that tree –

The bird flew at her. The Avon Lady raised the gun diagonally to ward it off, but the bird had turned into a fucking harpoon. The Avon Lady reacted by limbo-ing down and backwards, and the harpoon embedded itself in a tree behind her while she offered herself mental congratulations on her athleticism. But the harpoon was already melting into the form of a snake.

Rifle. Bang. Bang.

Two bullets into the snake. Bursts of prickling fire in The Avon Lady's blood, noradrenalin happy hour as she charged after the retreating animal, firing but missing now, and it dived down a hole between some boulders.

The Avon Lady circled the boulders, teeth bared, snarling.

"Fucking kill you," she muttered. But the snake did not reappear.

In the leaves nearby, she found blood and metal washers.

Back at the hotel, the night manager seemed to have changed ethnicity and height. There was no cable tv.

In the morning The Avon Lady woke up and went out to get a Pepsi and when she came back from the vending machine the hotel had turned into a tent.

The school was gone. The old women were gone. An old man played solitaire at a card table.

Fuck.

Laden with weapons and emergency rations, The Avon Lady took her MBA kit bag set off up the mountain.

She followed the stakes until she came to the red-ribboned exclusion zone.

Hesitated.

"What the hell," she breathed, and stepped across.

Somebody had drawn in crayon on the inside of The Avon Lady's corneas. A waxy orange box formed in her left eye. Within: tundra hanging overhead. Underfoot, roiling cloud and the sun a weak, fried-egg puddle. The monster was an elk made of knives and it walked toward her on tiptoe, upside down.

The Avon Lady remembered that she had always lived in this knife world and must fight with a blanket and an acid sprayer, which she had neglected to pack.

She could still see and hear and smell the forest.

In her right eye, a new box. All in black and white, a maze of metal ladders zebra-painted, extending in every possible direction. They frequently intersected one another in confusing ways. The monster was camouflaged to disappear among the ladders, but The Avon Lady could make out its shape, and by implication she knew that its body was a machine. It could crush you between the angles of its lattices when it folded.

Juice-stains of former victims made the whole place sticky.

Before The Avon Lady could remember or think anything more, the crayon-drawn boxes began to multiply. The visions and their concomitant mnemonic onionskins peeled away from one another like the accordion folds of a fan. Decadently, they splayed themselves before her.

At first these quasi-worlds were well-organized. They were aware of each other but each was captured within its own frame: the cast in the opening credits of the Brady Bunch. Only they weren't smiling.

Closer and closer. The Avon Lady could see each of the different versions of the monster. A snivelling old man with a fistful of wilted flowers and a machete. A batmobile. A blowtorch assembly with legs. A two-dimensional tiger with channel 13 fundraising extravaganza stripes. A red haze.

Multiple targets, thought The Avon Lady, and fingered the throwing star in her pocket. *Multiple weapons. Don't let it spook you.*

Closer still, until the neatly differentiated versions of reality began to surround her, and their frames tangled. The Avon Lady swung her sword but the multiplicities took pieces of her with them and her sword was broken into bite-sized chunks all going in different directions.

And there was nothing she could do about it.

Vertigo was just some weak green tea. This was some stronger shit, and The Avon Lady realized it too late. Her CNS wasn't built for this. Motor neurons weren't answering the phone. She could feel her toes but there was fuckall she could do.

The monster was all around her now, oozing in for the kill. Something cold touched her forehead and she wondered if this was what the other victims had felt before the monster drilled into their skulls.

A warm hand closed on her wrist, tugged. The Avon Lady felt the moist heat of the ecologist's breath. She stumbled backwards into the steadying presence of another human body, her face brushing the ecologist's close-cropped gray hair. The ecologist smelled like a cat.

"Let's get you out of here, little one," said the ecologist, and placed her forearm across The Avon Lady's collarbone. She pulled The Avon Lady backwards as if performing a water rescue. Back-pedalling, nearly at a run, over the pine needles and lumpy roots, went The Avon Lady and the ecologist, The Avon Lady stiff with fear or, at least, consternation.

The monster had dissolved as though never there at all.

Back at the tower, the ecologist took several books off a shelf and dragged out a battered tobacco tin. There was cocoa inside. While the milk heated, the ecologist said, "You must stay here. I can watch over you."

The Avon Lady started to demur but the ecologist cut her short.

"You've wounded it," she said. "It may lie low for a while, but you won't find your way back to the village. The mountain is in shards."

The Avon Lady was too exhausted and freaked to argue.

Half the tower was now crumbled to dust but the other half was immaculate except where some owl had left the remains of its prey dangling from a wall sconce.

"Why did you save me?"

Shrug. "I told you. I save lives."

"They said you are a witch. They call you Nikki."

"I don't call myself that anymore. Call me Jack."

"Jack. Jack the witch?"

An expression of bored tolerance hung on the ecologist's old face.

"I'm a healer. I've healed the monster. So many times, I lose track how many."

The Avon Lady stared. "But that's crazy. Can't you see the harm you're doing? What happened to Mo, anyway?"

Jack's glance flickered at the mention of Mo's name. But she didn't answer the question.

"I save life. I saved your life. Now, drink your cocoa."

Inside the tower were the remains of an enormous library. Books from floor to ceiling; books stacked on tables; books open underfoot. Everywhere books.

"What's all this?" the Avon Lady asked.

"Food," said Jack

"What?" said The Avon Lady.

"You should try it," said Jack. "Those corn flakes can't last forever."

The Avon Lady was suspicious of the books. They seemed to crowd round her. And the ecologist was right. The Avon Lady couldn't leave. The forest outside the tower had turned into a stir-fry of jousting realities. Presumably the monster was prowling the mountainside in some disjointed form.

And there was another thing. Maybe it was the fact that the ecologist had saved her life. Or maybe the ecologist really was a witch. Or maybe it was just the bond of being alone together, day and night, while the world outside shifted like a puzzle. Whatever the reason, The Avon Lady found that there was something about the ecologist.

An unglamourous strength. A solidity. And a warmth.

She felt safe.

But slippages were all around them. Carpets became sunrises and fingernail clippings became seagulls. Dust became moths that ate the carpets and when all the sunrises were gone, The Avon Lady and Jack sailed for a year on night's ocean. Bats flew around the ship's rigging and the salt opened the cracks in The Avon Lady's lips and the heavy brocade curtains of their room were always damp with mist. The tower glided in and out of fogs and the books pitched, wearily, in their mahogany shelves.

Every so often, The Avon Lady would make noises about going to finish off the monster. Getting up the courage. Et cetera.

"No," said Jack. "It's sick. It's in hiding. You won't find it, you'll just get lost and die."

"I won't," said The Avon Lady weakly, but she lacked the will to set out all over again. Not into that scrambled-eggs world the monster had left in its wake.

And so in time, she came to consume books, as well.

This wasn't very satisfying. If you took a book that you really liked, you ended up forgetting the book as soon as you'd digested it. So it was as if you had never read it. And if you restricted yourself to books you didn't like, then you had nothing more than the satisfaction of knowing that the books you hadn't read still existed.

The Avon Lady thought it was worst of all when she inadvertently gobbled up a book that turned out to be incredible, mind-blowing, world-altering. Because, of course, it was no sooner consumed than it had disappeared totally from her memory.

The entropy of this was hard to take. Every time she stole into the periodicals section for a snack, The Avon Lady would look up and down the shelves and wonder how long the two of them could last this way.

"We can't remember the books because we have left ourselves inside," Jack said, once.

One day, she jolted from a dream of blueberry muffins to hear Jack talking to someone. In the bathroom.

"I know you're hungry. And I know she made a mess. But you can't have her."

A pause; then:

"She is not the same as the other one. Don't threaten me."

Beat. Whispering sound. Jack said:

"Everything will be okay. It will be different this time. Trust me."

The Avon Lady heard the toilet flush and she scurried to the other side of the library where her tea had gone cold. While she wondered what was going on, rain rattled on the windows but did not fall through the open part of the roof. The Avon Lady pressed her mouth to the gold foil rim of her tea cup, without drinking.

Later, she lay with her fears soft in the stretching night. All around her, beyond the blur of candles, beyond the sound of Jack breathing. Fear of the monster. Fear of what she had to do to the monster. And whether she could do it.

Because The Avon Lady and Jack were coming to an understanding.

No: something more and something less than an understanding.

Something that lived in small gestures and the way they inhabited one another's glances. Something that, in the naming of it, would have been crushed because it was too young and fragile to survive the process of identification.

And the something was growing stronger all the time.

The something scared The Avon Lady.

"People eat meat from cows they have slaughtered," The Avon Lady said to Jack. "They buy it in packages wrapped in plastic. And at the same time they keep cats and clean up their shit until they die, and then they bury them in pet cemeteries. And that seems to be okay."

Jack didn't respond. She was reading something.

"And they keep rabbits. And they even keep rabbits and cats together – my grandfather did. Did you know rabbits and cats can get along?"

"What are you saying?" muttered Jack, glancing up from the pages of a Dr. Seuss biography.

The Avon Lady found that she couldn't answer.

One day, abruptly, the tower struck land and a hazy light coughed a few times before settling in the skylights and windows.

"What's happening?" asked The Avon Lady, even though it was obvious that the long night was over.

Jack went into the kitchen and began peeling a heap of potatoes that had not been there before.

"Has the monster died?" The Avon Lady asked, elated.

Jack shook her head.

"I told you I would heal it."

"Heal it? How?"

"All those books we read."

"I thought you said those were food."

"Not for us. For it. But it can feed itself now."

"You tricked me."

"You tried to kill it. Now you have repaired some of the damage."

The Avon Lady seethed. "You're so stupid, Jack. Don't you understand that the monster is ruining the continuity of the world? It kills people. It fucks with reality. It's got to be eliminated. I'm sorry, but it's got to be done and I've got to do it."

Jack's blunt features showed no sign of compromise.

"I was put on this earth to heal," she said. "It's all I know how to do. Don't ask me to do different."

"God damn it, Jack. You'll be sorry for this one."

Jack dropped the potato and the knife and turned to face The Avon Lady. She was bigger than The Avon Lady and her wiki-tiki eyes went even wider than usual.

"Now I'm going to tell you what to do. You go down that mountain, you get in your rentacar and you *go*. Get out of here. You were lucky last time. Believe me, you don't want to end up like Mo."

"Aha. What happened to Mo?"

Jack broke eye contact. She waved the thought of him aside with a chunky hand. "He couldn't understand. All he knew about was killing. You're smarter than him. So I'm telling you, go. Now. I've made you an opportunity. Take it."

Jack strode to the door with heavy man-steps. She flung it open.

And the Avon Lady saw that they were back on the mountain.

She stumbled out into the wood. Now the red-ribboned marker was planted just outside the tower gate. There was just enough room for The Avon Lady to slip past.

She switched on her cellphone and got a signal. There was a message waiting for her from her supervisor.

"What the fuck are you doing up there? We got a quadruple hit in your area."

The Avon Lady listened as he explained. The most recent victims had been tourists, a family of four who had wandered into the forest in search of mushrooms.

Jack came out blinking into the sun.

"Don't do it," she said. "Go home."

But The Avon Lady shrugged aggressively past her into the tower, already jerking the bathrobe off her shoulders.

She gathered her weapons and managed to get to the scene before the locals had taken the bodies away. The father had died a little distance away, but the mother and children had fallen almost on top of one another. All of them had been killed by characteristic monster head wounds, like drill-marks from above: trepanation gone wrong.

They looked fine, otherwise. Healthy children. Ice cream stains on the boy's t-shirt. The girl had a Dora the Explorer belt. The Avon Lady kept expecting them to move, to speak. But they didn't.

The sheriff walked around taking photographs. Her nails were painted with the instant-hardening varnish that The Avon Lady had brought. The Avon Lady put her hand over her own eyes. She did this as if she could make the whole thing not happen. No wonder the locals veiled not their faces, but their eyes.

When The Avon Lady got back to the tower, Jack was reading. She didn't look up.

In a ghost voice The Avon Lady said, "I've just seen two dead children."

Jack nodded.

The Avon Lady was filling from the toes upward with vitriol and a peculiar, hollow echoing noise. She heard herself sniff, a small, derisive sound. Inadequate.

"Are you going to say anything? Do you seriously think it's okay to let this thing run free when it's killing innocent people?"

Jack kept reading. The Avon Lady could see her eyes flickering across the lines of text. The *Bhagavad-Gita*.

"Hey! Answer me!"

Jack closed the book and closed her eyes. She was shaking. Her nose was turning red.

"Don't make me cry," she said. "It won't do any good. Some things just are the way they are. The mountain is what it is. I can't help that."

"But all this time, I could have been hunting. You distracted me."

"Distracted you? From what? Getting yourself killed?"

Bitterly, the Avon Lady sighed. "Look, I appreciate how you saved me that time, but I've got a job to do here."

"I told you from the beginning. I'll fight you every step of the way."

"Are you the monster?" The Avon Lady blurted.

"I don't know what the monster is," said Jack.

"That's not a real answer."

"It's the only answer I have."

"Well, I'm going to kill it. Whatever it is. I don't know what game you're playing, but you didn't see those kids. Just lying there."

"Please. Don't." And Jack looked at The Avon Lady out of wrinkly eyes in a doughy face. Ungroomed eyebrows and a big mole on her cheek. "I love you."

"I love you, too. That's why I'm going to take you out of here. After."

"You must know that isn't possible."

With a meaty hand, Jack turned the page of the book she was reading. The page trembled audibly.

"Don't you dare disappear in that book. How do I get through to you?"

"I'm a healer. I don't kill."

"You think being a healer makes you the good guy? It doesn't. I'm not the bad guy here. You are. I'm doing the good thing. You're the bad guy, Jack. But it's not too late to change your mind."

"I tried to save you from it, and I'll try to save it from you."

The Avon Lady said, "I could understand your attitude a lot better if there was a reason for what it did. If it was killing for food. If there were steps people could take to avoid being attacked. But it's nonsense, the whole thing. I've seen a lot of different kinds of monster. And the monster you're protecting just kills people and fucks with reality to cover its tracks."

Jack shook her head. "You don't understand this place. I lived here all my life. You say, *fucks with reality*. But to me this *is* reality. The world changes. They say it's different in books, but I wouldn't know."

"Yeah,' said The Avon Lady. "That's the whole point. What good is a book if you forget the words as you go along?"

"They're good for healing," said Jack. "Words are a gentle substitute for real paradox. But I forgot. You only care about killing."

"You got that right," The Avon Lady grunted, and began loading her weapons.

Only a few steps into the exclusion zone, The Avon Lady found the monster waiting for her. It was hanging from the tree branches as if it had been blown there: a homely-looking patchwork quilt sewn all in warm tones. Amber and russet and gold. Just lovely.

"Get the fuck out of that tree," The Avon Lady shouted, unslinging her crossbow. She let off two bolts in quick succession, and the quilt shuddered. It dropped to the ground.

That was too easy.

Adrenalised, snappish, The Avon Lady stalked forward. Scared to shit.

There were voices in her ears, plastic-sounding: TV from the next room. Splotches of colour disrupted her peripheral vision, like light-spoilage on film. With a rushing sound, the quilt came towards her. A big, dirty mouth, opening.

The Avon Lady ducked and spun; not quick enough, though. She caught the grey smell of death, and numbers flashed before her eyes like a stock market report. She was beneath the billowing underside of the monster. She drew her sword to fend it off. Fractions marched towards her in formation.

They would cut her apart.

They would drill her skull.

The Avon Lady looked into the erasure of herself and swung the sword –

The monster swept away like a matador's cape and fell. Jack stood there, holding one corner.

"Stand back," said The Avon Lady. "Me or it. One of us has to go."

"Not if I can stop you."

Kimono flapping, Jack planted her bare feet in last year's leaves and spread her arms. She'd dropped the patchwork quilt; it lay quiescent on the ground, quite devoid of visual effects.

"Get out of the way," said The Avon Lady. The inside of her mouth tasted like mustard on a baseball game pretzel.

"I can't do that. Now go, and save yourself."

The Avon Lady threw the javelin. Jack tried to deflect it, but she was too slow. The javelin lodged in the middle of the quilt and stuck there, quivering. The Avon Lady tasted chocolate.

The quilt thrashed a little. *Playing the pity card,* The Avon Lady thought. She was scared. She remembered what the thing could do, if it wanted. Inside her left ear came a blast of pop music. Justin Timberlake. Or maybe Timbaland. Or both. She shook her head like a waterlogged swimmer.

"You're hurting it," said Jack. "Don't do that. We must save it."

She bent and pulled the little book out of her breast pocket.

The Avon Lady took a few paces forward. She mustn't hesitate. She drew the broadsword, respectfully aware of its weight and edge. Stepped around Jack. Quilt still lying there playing wholesome Quaker meeting. The Avon Lady hacked at it. She stood on the edge of the quilt and chopped downwards with the extravagant blade. There was a high-pitched shredding sound. A Swiss Army knife would have had more effect, but The Avon Lady liked the big sword. Big swords said battle, not murder.

The tastes on The Avon Lady's tongue began to mutate and tug at her memories like a billhook pulling down vines. Formaldehyde and bakery cookies and oregano and semen and aluminium. The crash of music colliding with music within infinitesimally small slips of time. Would not be confined to ears nor even head. And the grammar of her own thoughts, unchecked, breaking. Not that would monster ever Pele's service station pitch the into or bitumen reading that excavation which monster of renewing ecologist monster in and and and and monster.

Jack grabbed the edge of The Avon Lady's sword, severing her own fingers. The Avon Lady hesitated, afraid to pull the sword back, afraid to thrust it in. Something brown flashed in front of her eyes, and then she found herself on her knees. On the quilt or shreds thereof. The quilt was disappearing into the hole at the top of Jack's head. Or appearing from it. Emergent, merging, uncertainty a matter of mere direction and impossible to know that now.

The Avon Lady's head a profusion of unnameables. And the quilt stuffed itself into Jack or vice versa, as above.

Jack had blood in her eyes, but she spoke quite clearly. "I'm buying you time. There will be a road. Get out of here. And whatever you do, don't kill it."

The Avon Lady jerked her sword from the monster's body. Jack was thrashing, ecstatically or otherwise. The Avon Lady stepped back. Sequence fucked and timing still, but earmusic dissipating now and only new leather smell her throat in. She stepped again back. Aware of a rushing darkness around her – no, not darkness but some other absence. A sucking void.

Jack lay open-eyed, inert, and the patchwork quilt was made of book covers now, everything from *Thomas the Tank Engine* to the *Bhagavad-Gita*.

Jack was dead.

The quilt stirred, weakly. Then it picked itself up, tore into a murder of crows, and flew severally away.

There followed a period of more than usual confusion in The Avon Lady's mind. Then she bared her teeth and ran after it.

"How...dare you," she panted. *"Kill...you for...sure...this time."*

But the pieces of the monster went in several directions. Before The Avon Lady's eyes, the forest divided like a Magritte painting and off went the monster, everywhere at once and nowhere, while The Avon Lady stumbled through a slideshow of tree trunks. Vertical lines, converging, and she whirled in a circle.

Sword.

"Show yourself, you fucker."

No movement. The Avon Lady scanned. She'd find the thing. As long as it took, she'd find the creature. Avenge all the deaths.

She heard a cracking noise and whirled. An old iron cannon squatted within ferns. Its round hole pointing at her, blind. She smelled smoke...

...dove to her left as the cannonball hurtled toward her. Time so slow that she could see the ball spinning in the air.

She lost hold of the sword. Rolled in the leaves, scrambled up, reached for a throwing knife. Whatever that was going to do against a cannon...

But the cannon was a young deer, fleeing. The Avon Lady stumbled after it, thinking of nothing but placing her feet among the twisted roots and hidden clefts that lay beneath the leaves. Thinking of nothing but breathing.

She tracked the fugitive downhill and it kept changing shape. An arrow. A swarm of bees that turned and attacked her until she sprayed them with mace. A monkey. Then – wearily, maybe – the monster became a dry maple leaf and disappeared among many others.

The Avon Lady halted. She kicked at the leaves. She stamped them. She got out her gun, but there was nothing to shoot.

She couldn't accept what was happening. Jack was dead. Like some unlucky lion-tamer. She had taken care of this evil thing, and it had killed her.

"Rip my heart out," The Avon Lady snarled. *"I'll get you back for taking her. I'll get you."*

The Avon Lady must have come halfway down the mountain. She was near the edge of the wood. There was light here.

Something white gleamed through the trees, overhead, just beyond the forest's edge.

The Avon Lady gripped her gun and stalked forward.

Light bleached everything beyond the trees. And at the forest's edge, in silhouette, waited the monster. It looked like a bear, up on its hind legs. Or possibly a gunnery sergeant.

Or a bread machine.

The Avon Lady gripped her pistol in both hands. The monster didn't move. It was in her sights.

This was the time. If she was going to shoot it, she had to shoot it *now*.

The Avon Lady hesitated.

Jack had died to protect this thing. Jack's memory clamoured for audience.

Whatever you do, don't kill it.

The monster was a blackberry bush. A lamp post. A sponge.

The Avon Lady squeezed the trigger.

Too late.

The bullet ricocheted off a rock and thudded into the leaves.

The monster sat nearby, a toy submarine, unmoving.

There was time for another shot. But The Avon Lady had spotted something.

The white thing that she'd seen moving overhead was a tall, revolving sign that read, 'Pele's.'

The sign came with Pele's service station and the service station came with a road.

The toy submarine turned into Jack, who was no longer Jack, but who nevertheless repeated:

"There will be a road. Take it."

The Avon Lady held the gun with both hands. She was trembling.

"Cheap trick, monster," she said, and again she pulled the trigger.

Before the bullet could hit home, Jack's form broke up into a swarm of bees. They came after The Avon Lady, zeroing in on her head. She ran.

She ran past Pele's service station and on to the road. Nearby, kids were playing soccer in the school yard. They shouted at her and pointed as she passed, but she didn't look back. She ran and soon she came to the tower; now it stood right beside the road, and it seemed to have been repaired. There were no crows.

The Avon Lady's phone rang. Her damned supervisor. She pelted towards the tower. The phone wriggled in her pocket until eventually the call went to voicemail.

The tower looked almost spiffy. It was modern now. She must have made a mistake; this couldn't be the same place. But the sign read, *Ecological Field Station.*

The Avon Lady barged in and slammed the door behind her. She could hear the bees outside for a few moments. Then silence. She looked around.

The shelves and the curtains were gone. There was only one book left, and it lay on the tile floor.

The Avon Lady picked it up. Brown, plain, its cover a woven fabric that felt rough to the touch. It fell open. The Avon Lady read.

"I am the ecologist."

"Jack?"

"No. I am the ecologist. Jack was a local woman who helped me when Mo wounded me, almost to the death. She saved me. She saved the mountain. But now she is dead, too."

"You are the monster."

"I am the ecologist."

"Are you going to finish me now?" said The Avon Lady.

"I could ask the same of you."

"I can't even see you."

"I am only a book," said the ecologist.

"Ah, but what's inside you?"

And there was the sheriff, with gleaming opalescent nails.

The schoolboys.

The motel clerk.

The rental car.

Her cell phone.

Steam rising from tea.

Crows.

And The Avon Lady still held the book in her hands, because those things were only words.

The ecologist said: "I live on the seam. Like bacteria live on volcanic vents. This is the place where the world ends, and I process its energies.

"Death surrounds you on all sides," said the ecologist. "It can come galloping for you any time it wants. The end of the world is much bigger than death. You are lucky I am here to keep it back."

"You drill into people's heads," The Avon Lady protested.

"I am only hungry for their paradox," the ecologist said.

"But you're killing people."

"If they were to carry the end of the world away with them, they would cause the world to unravel. So which is worse? I groom the edges of things. I make them curve nicely. I keep the balance."

"You were hurt. Jack said so. There was a long night."

"You had many weapons. I was injured and I could not feed. The world was imperilled. Then Jack gave me books. I felt better, and I resumed my normal appetite."

"Appetite. A family of four. You opened their heads."

"People should not come here. The locals don't ask questions. They take what you call slippage for granted. It is normal to them. But outsiders, like you. Nothing but trouble."

The ground shook as if a subway train had passed beneath, and steam rose. Doors opened and shut in the forest, outside.

"What's going on?" said The Avon Lady, alarmed.

"I am always hungry. It is always the end of the world. I have much work to do."

"So do I," said The Avon Lady. "How about a final showdown, you and me?"

"You cannot win. If you destroy me, the world will be fatally untangled."

The Avon Lady stared at the pages of the book for a long time. She perceived the truth in this.

"I don't know what to do," she said.

"I have a proposition," the ecologist said.

"Oh?"

"I need protection."

"From people like me?" asked the Avon Lady.

"Exactly. You are a dangerous fighter," the ecologist said.

"This was your plan all along."

"Close the book if you don't like it," said the ecologist.

The Avon Lady closed the book inside the book. But outside the book, or maybe inside it, hard to say really, she was still reading. This trap repeated itself forever.

"Now you can't leave," said the ecologist. "Because if you do, you will take the end of the world with you. Everywhere you go."

So The Avon Lady stayed, and more paradox crowded into her head, and she left. And the world fell apart before and around and within and between her. And she stayed. And left and stayed.

And after a while of that, she could not tell the difference.

Alone in the tower, she polished her weapons, in case someone like herself should come, and want to fight. She kept them ready. Because that was what The Avon Lady was all about. Fighting.

The doorbell rang.

The Avon Lady put the book down and opened the door.

A guy was standing there. He was carrying a fishing rod and bag, and a map. He grinned at her.

"I'm Sven from the EBU," he said. "Are you the ecologist?"

"No," The Avon Lady whispered. "What do you want?"

"I'm pursuing a rogue agent. I have to bring her in, and finish the job she was sent to do."

The Avon Lady opened the door.

"Come in," she said.

He left the fishing rod outside, but when he dropped his tackle bag The Avon Lady heard the clatter and thud of diverse weaponry hitting the floor.

"Uh, the rogue agent would be me," said The Avon Lady.

Sven insisted on looking stoical. He took handcuffs off his belt.

"Then you better put these on."

"I would, but I can't. I'm trapped in the book."

"What book? That book?" Sven swaggered over to it, his footfalls heavy in the empty tower.

"If you save me I will let you go," the ecologist said. "Paradox and all. I promise."

Sven opened the book and ripped it in half.

Transistor radios rained from above and all yellow drained from sight.

"Cut that out," said the Avon Lady. "You don't know what you're doing."

"I got my orders," said Sven.

"Boy, you're stupid," the Avon Lady said. "Was I ever like that?"

"Somewhat," the ecologist gasped. "Save me!"

Sven got The Avon Lady's forearm in his grip. She didn't even try to pull away. His arm was almost as thick as her leg.

"How about you come quietly," he said.

"I can't! This is going to cause trouble, Sven. Tell the OBO I quit."

Sven started to drag her across the floor. She slid. It was like being a water skier. Nothing she could do. He pushed her to the wall, which had turned into a stack of race car tires.

"Just stay there. This is between me and the monster."

He grabbed the book again and tore off the covers.

"No!" cried The Avon Lady. To the ecologist, she said, "Why don't you change? Why are you letting him do this?"

The ecologist said, "I can't change. He has followed you inside. This is what I am."

The ceiling whirled purple with Armageddon clouds and crowds of faces in shipping containers and an excavator reaching into a quarry. And mice. Sven continued to abuse the book of the ecologist.

The Avon Lady attacked him with her fists and feet. He threw her off and she came back. He threw her off again.

"It's just slippage," he grunted. Her arms stung from where he'd blocked most of her blows and her teeth were rattling from being thrown. "Disregard it."

The Avon Lady could not answer because she was badly winded. She felt sick.

Then Sven opened his tackle bag and got out a morning star. He whacked the book like an urban mom going after cockroaches. Little chunks of paper and cloth flew up in the air.

There came a rumbling sound from below them.

"Please," gasped the ecologist. "Not the morning star. Its name opens the world."

Sven stood back to look at his handiwork. The ecologist lay on the floor, slashed and torn. Sven flexed his grip on the morning star. He was going to go again. The Avon Lady looked out the window.

The sky was slate washed pink, and Venus cleared a horizon that was no longer mountain. A horizon devoid of trees, and gleaming.

"No!" cried The Avon Lady, terrified. "It's the end of the world. Don't attack, Sven."

She had seen that the tower was built on a plastic jar grubbed with fingerprints, and the earth was branded with the words *Made in Taiwan,* and the morning star was ascending. The base of the tower was crumbling; this was the sound they could hear. Everything shook. The morning star was getting brighter; there would be no sun. The world was spinning towards the brightness of the weapon.

The Avon Lady launched herself at Sven's legs. The morning star came down on her back and dug chunks out of her flesh. Sven and the Avon Lady hit the floor. She bit. She scrambled and twisted, all her energies intent on getting that weapon off him.

"What the fuck!" Sven yelped, trying to get up. The Avon lady head-butted him and his nose flattened beneath her forehead with a wet sound. He loosened his grip on the morning star and she grabbed it, hurled it away into the whirling brightness that was within and without the tower. Then she turned to the book, to see what was left of it.

"What's happening?" Sven demanded. Blood dripping from his nose. He was staggering towards his bag of weapons, falling and then getting up, as the world lurched away from the brightness of the morning star. Grey indeterminacy forming now. In the outside and under. It. Objects appeared and disappeared from the room. Walls became buckles as an indicator of their almost-fallingness.

"Don't die," The Avon Lady whispered to the ecologist. "I believe you now. I'll heal you. I'll try. Tell me what to do."

"Books," the ecologist said. "Jack used words to save me. They can easily pass across the boundaries of the world."

"There are no more books," said the Avon Lady, looking around the bare tower. "Words…."

She cast about in a panic. Her gear, all weapons; no good here. Her CVS bag – but that was only letters. She dumped out the contents.

Meanwhile Sven was checking about his person as if looking for his wallet. "I got a Berenger here somewhere. That should take care of it."

"Foundation!" cried the Avon Lady, and brandished the little taupe jar in triumph.

The makeup vanished, and with grinding noises the collapsed tower began to straighten.

Outside the windows, trees rose from the ground, revenant.

The sun squeezed through the slate and obliterated the morning star.

"Concealer!" added The Avon Lady, waving a little stick.

The ragged book was no longer there. Instead, the ecologist sat up as if rising from sleep. The ecologist was a stunning girl of sixteen, wearing a party dress. She looked at Sven, assessing.

"I will have to have him," the ecologist said.

Sven grinned back, bloodily.

"She looks good," said Sven. "She's beautiful. But I got a job to do. What happened to the monster?"

"It's in your head," The Avon Lady told him. "Or soon it will be. By the way, may I introduce the ecologist?"

"How do you do," said Sven.

"I don't actually know," the ecologist replied. "How I do."

The Avon Lady took this opportunity to bolt from the tower. She charged out into the forest and there were many doors, opening and closing, among the trees and sometimes inside them.

"Go through every door at once," the ecologist called after her. "Open your head, and you will survive."

It was true. And The Avon Lady escaped at last.

Yet everywhere she went afterward she brought nail-cuttings of the world's end with her, so that streets changed their names midway and some weeks had two Thursdays. Everywhere she went, a little bit of strangeness followed after her, like a shadow.

Maybe this has happened to you.

Tricia Sullivan was born in 1968 in New Jersey and published her first novel, *Lethe*, in 1995, the same year that she moved to Britain. Her further novels include *Someone to Watch Over Me*, *Dreaming in Smoke* (which won the prestigious Arthur C. Clarke Award in 1999), *Maul*, *Double Vision* and *Sound Mind*. She lives in Shropshire with her partner Steve Morris and their three children. Tricia writes all too few short stories, so those that she does produce are always worth celebrating, particularly when they are as good as this.

Also available from NewCon Press:

CELEBRATION

An anthology to commemorate the 50th Anniversary
of the British Science Fiction Association

Edited by Ian Whates, with an introduction by Pat Cadigan.

Features original fiction from:
**Brian Aldiss, Stephen Baxter, Jon Courtenay Grimwood,
Molly Brown, M. John Harrison, Christopher Priest,
Dave Hutchinson, Ian R. MacLeod, Ken MacLeod,
Alastair Reynolds, Adam Roberts, Martin Sketchley,
Kim Lakin-Smith, Brian Stableford, Tricia Sullivan,
Ian Watson, and Liz Williams.**

Available now in both hardback and paperback from
www.newconpress.com

disLOCATIONS

edited by Ian Whates

A signed, limited edition:
50 hardbacks, 500 softbacks

Every copy numbered and signed by all contributors.

*Two stories & cover art shortlisted for the BSFA Awards
***Two stories selected by Gardner Dozois for his 'Year's
Best SF' anthology.**

www.newconpress.com